Misbehaviour
A Collection of Women Up to No Good
From Black Lace

Look out for other Black Lace short fiction collections:

Wicked Words 1 – 10
Quickies 1 – 10
Sex in the Office
Sex on Holiday
Sex and the Sports Club
Sex on the Move
Sex in Uniform
Sex in the Kitchen
Sex and Music
Sex and Shopping
Sex in Public
Sex with Strangers
Love on the Dark Side (Paranormal Erotica)
Lust at First Bite – Sexy Vampire Stories
Seduction
Liaisons
Sexy Little Numbers – Best Women's Erotica Volume 1
The Affair

Paranormal novella collections:
Lust Bites
Possession
Magic and Desire
Enchanted

Misbehaviour
A Collection of Women Up to No Good
From Black Lace
Edited by Lindsay Gordon

BL

This book is a work of fiction.
In real life, make sure you practise safe, sane and consensual sex.

Published by Black Lace 2009

2 4 6 8 10 9 7 5 3 1

Office Sex © Justine Elyot; Icing on the Cake © Janine Ashbless; The Renaissance of Lisa Galley © Gwen Masters; Torment So Refined © ADR Forte; The Student © Alegra Verde; Our Scam © Eva Hore; Concerning Etiquette © Rhiannon Leith; The Distraction © Portia Da Costa; Alley Cats © Jennie Treverton; Phone Sex © Sommer Marsden; Girls' Talk © Chrissie Bentley; To Protect and Serve © Kimberly Dean; Flexible © Charlotte Stein

First published in Great Britain in 2009 by
Black Lace,
Virgin Books,
Random House, 20 Vauxhall Bridge Road,
London SW1V 2SA

www.blacklace.co.uk
www.virginbooks.com
www.rbooks.co.uk

Addresses for companies within The Random House Group Limited can be found at:
www.randomhouse.co.uk/offices.htm

The Random House Group Limited Reg. No. 954009

Distributed in the USA by Macmillan, 175 Fifth Avenue, New York, NY 10010, USA

A CIP catalogue record for this book is available from the British Library

ISBN 9780352345189

Typeset by Palimpsest Book Production Ltd, Grangemouth, Stirlingshire

Penguin Random House is committed to a sustainable future for
our business, our readers and our planet. This book is made from
Forest Stewardship Council® certified paper.

Printed and bound in Great Britain by Clays Ltd, Elcograf S.p.A.

Contents

Office Sex
Justine Elyot

Why, when the time accurate to a millisecond ticks away on the screen before me, do I still find myself watching the clock? Something about the stiff vibration of the minute hand compels my eyes, or maybe it's the effect of years spent at school in the same pursuit. Is it habit, or do I prefer the clock to the screen?

Who cares anyway? Usually he has been into the office by now. This is the latest he's left it by a good ten minutes, and I'm beginning to feel antsy. I keep clicking the screen, refreshing it for no good reason, so it looks as if I'm doing something productive, but really I'm wondering whether I could phone or email him on some pathetic pretext, just to make sure he's in the building.

But then, that would make him think I care, and I don't want him to think that. I don't want him to realise that this daily ration of furtive eye contact and quasi-accidental touching is at all important to me, because then it would probably stop, and I'd have to think about getting a life. Or a 'normal' boyfriend.

I chuckle under my breath at the concept of 'normal' and tip my half-cup of paperclips onto the desk. Time for some Clip Art. I link them together to make two rough stick-figure shapes and flatten them out on the veneered wood. What shall it be today? Doggy style perhaps. Paperclip figure 1 bends gracefully, clinky metal arms hanging down, while Paperclip figure 2 (extra clip for height) stands behind. I think his arms can cross in a diagonal, so that they rest on figure 1's back. Ah, primitive but surprisingly pretty to look at. I try to cross my legs, which is hard work in the progressively shorter and tighter skirts I have been favouring lately. Before the left and right limbs can cross, there is a low rumble in my ear which makes me leap off my chair, sending it skittering on its castors across the office.

It is *him*, clearing his throat behind me. The bastard has come in through the fire escape door at the back of the office.

He has a hand lightly on my back, preventing my impulse – to flee to the Ladies' and beyond – from taking effect.

'If that isn't flagrant misuse of company property, I don't know what is,' he says, his voice perfectly mingling amusement and disapproval in that uniquely come-hither-but-only-if-you-can-handle-it way.

I just glance at him from under radically lowered eyelashes and curl a bit of lip. Should I apologise or flirt? I'm not sure, so I wait for his next signal. The other four desk jockeys in my bank of workstations are trying their best not to rubberneck blatantly, but I know what the water-cooler conversation will be today.

At that very moment, my bloody screensaver chooses to make its appearance; usually I can hastily return it to the default setting whenever anyone important crosses the threshold, but the boss's sneaky entrance has thrown me into confusion. 'MR MORRELL IS HOTTER THAN HELL' ambles across the screen, in no hurry to pass by and spare my blushes. Childish, I know, but I've only been here three weeks and nothing wittier has occurred to me yet.

I shut my eyes and await my P45.

Instead, I am told that the stationery cupboard needs re-organising, and I seem to be just the person for the job.

I open my eyes and stare blankly at Mr Hotter-Than-Hell Morrell. It's true though. He is almost impossible to look in the eye without salivating. I want to put out a hand and grab him by the tie, drawing him into a passionate lambada across the beige expanse of the office. The only reason I watch *Strictly Come Dancing* is so I can imagine it is Morrell spinning me around the floor in thrall to his body, our eyes locked, our pelvises conjoined. Also because I like the use of the word 'Strictly' in the title. Kinky!

'You know the way, I assume?' he says, raising an eyebrow and gesturing to me to turn around and march. My route will take me through the office, past the vending machine, lifts and toilets, to the other side of the landing. Just a short hop on an ordinary day, but in this alternative reality it seems like the London Marathon. At least I get a chance to practise the Marilyn Monroe wiggle I read about in some magazine. I put each high-heeled foot in front of the other, forcing my arse to sway and strain against the constricting seams of my inappropriately short skirt. The thought of him following me, watching my bottom, is arousing and I can feel my nipples start to chafe against my scratchy lace bra.

Once we are out on the landing, my heels echo clickily on the shiny floor; I have to slow down to make sure I don't go arse over tit. One of my fellow temps emerges from the Ladies' and looks us both up and down curiously before scurrying back into the office.

The door of the stationery cupboard looms towards me; I turn the handle and lead us inside, flicking on the light. It is the size of a small room, carpeted, with banks of metal shelves covering three of the walls.

I hear Mr Morrell shut the door, then take a quick breath when I hear a sound like a key turning in a lock.

'Turn around and face me,' he says. He is standing, arms

folded, a pinstriped sex god with a key dangling from the fingers of one hand. He puts the key into a pocket, withdraws a BlackBerry and, with total deliberation, switches it off before replacing it.

It seems I have become Priority Number One, marked 'urgent'.

Oh, what on Earth is in store for me, in the stores?

'That's a very short skirt you're wearing,' he remarks. 'I'm not sure it's entirely appropriate for the workplace.'

'Oh . . . aren't you?' My conversational faculties have taken an early coffee break.

'I'll give you a choice, Hannah. You can go home, get changed and come back here in a longer skirt. Or . . .' The pause is just long enough for me to wonder if my heart is still beating. '. . . you can take it off. Here. Now. Which do you choose?'

Oh, I *hate* choices. It takes me half my lunch break to pick a sandwich filling. This, though, is one of the easier decisions I have faced in life. The set of his jaw, the angle of his eyebrow, make it for me.

Fumbling fingers unclip and unzip; the brief strip of charcoal flannel slides over my hips and down to the floor, the nylon lining crackling static against my stockings as it falls.

'Plucky,' he says, smirking slightly. 'I like that. I like it a lot.'

Only now does the implication of what I am doing sink in. I am standing in front of Morrell – my boss – in my tarty underwear. In a stationery cupboard. A *cold* stationery cupboard. My hands reach down to cover my goose-pimpled thighs, but he tuts and shakes his head. He swirls a finger in the air, the circular motion suggesting that I am to give him a twirl.

I remove my hands and perform a slow 360-degree turn. The knickers I am wearing are sheer and black with a red bow

4

on the front. While not as revealing as a thong, they are cut high at the back, the filmy lace shearing away up to my hips so that most of my bottom cheeks elude coverage.

'Good,' he says eventually, then after another excruciating pause, 'Shall we make a start then?'

I laugh nervously. 'A start?'

'This stock inventory I have in mind. Why don't you count the scissors in that box and then bring a pair to me.'

This was *not* what I had been expecting him to say. Wrong-footed, suspecting trickery of some kind, I go over to the box of scissors and count nineteen pairs, conscious all the time of his eyes upon my bum cheeks, then take the nineteenth gleaming pair of stainless steel snippers and hand them to him, nonplussed.

'Didn't anyone tell you to offer the handle, not the blade?' he tuts. 'Stay there. I want to make sure these are in full working order.'

He reaches down to the top button of my white work shirt, tugs on it and then, heartstoppingly, snips it off.

'Hmm,' he says, putting the button in his top pocket. 'It seems fine ... but we have to make sure ... we can't do things by halves at Morrell & Co ... yes, I think I'm satisfied now.'

With each murmured phrase he shears another button away from the placket until my shirt hangs open, revealing my bra in its gauzy glory.

'You might as well take that off,' he observes, handing me the scissors. 'And put these back.'

Reduced to my wisps of underwear, I retreat to the shelving, pressing my back to it for rickety support, feeling like a small animal, vole or something, cornered by a fox.

'Now then, Miss,' he says, folding his arms and switching his stern look to its highest setting. 'Somebody here needs a lesson in the proper use of my time and my property. I don't tolerate wastefulness or clock-watching here. Do you have anything to say for yourself?'

His tone is making me feel weak; I lean back, hoping my heels will support me as they dig into the carpet, and half-whisper, 'I'm willing to learn, Sir.'

He approves of the reply, smiling broadly, before returning to boss mode. 'I'm sure you are. Now is the time to prove your commitment to the company, and your loyalty to your manager. But first there is a small matter of correction for your misdemeanours . . . and how better to correct an employee than with . . . correction fluid.'

For a second I'm not sure what he means, and wonder if he is making an obscure reference to his sperm. I am all set to give the man a spectacular blow job, dithering by the shelves, but he shakes his head and indicates a clutter of liquid paper bottles behind me.

'Oh! You want one of these?' I can't quite believe it, but he nods and holds out his hand.

'Yes. Now stay there, quite still.' He approaches me, unscrewing the cap. I have nowhere to run, pressed up there against the metal struts, bars of coldness against my naked back. I breathe in sharply as he applies the brush to my right breast, just above the cup of my bra. He is . . . writing something. It is ticklish, and I squirm a little. The fluid chills my skin in a room that is already unheated, and I am conscious of my nipples, hardened to soreness in their sheer casing.

'I need a little more space to fit the full message,' notes Morrell, and he yanks down the cup, chafing the crimson crest of the nipple so that I emit a quick 'ooh'. I look down and read, upside down and backwards, the word BAD, underneath which he is painstakingly tracing out a G and then an I and then an R and finally an L.

'Judging by the state of these,' he says, pinching slightly at the nipple before running the pad of his thumb across it, 'I'm not far wrong. Am I?'

'No, Sir,' I wheeze, shutting my eyes and throwing my head back, rolling my neck against the metal, while he repeats the procedure with my left breast.

He must be able to smell me, I think desperately, conscious of how my knickers are flooding with my arousal juices. He must know he can do what he likes to me.

'Now then,' he says, giving my tits a tactile examination. 'While we're waiting for that to dry, let's move to the next stage of your punishment, shall we?'

Yikes! Punishment? I cast my eyes around the room, noticing several types of stationery I would not want much to do with. Hole punchers. Staple guns. Drawing pins.

He does not ask me to fetch anything though. Instead he instructs me to turn around, facing away from him, and bend over so that my hands are on the lowest shelf.

Oh, those words ... *bend over* ... taking me back to one of my oldest fascinations. Though corporal punishment in school was outlawed by the time I reached secondary age, I had often imagined how it must have been to be called up to the teacher's desk and ordered over for a taste of the slipper or the strap or even the cane. The ritual, the humiliation, the idea that everybody would *know* – oh yes, that had been a fantasy to be savoured, slowly, drawing out the detail, on many a long night.

I swallow, then slowly lower myself, pivoting at the waist, until my hands reach for the lowest sheet of metal and grip it. My spine is sloping downwards, creating maximum upthrust of arse, and although my knickers are still scantily on, I imagine he can see the clenched nutmeg shape of my mound through the filmy material.

7

'Spread your legs a little,' he commands, and then he *definitely* can – and not so clenched either. I jump and almost lose a shoe when he unexpectedly twangs a suspender strap against my thigh. 'Keep still,' he growls.

There is a hand, two hands, large and warm, on my goose-pimpled bum cheeks. They feel good, cupping the globes, brushing the skin like one of those anti-cellulite mitts but much, much better, tugging at the frilly edge of the knickers, pinching and kneading. I am gushing, the scrap of fabric sodden, and I try to push myself back towards his touch, greedy for as much of it as I can get.

His hands fly away from me, then I feel the top of my knickers pulled ruthlessly taut – a wedgie, no less! – so that the black material disappears into the crack of my bum. I yelp at that, and then I yelp louder as his hand returns, no longer the giver of pleasure but of pain. It deals a sharp smack to my right side then my left. The sensation is intense, but brief, the burn dying down almost immediately, outlived by the shame of my position.

'Do you think you deserve this?' asks Morrell, his tone making it clear how he thinks I should answer.

'Yes, Sir,' I quiver dutifully.

'Yes, Sir. I should think you do. Ask me for it then.'

Oooh, the *bastard!* I want to feel more of this tingling, but I'm not sure I can frame the words he expects from me.

'Ohhh . . . Sir!' I protest.

'Ask me.'

'I can't.'

'You can and you will. Tell me what you deserve.'

My mouth fits itself reluctantly around the words, muttering them. 'I deserve a . . . a good spanking, Sir.' *A good spanking*, a phrase I have often heard in my imaginings, sounds weird and foreign in my actual voice. It makes me want to giggle with mortification.

'Indeed you do,' he says, and there is a hint of smile in his voice amid the grimness.

I grit my teeth, bracing myself for the next strike, but it is slow in coming. Not until I have finally unclenched my buttock muscles and tried to look back does the stinging onslaught resume. His technique blends speed and accuracy to a degree that finds me hopping and hissing in very short order. My cheeks and upper thighs are peppered with the fast-falling smacks, their pattern unpredictable but their impact never less than yelp-provoking.

Somewhere between the sharp report of each smack and my own yowls of surprised pain, I am expected also to listen to some kind of lecture taking place above and behind me.

'My property is to be respected,' is one phrase that does not drown in the crack-smack-ouch filling the air. 'You will learn that I do not tolerate slapdash work or lax attitudes,' is another. Periodically I am expected to contribute a 'Yes, Sir' or 'No, Sir' and I am vaguely grateful that no more verbose expressions of contrition are called for. I am far too busy concentrating on the slow heating up of my rear; like an electric hob ring I imagine it beginning to glow, first faintly, then a vibrant orange, then an unbearable beacon red. Oddly enough, the same effect seems to be transferring to my crotch. Hot and swollen, though mercifully missing the soreness, it is making its presence felt quite insistently.

When he stops I miss the size and weight and heat of his chastising hand immediately, and even push my bum out in a silent plea for more.

'You blatant little tart,' he says, pressing a fingertip to my throbbing flesh, no doubt admiring his handiwork. 'You enjoyed that, didn't you?'

'Mmm, of course I didn't, Sir,' I murmur, swivelling my hips a little in invitation. 'I've learnt my lesson, honest.'

One finger drifts down the line of my bunched-up knickers in the crack of my arse, stopping at the puddle of lust between my legs.

'You're very wet down here, aren't you? Eh?'

'Er, yes, Sir.'

'Why is that, do you think?'

'I . . . not sure, Sir.' I know he is going to make me say it. I really don't want to.

'I need an answer, Hannah. Why are you so wet between the legs?'

Oh, for God's sake, I wanted a shag, not a bloody interrogation. I hunch my shoulders sulkily and say, 'No idea, Sir.'

'Oh dear. I don't think you have learnt your lesson, have you, Hannah? You need to brush up your communication skills. Well, let's see . . . Hand me one of those rulers from the top shelf.'

I stare at him, biting my lip. My arse is sore enough as it is – does he really mean to . . . ?

'A traditional six of the best might prove sufficient incentive to untie your tongue,' he clarifies.

Wow. The full-on schoolgirl fantasy. My curiosity is stronger than my fear, and my arousal stronger than both together, so I reach up and take one of the rulers. It is thirty centimetres long and about half a centimetre thick, made of Perspex. 'Shatterproof' is proudly proclaimed across the centre.

I hand it to Morrell and he slaps it rather terrifyingly in his palm a few times, then bends it backwards and lets it flick back into place.

'Oh yes,' he says, 'this will do nicely. Firm but flexible, and capable of producing a serious sting. A little like me.' He grins demonically. This is almost too exciting; my heart is bumping about my ribcage like a pinball. 'Back into position please.'

My bottom, still hot from the spanking, resumes its vulnerable pose. I try to work on my breathing – keep it even, keep it regular.

'You will have to count these, Hannah,' says Morrell. 'I have been known to miscount . . . I can get carried away . . .' So he has plenty of practice at this kind of thing then. I suppose you could say that that's a good thing.

The wait is almost more excruciating than the first blow, when it comes. He takes his time preparing, flipping the ruler through the air, then tapping it lightly against my bottom, testing it for resilience perhaps.

The first stroke shocks me; it falls hard and loud across the broadest part of my bottom, a white stripe of exquisite pain. I wonder if the people in the distant office can hear my howl of outrage, which ends in a broken, 'One, Sir.'

'Felt that, did you?' His voice drips with sadistic glee. 'There's plenty more where that came from.'

The ruler whaps down again, directly beneath the first line of fire. I rock back and forth on my legs a little, wondering if I can keep position for the next four. If they are all as hard as this, I don't think I'll be able to do it.

'I didn't hear your count.' Morrell's voice seems disembodied, a distant thing now.

'Oh . . . two, Sir.'

'Hmm, well, just for that . . .' He flicks the ruler, lightly but sharply, between my legs, stinging the insides of my thighs. Their dampness accentuates the pain. 'Don't forget again,' he warns me.

On the next stroke I almost pull the shelving over, so fiercely do I have to cling to it to maintain my humbling stance. It falls directly on the tender spot between bum cheek and thigh top, searing like a brand, making me wonder how long the marks will last.

'Oh lordy lordy Lord. Three, Sir,' I wail. Are we really only halfway through?

He takes a break to pull my knickers down to my knees, where they are stretched so tight their elastic digs into my skin, cancelling out the relief to my scratchy rear cleft. I wince in anticipation of the fourth stroke, but it is slow in coming. Instead, Morrell places the flat of his hand beneath my pussy lips and slowly moves it up and down, rubbing against my swollen clitoris in a way that is teasingly gentle until I have to jam myself down into his palm, desperate for a firmer touch.

At once he withdraws his hand, tutting, and puts it to my nose.

'What do you smell?' he asks.

'Myself,' I hedge.

'More specifically, Hannah, or I shall have to add to your punishment.'

'My . . . juices.'

'Juices? What sort of juices?'

'Oh, oh, sexual lubrication juices,' I fluster.

He laughs. 'Why would your body be producing sexual lubrication juices, as you call them, when I am whipping you? Do you have an explanation?'

'No, Sir.'

'Think about it. I might let you off a stroke if I like your answer. Or would that disappoint you?'

It makes sense now that Morrell would be hotter than hell. Because he lives there. He is the devil.

'Because . . . oh, because I suppose it must be turning me on.'

'I suppose it must be,' he muses. He moves his hand down so that it rests against my lips. 'Lick it. Tell me what it tastes like.'

Obediently, I slip out my tongue and lap at his lifeline for a few seconds.

'It tastes pretty much the way it smells,' I report. 'A little salty, but that could just be the natural flavour of your hand.'

He laughs again, and is still laughing when the ruler cracks its fourth wicked blow, catching me completely off guard so that I leap up, shrieking and clutching my bottom.

'Four, Sir!' My count has an indignant tone. He pushes me right back down and is swift with the fifth, laying it on the top of my thighs for maximum ouch effect.

At last, the final stroke; relief tinged with disappointment and excitement about where we might be heading next floods my head, until the pain drives all other emotions out again. His hardest, cruellest blow, back across the spot where the first was laid, breaks the ruler in half.

'Aaaaaaaaaaargh, six, Sir,' I yowl, my knuckles whiter than white, my legs trembling.

'Good girl,' says Morrell. 'Your debt is paid. And those rulers really are shatterproof, if not unbreakable. You'll have to order a new box. No, don't move. Stay there. I'm enjoying the view.'

One fingertip travels the scorched terrain of my well-thrashed bum, climbing the raised strips and descending into the less reddened valleys, tracing patterns. It feels sore, but nice, and much nicer still when the finger reaches my wide-open slit. More fingers are called into service, exploring each fold and crevice, rubbing and flicking my longing clit, circling the hole that I hope to have filled before long. One digit spears it with a luscious sucking sound.

The man who is fingering me chuckles and says, 'I think you enjoyed that almost as much as I did. Didn't you, Hannah?'

'Yes, Sir,' I sigh, pushing down on him, lost in the swirl of sensation his other fingers are producing with their clitoral manipulations, drowning sweetly, feeling the pressure build and build and build and then . . .

He takes them away.

'Not yet, dirty girl,' he says. 'You haven't thanked me properly for your punishment.'

'Right. Oh. Thank you, Sir.'

'That isn't what I meant. Kneel down in front of me.'

A little dizzy from breaking position, I do so, grateful that the cupboard is carpeted, although it is that rough, scratchy kind of office covering that produces the worst carpet burns. From this position, Morrell looms high above me, a towering inferno of sex, still impeccably suited and booted in contrast to my nakedness.

I reach up and unbuckle his belt, wondering how that would feel on the tender flesh of my whipped bottom, then wondering why I even want to know. I unbutton his fly, push the waist of the trousers down, steering wide of the substantial lump in front, letting them drop to his ankles. That really is a bulge and a half. I reach wondering hands up to feel its steely weight inside the silk boxers, which are tellingly stained, before pulling them down too.

Now I have a problem. I cannot get his cock – which is pretty similar in length to the late-lamented ruler – into my mouth from this position. He is too tall. The most I can hope for is to give his balls a tongue wash. So this is what I begin to do, approaching my task with reverence.

'I need a chair,' he says, taking a red plastic number from a stack in the corner and sitting astride it. 'You can kneel between my knees, come on.'

I proceed to give him the first blow job I have ever given my full concentration; his magnificent tool demands no less. Nothing quick or perfunctory about this; no back-of-the-mind shopping lists. I do everything the magazines recommend, from massaging his perineum to flicking my tongue against his frenulum; I even hazard a deep-throat, but I don't think there is a throat deep enough for him.

His legs twitch; he moans and clutches at my hair and I feel rewarded, his pleasure my prize. I have already decided to swallow, but before the crisis approaches, he yanks me off his cock by the roots of my hair and whispers, 'No. I want to fuck you. I want to make you come. I want to hear you beg for mercy.'

'Mercy,' I whisper, mesmerised by his low-spoken words.

'Yes, like that. Now go and get that box of OHP transparencies. And a roll of parcel tape.'

What? Is there no end to this man's fiendish imagination? I hope not.

I'm guessing that the parcel tape presages a spot of bondage, but I can't figure out why he could need OHP transparencies. In the event, he doesn't – he just needs the box, a large, flattish square. He puts it in front of the chair.

'That should do it,' he says, eyeing me and the chair in a trigonometric kind of way. 'Now stand on the box and bend over so your hands are at the top corners of the seat. Good.'

He tapes my wrists to the chair legs, repeating the process with my ankles. Up on the box with my red arse sticking out, my sleeve is now at the ideal height to take his cock. He will need to keep a good hold of my hips, though, if he doesn't want to push the chair over. That would be the highlight of the Accident Book, for sure.

'Perhaps I'll tether you with this next time,' he says, pulling the tie from around his neck and dangling it in front of my nose. Next time. I like that. His jacket and tie drop to the floor, but he does not remove his shirt, opting only to unbutton the collar. He has those bands round the elbows; I always find that strangely sexy. Lovely cufflinks as well.

Now he is moving around behind me; one hand travels slowly up a captive thigh while another brushes my dangling tits. He pinches at the nipples, coming closer, fingering my clitoris, and now his hard cock is between my thighs, rocking back and forth, getting wetter and thicker. My position, head hanging down, forehead on the chair seat, means that I can see through my legs. I can see the head of his cock, slipping and sliding between my swollen lips; I can see his hand squeezing my breasts. Oh, put it in, put it in, put it in, I silently beg, and then I remember what kind of man he is – silent begging is no good to him.

'Please put it in, Sir,' I gasp.

'Put what in, Hannah?'

'Your cock, Sir. Please put it in. Please fuck me.'

'Put it in? Here?' His thumb prods my startled arsehole and I squeal.

'No! Well, not now.' I have never done that before, and I'm not sure I want to try it while gaffer-taped to an office chair until I'm a bit more used to the idea.

'So where do you want me to . . . put it in? You'll have to tell me. We need all communications to be clear and unambiguous, Hannah, don't we?'

The swine is directly quoting something I said at the Monday meeting. I would laugh if I wasn't so insanely horny.

'In my, oh, my pussy, or my cunt, or my vagina, or whatever,' I blither.

'Yes, that was suitably unambiguous,' he approves. 'Good. Now prepare yourself for a good, hard shag. You aren't going to be walking straight until the weekend.'

Yikes, it's only Tuesday. With one clean smooth thrust, his shaft is embedded deep inside, stretching me as I've never been stretched before. He stays in up to the hilt for a little while, waiting for me to habituate to the unfamiliar girth, jiggling and swivelling. His hands are clamped to my hips and his abdomen presses against my lower bottom and thighs, heating them up again where they had begun to cool off.

He draws back, slowly, very, very, slowly, so that I feel every inch travelling down the tunnel. He almost pulls out, and I voice an inarticulate protest, but then he slams back all the way, knocking the breath out of me for a second. And we're off!

His pace is measured at first, nothing too wild, a languid see-sawing accompanied by plenty of little finger-dances across my nipples and clit, but he has to cut down on those when the tempo increases. Soon each thrust is vividly felt, pounding broad and hard, causing the chair to wobble and my breasts to swing like out-of-control pendulums. The friction is divine and intense; his cock seems to get ever thicker, stretching me, splitting me, owning and controlling me. He wraps an iron arm around my stomach, keeping me and chair in place, while he uses the other hand to prise apart my bum cheeks, opening me impossibly further, gaining the angle he needs and I crave.

'One day,' he tells me, his voice strained with effort, 'I'm going to bugger you. I'm going to bend you over, tie you up, strap your arse till it's sunset red and then give it a good reaming. Would you like that, Hannah?'

'Nnrgh,' I say.

He slaps my bottom. 'I didn't hear you.'

'Yes, Sir,' I pant.

'I thought so. I've always thought . . .' He punctuates each phrase with a ragged breath. '. . . Ever since you joined the company . . . that there's a girl . . . who needs a good seeing-to . . . by a man like me . . .'

'Have you?' I ask, enthralled at the idea, pushing back on his hard rod, sucking him all up.

'Oh yes, Hannah . . . your tight skirts . . . your high heels . . . your "fuck me" eyes . . . you little trollop . . . you need it, don't you? . . . and now you're getting it . . .'

I can hardly contradict him. I am, in just about every sense, 'getting it'. His nails are digging into my hips now, his speed increasing. Between my legs, the scene is blurring; I see the root of his cock whipping in and out, feel the slap of his skin against mine, hear the slicking noise his thrusts provoke, smell the warm, heady scent of our combined juices. My legs are starting to give way; one heel has punctured the cardboard of the box I am standing on and is making an indentation in the plastic transparencies within; I am hot and sticky and sweaty with exertion, even though I am taped into immobility.

He finds the spot and I scream, bucking the chair back and forth, alight with orgasmic electricity, then he roars, pinches my hips so hard I fear his nails will break off in them, sends one final body-shattering stroke to the target and then collapses limply over my sloping back. My legs want to melt but they can't because of the tape that secures them to the chair, so I flop sideways, hoping he will catch me. He does, skilfully managing to turn the chair on to its side on the floor, where we lie, spent and exhausted, in a spoons position.

Then there is a knock at the door.

We ignore it, lying silently. I know the door is locked, but I can feel Morrell's heart thumping against my back.

A cough. A trying of the handle.

'Is everything all right? Is there anyone in there?'

It is Sharon, one of the girls from the office. She knocks again.

'Maybe something fell off a shelf,' says another voice. Her friend.

'It was people, I'm sure,' says Sharon's muffled voice. 'Sounded like they were in pain.'

'Maybe it was coming from the loos?'

'Well . . . I don't know. Maybe. Where's Hannah got to?'

'Dunno; Morrell marched her off. Maybe he's given her the boot.'

'Or he's giving her one . . . ooh! Do you think . . . ?'

'Shit! Let's get back to the office.'

Their heels scuttle clickily off and I exhale again. As does Morrell. And then he kisses me.

'Unfortunately, we do need to get back to work,' he says into my ear, his voice low and caressing. 'Perhaps next time we'll use my office. That could be just as much fun. I have a very big desk, you know.'

'Next time, eh?' I sigh, then I suck in my breath when he starts untaping my wrists. You could wax your pubes with that stuff. I am examining the red cuffs of sore skin above my hands as he talks.

'Oh yes, I think so. I might have it written into your Job Description. Personal services to the manager, no fewer than three times weekly.'

'That could come under "Other Duties As Required", I suppose.' Damn it, my stockings are laddered now.

'Yes. And instead of Dress Down Friday, we could have Get Undressed Friday.'

I giggle. 'Are there any tissues in here?' I ask, squinting at the dark shelves.

'No tissues,' he says. 'I want you sitting at your desk – if you can still sit – in sticky knickers for the rest of the day. I want the other girls to smell it on you.'

'You pervert.'

He raises an eyebrow. 'Is that any way to talk to your manager?' he asks. 'Do I need to test another of these rulers to destruction?'

'Maybe not today, Sir,' I concede. I pull my knickers back up, but he stops me, placing a Post-it note on each pink bum cheek.

He leans over and writes on them in green felt tip pen. 'What does it say?' I ask, craning my neck to read.

'"Spank me",' he says. 'Keep those there until you get home.'

'Oh, OK.' I pull the knickers carefully over the notes, making sure not to detach them from my skin, picturing the tasteful colour contrast they must make. My skirt is next, up over my laddered stockings, then I try to button my shirt up over the hardened correction fluid message on my breasts. Except . . . no buttons. Morrell chuckles, then reaches for a stapler, tacking the shirt together haphazardly. I stare at him wildly – surely he can't expect me to wear this in the office? – but he simply smirks and nods.

'Don't forget to order those rulers,' he says, as I turn to him, uncertain how to end this strange interlude. 'And I want to see you in my office at close of play. I want to check that Post-its, stained knickers and Tippexed tits are all still intact. Do you understand?'

'Yes, Sir.' I grin blushingly.

'Good. Now get back to work, and no more slacking.' He sends me on my way with a light pat to the seat of my skirt that still manages to make me wince.

What a long work day it proves to be.

I can barely sit on my swivel chair; my bum throbs, and rustles every time I shift; my knickers are cold and slimy against my sore and swollen pussy and I have to avoid crossing the office for fear that the spunk has stained my skirt. My laddered stockings would be bound to draw comment too.

Inferences are made around the workstations; I often catch heads bowed behind screens in muttered conversation, then raised to look at me. Sharon, sitting opposite, comments loudly to her neighbour that she might buy an air freshener at lunchtime.

I soldier on, working harder than I ever have before. Morrell's unusual management techniques are certainly improving my productivity.

They haven't cured my clock-watching though.

Justine Elyot's erotica collection *On Demand* is published by Black Lace in December 2009. Her short fiction appears in the Black Lace anthologies *Liaisons* and *Sexy Little Numbers – Volume 1* .

Icing on the Cake
Janine Ashbless

It was going to be a lovely wedding cake. After days of baking and icing I was starting to feel some confidence: none of my nightmares had come true; nothing had burned, fallen off, or failed to dry. So far, anyway. I touched the heavy wood of my kitchen table top with cornflour-dusted fingertips to make sure of my luck.

Oh, that cake: three tiers of fruit cake, each painted with sieved apricot jam, blanketed with marzipan – OK, so no one likes marzipan but you need that firm base for the icing above – and plastered with three layers of royal icing smoothed to a perfectly flat glacial finish. Three layers, I might point out, each one of which had had to dry for a day. It was only after that that I'd been able to start on the filigree decoration. This cake had been the focus of my life for over a week.

Still, Helen was going to love it. And I'd be there to see it on her wedding day, when it would be the focus of attention as she and Pete posed for photos, ready to plunge the knife into that snowy crust.

I scratched my nose, leaving a dusting of white, which I tried to wipe off with the back of my hand, and then stretched my back. I was trying to alternate making the sugar-paste roses – I planned a cascade from top tier to bottom – with piping the detail on the panels of the cake, because the latter involved a lot of bending over and steady handwork. Helen was from a

Scottish family so I'd pricked out a design of interlaced Celtic knotwork all over the smooth surfaces, which had to be filled in using an icing bag with a fine No 1 nozzle.

No one could accuse me of not trying.

I stuck my fist into the small of my back then and knuckled my spine. I knew I was, in a way, putting in too much effort. I mean, cake decoration is a hobby I enjoy and I'd volunteered to make it as my present to the newly-wed couple, but it was an astonishingly time-consuming job. It was my first wedding cake and I was beginning to appreciate, just a little, why they are so damn expensive to buy. Helen isn't even one of my closest friends to deserve such dedication. I hadn't even been invited to her hen night. Well, I was originally, when it was supposed to be a weekend of drinking and roller coasters at Alton Towers, but then, when her mum suddenly decided to pay for her to fly out to New York instead for some shopping, I hadn't been in the elite asked to go with her.

That still rankled a bit, but I wasn't going to bear a grudge. Helen always gets forgiven, whatever she does or fails to do. She's just one of those people – blonde, perky, impetuous and with an iron will before which men and women alike just crumble. She's always forgiven by everyone, whether she forgets something she's promised to do or takes a favour for granted or breaks a heart.

By now the cake wasn't about Helen, though. It was about me making something I could forever be proud of – and about everyone else admiring it too. That was worth a few back twinges and stiff shoulders, surely?

'Coffee,' I said to myself, putting down the paper bag full of white icing.

That was the moment the doorbell rang, and I groaned under my breath. I wasn't expecting anyone and I wasn't exactly dressed to receive visitors; after showering that morning I'd just pulled on a pair of bright cotton beach trousers and a sleeveless top. I hadn't even bothered with a bra. And everything was dusty with icing sugar by this point, too. I beat ineffectually at my clothes then went to answer the door.

It was Pete, the groom, standing on my doorstep. I smiled, surprised. 'Hi.'

'Hey, Suze. Helen asked me to bring something round.' He held up a small but curiously expensive-looking paper bag.

'Oh, right?' I liked Pete. Like Helen and me, we'd known each other for years: we were all in the same social circle. He wasn't a complicated guy, just a regular bloke. He trained with the TA at weekends and, though he worked at a desk job in between, he was in better shape than anyone else I knew. He was also cute, with a neat mat of close-cropped blond hair and eyelashes that stuck together in incongruously dark triangles, drawing attention to his blue eyes.

Four words for Pete: *Out. Of. My. League.*

No wonder Helen had been the one to nab him.

'It's a cake-topper, she says,' he explained, looking a little embarrassed. 'She bought it in New York.'

'Oh. You'd better bring it in then.' I waved him through into the kitchen. 'You want to put the kettle on?'

'Yeah, OK.'

'How's things?' I asked absently, extracting from the paper bag an embossed cardboard box while Pete busied himself finding mugs. 'You feeling ready for the big day tomorrow?'

'I'm shitting bricks,' he said cheerily. 'Hey. Is that the cake?'

He'd done well to spot it camouflaged in the mountain of bottles and tubes and spatulas and basins all over the table top; I'm one of those people who gets *everything* out when I'm working on something. 'That's the bottom tier; the rest is in the cupboard. I've got to finish the decorative bits on the sides, then a load more roses, and I can put it all together.'

'It looks amazing.' He came up and examined it closely. I felt my heart warm a little at the praise. 'Look at all that detail.' He poked with a finger in the air above one of the roses. 'Are the flowers edible too?'

'Yes; they're icing.'

'You're kidding; they look real.'

I moved to the marble slab where I'd rolled out a sheet of icing. 'It's not that difficult.' I used a cutter to press out a few petals, then demonstrated how they were furled together. 'Look, like this. You just keep adding petals until the flower's big enough. Then you leave them to dry, and then you paint them with food colouring.' My roses were to be flushed with pink at the petal edges; it'd look striking, I thought, against the pure white of the base cake.

'Shit, Suzie.' He grinned. 'That's great. Helen's going to be knocked out.'

'You think so?'

'I know it.'

'And she wants this on top?' I cracked open the box at last. The glitter of crystal met my eye. 'Right,' I muttered. It was a pair of dancers, cut in multifaceted glass. I lifted them out, wishing I had the guts to drop them on the floor: a woman in a full romantic ball gown, a dashing man bending her in his arms. 'She got this in New York, you say?'

'Yes.' Pete didn't look any more impressed than I felt. 'It's a bit Disney, isn't it,' he admitted tactlessly.

'A bit.' Oh God NO, not on MY cake, was the actual thought running through my head. Unfair, sure, but I had the whole decoration worked out already, without this glitzy topper being part of the scheme. Besides, it was going to be out of scale.

I pulled a face. 'Hold on; I'll have to get the top tier out and have a think.'

Pete busied himself making two cups of coffee while I unboxed the smallest cake, set it up on the table and stared at it grimly. The relief work was already done on this tier – piped, dried and, on the very topmost surface, picked out in gilt. All it was waiting for was the spray of roses.

'Wow. That looks complicated.' Pete presented me with a mug.

'It's just gold leaf,' I said, showing him the packet with the metallic film in it. 'You sort of stick it on with liquid glucose.' I'd been nervous that the gilding was bit too much, to be honest, but it looked good right now – just when I was going to have to trash it.

'Real gold? You can eat it?'

'Yes – gold's inert. And it's really thin.'

'Ah. Like in the vodka.'

'That's right. How did the stag party go, by the way?'

He rolled his eyes. 'You'll all find out during the Best Man's speech.'

I smiled, but I wasn't really distracted from my main problem, which was how to fit the damn cake-topper into the middle of that complicated linework. Putting my coffee aside I stooped over the cake, resting one elbow on the table top for firm balance, lowering the crystal ornament to the icing to see how much area the base covered. Pete gave an odd sigh.

'You remember the party at Elliot's dad's place,' he said wistfully from behind me.

I smiled. 'Oh yeah. Though I'm surprised you do. You were that drunk . . .' I could just carefully pick out the relief icing, I told myself, stick the dancing couple down, then disguise the horrid juxtaposition with lots of little icing roses.

'I wasn't.'

I lifted my eyes from the cake briefly. 'Hey. I remember what you were saying to me that night.' We'd ended up somehow in the wicker sofa in the conservatory, that evening a couple of years ago, and we'd come surprisingly close to getting off. 'You must've been drunk.'

Well, he must have been. I'd just laughed him off at the time.

'I said I wanted to fuck your beautiful bum,' he said softly. He was standing *right* behind me as I was bent over, I realised suddenly. Close enough that I could feel the brush of cloth on cloth – then the exploratory bump of his weight against me. 'I wasn't drunk.'

My hand started to tremble and I put the figurines down carefully. 'Um,' I said, not as quick-witted as I liked to think myself.

'You have got a lovely bum,' he pointed out, putting one hand on my arse cheek, with reverent appreciation. All the blood seemed to leave my head and flood down into my body, charging my lower regions with heat. I could feel the flesh between my thighs grow heavy, and my legs correspondingly weak.

'Shouldn't you be thinking about Helen's bum right now?' I asked, my voice coming out all husky and plaintive.

'What bum? She's been on this sodding diet for months – no bread, no alcohol, no chocolate – and she looks like a string bean. She hasn't *got* an arse any more.' Both his hands moved on my cheeks in warm caressing circles. 'Not like you. God . . . this feels good.'

If I'd been capable of thought I might have tried to come to grips with the peculiarly male notion that less is not in fact more, but thinking was, it seemed, no longer one of my strong suits. I was too busy feeling the shockwaves of sensation washing through me with each flex of his grip on my cheeks.

Too busy trying to sort out the alarm and the glee that were battling it out in the empty shell of my skull. With a little groan of relief, Pete pushed his groin and thighs up against my long-coveted butt, and I could feel the hard challenge to my cushioning softness. Like – really, seriously hard. The kick of arousal that shot through my guts was like a jolt of electricity. I barely had the sense to push the cake a few inches further away towards safety. 'Oh God,' I said. What I meant was, You really mean it! You really do!

'Oh yes.' He ground his hips against me.

Pete, of course, had an excuse for all this. His forebrain paralysed by pre-wedding panic, it was his lower brain that was in charge. So what was my excuse? Getting one over on a friend who had always put me in the shade? Getting a slice of a seriously hot man beyond my normal aspirations?

Maybe the truth is that I'm simply a bit of a slut, when I get the chance. Well, how should I know? – it's not like other women's blokes are chucking themselves at me all the time.

'Suzie,' he murmured with pleasure, taking me by the hips and wriggling up against me snugly. 'You've got such a lovely fucking arse, I've wanted it for years, and –' He paused, then leaned in to murmur in my ear, 'And you're not wearing any knickers, are you?'

'No,' I whispered.

'Lucky me.' He tugged at the elastic waistband of my trousers, baring my hips, the swell of my bum, the cleft between my cheeks, right down to the tops of my thighs. Then he worked my bum against his crotch, back and forth over the rigid length of the erection that fought the confines of his own clothes. I loved the way he manhandled me; I loved his greed and his delight. I straightened up against him, bracing my hands on the table, my back to his warm chest.

'I'm not wearing a bra either.'

God, that got him going. He grabbed at my tits through the thin cloth, squeezing and mauling them like he was discovering boobs for the first time, while his hard-on ground into my backside and I gasped encouragement. Then he found that he might as well stick his hands up under my shirt, and then he pushed the top up to bare them, tugging at my nipples and rolling them between his rough fingers. 'Great tits,' he grunted, 'great arse.'

'You like them?' I pulled my top off over my head and flung it behind us; I think it landed in the sink. Then I scraped my nails down his neck, provoking him into squashing my tits together into one luxurious bosom and pinching my nipples until I squeaked.

'Fuck, yes,' he groaned. Like I said: there was nothing complicated about Pete. He whirled me round to face him then, picked me up and plunked my bare arse on the table – God knows what the food hygiene people would have had to say about that – and for a second just goggled at my tits. I cupped them in my hands and lifted them for his inspection, and Pete fell into my breasts, plunging his face into my cleavage and taking great wet mouthfuls like he would eat me all up. I had to cling to him just to stop myself falling over backwards among the sugar flowers and the bottles of colouring. His hot sucking kisses on my tits sent me crazy, my nipples standing up like jelly sweets in response to his tongue and his lips and his teeth. When he lifted his head from those glistening orbs there was a hungry, wicked look in his eye.

'Don't stop,' I said, pouting.

Grinning, he grabbed the icing bag and turned the nozzle on my left tit.

'Pete!'

'Hold still.' A thin line of sugar icing squirted out as he squeezed, and he drew a spiral round and round my flushed, swollen nub of flesh, capping it with pure white. With almost comic precision he did the other one too.

'Got a sweet tooth?' I giggled.

He squirted icing into my mouth in answer, then kissed me, the sweetness melting on our entwining tongues. Then he bent to lap the icing caps off my breasts. I scrabbled for a small pot on the table beside me; by the time he released my nipple I had the cap off.

'Try this,' I gasped, using my fingers to paint it on my boobs and breastbone. It was liquid glucose, a pure clear syrup, incredibly sticky and sweet. He ate it off my tits and followed the drips down my belly into the fuzz of my sex. I slopped a dollop on my pussy lips and he tore off my trousers to part my legs, kneeling to bury his face in my muff and tongue me. I'll say this for Pete: he knows how to eat a woman. I wrapped my bare thighs around his shoulders and raked my sticky fingers through his short hair while he gobbled me until I squealed and bucked and came so hard that the table shook and bottles toppled.

He took a moment to draw breath after that, rising to his feet and giving me a dark, sticky grin. He stroked the bulge in his trousers and my fingers joined his.

'Shall we go to the bedroom?' I suggested, dizzy but wanting more.

'Good idea.' But when he lifted me off the table he stopped dead. I turned my head to look. He'd sat me down in a thin drift of icing sugar, you see, and when he peeled me off it left a perfect imprint of my two bum cheeks on the table top.

'That's it,' he said under his breath, as if I'd provoked him beyond endurance. He turned me again and pushed me face down on the table top, my white-powdered bum presented to him. Sugar roses crunched and crumbled; the cake missed being squashed by an inch. 'Spread them,' he said, like I was one of his weekend soldiers. I did, spreading my thighs. He ran his finger down the cleft from my tailbone to the wet juicy melt of my sex, then back up to the pucker of my bumhole, circling it, making me squirm with terror and delight. 'This is what I've wanted, Suze,' he said, sounding almost mesmerised, 'to fuck your sweet arse.'

I blushed all over, but I answered 'Yes,' nearly in pain with wanting him inside me.

'Just relax.'

Spread naked across the detritus of my cake-making, that wasn't going to be easy, but he stroked me one-handed as he adjusted his clothes, raising me to the boil. Then he went for something that surprised me – the icing. Not the bag, but the sheet of royal icing I'd rolled out earlier. He lifted it from the marble and laid it on me between my spread cheeks, all down the length of my split, covering my bum and my pussy. I gasped, taken beyond every familiar sensation by this new game. *Cold. Heavy. Soft.* He moulded it to my most intimate shape with his fingers, strangely gentle. Then he spread my bum with his hands and knelt behind me and pressed his face to my behind.

He licked his way to my bum-hole through the icing, the sweetness melting on his tongue, and as I realised what he was doing I cried out but he soothed me with his firm hands and kept going. As the sugar warmed and softened, so did I. As it turned from solid to liquid, so did I. I felt his warm breath and his caressing tongue and before I knew it that tongue wasn't outside me but insinuating itself within, and I was dissolving like wet sugar under his kisses. One of his hands pressed my pussy through the icing veil further down, and that bit was melting too from my wetness. So intense was the sensation of his tongue in my hole that I came then and there, not fiercely but in tremulous waves, and then he stood and pushed his hard cock through the slippery slush of sugar and sex, trying for entrance. I felt the thrill of his cock head pushing on my dilated ring.

I was concerned he'd be impatient, he was so hungry for my arse, but I needn't have worried. He'd waited years for this and he wasn't in any rush to get it over with. Every fraction of an inch that I yielded made the effort worthwhile. The little noises I made in my throat – part protest and part surrender – urged him on, until he was suddenly inside, sliding frictionless past all resistance. Fucking my sweet, sweet arse, and groaning with gratitude and triumph.

And then coming.

I didn't come while he was fucking my bum; it was far too intense an experience for me to be able to lose myself in orgasm. But I came afterwards, a couple of times. We ended up on the kitchen floor, butt-naked and covered in sugar both sticky and powdery, crushed sugar-paste rose petals littered about us. I piped icing trails all the way down his chest and belly to the tip of his cock, then licked them off. I sucked his big handsome dick back to hardness and wrapped it lovingly in gold leaf: the pride in his face as he looked down at himself was a picture I'll treasure. Then I rode his golden cock, my undieted bum cushioning each plunge, my boobs bouncing, sugar in my hair and sweat glazing our skins, while he thrust up to meet me. It was wonderful.

I was covered in flecks of gold after that one. Gilt, but no guilt.

Luckily the main body of the cake came through it all unharmed. I did have to give up on the sugar roses and use fresh ones, but no one noticed. Not even Helen.

Janine Ashbless is the author of the Black Lace novels *Divine Torment, Burning Bright* and *Wildwood*. She has two single author

collections of erotica, *Cruel Enchantment* and *Dark Enchantment*, also published by Black Lace. Her paranormal erotic novellas are included in the Black Lace collections *Magic and Desire* and *Enchanted*. Her short stories are published in numerous Black Lace anthologies.

The Renaissance of Lisa Galley
Gwen Masters

Written in red marker on a stark white background, the note was short, clear and to the point:

STAY AWAY FROM MY HUSBAND.

Lisa stared at this note while she sipped on her Martini. The waiter discreetly brought another during the time she contemplated the little piece of paper, the one she had found stuck underneath the windshield wiper of her car. It was anonymous and safe, and those things also made it slightly disturbing.

When the waiter brought her food, she showed it to him. He smiled, shifted his weight from one foot to another, uncertain whether to laugh or look appropriately sad.

'This,' she said, rattling the paper, 'should be the picture next to "passive-aggressive" in the dictionary, don't you think?'

The waiter nodded, solemn. She balled up the paper and flipped it to him.

'Trash that, if you don't mind.'

She watched her cell phone while she ate, waiting for it to ring. Paranoid, she knew. She briefly flirted with the idea that someone had chosen the wrong car on which to leave that note, but she was too smart for that. Any woman with a cheating husband would check out her facts like a detective trying to solve a career-making case. Wifey had pinned the right car.

But which wife was it?

That night she lay in bed while Rich, the only man she had never slept with, sat in his chair in front of her, strumming his guitar and listening to her rant.

'How can I do what she wants me to do if I don't know who she is?' Lisa asked. 'I would gladly stop sleeping with her husband if she had the balls to say it to my face. But I'm not going to stop sleeping with all three of them!'

Rich rolled his eyes. 'Sweetie, you wouldn't stop anyway. You would invite her to watch.'

Lisa smiled as she remembered one jilted wife who had taken her up on the spur-of-the-moment offer: the way the woman had perched on the chair with her long cigarette, perfectly controlled, knowing her presence was the one torture her husband never dreamed she would have devised.

'Fuck her properly,' the wife said to her cheating husband, 'or I'll leave you.'

So far as Lisa knew, the husband and wife were still together. Lisa had broken off the affair after that night, and it wasn't only because the wife had asked her to do it. The illicit thrill was gone, and she was all about the thrill. She could get her kicks elsewhere.

'Anyway,' Rich said, 'you've got no heart, Lisa. You won't stop fucking married men until the day they put you under. Even then, it will probably be thanks to a gunshot from somebody's wife.'

Lisa stared at the ceiling fan. 'I've got a heart.'

Rich played his guitar and didn't answer.

'Wanna fuck?'

Rich snorted with laughter. 'Have you grown a dick?'

'Working on it.'

Rich rose from the chair, guitar in hand, and leant down to kiss Lisa on the forehead. 'I'll say this,' he murmured against her skin. 'You might not have a dick, but you've got balls, baby. Big ones.'

The next day was Tuesday, which was always John's day to come to her. During the summer, his wife thought he was playing golf. During the winter, she thought he was working long hours to prepare his accounting firm for the next tax season. Lisa had often thought his wife was one of three things: overly indulgent, blind or having an affair of her own.

John closed the door behind him and gazed at Lisa. She was spread out on the bed in a flimsy teddy, the blue one, because it was his favourite colour. She made it a point to know such things about her men. She also knew not to be coy, to just get down to it, because John liked his sex hard and fast, then made up for it with an hour of cuddling and pillow talk.

'Fuck me,' Lisa murmured, and that was all it took. John was out of his suit and all over her bed before she could say anything else. He climbed between her legs, cock in hand, and slid into her with a slow, long moan. The next thrust was hard, ramming her. Lisa lifted her hands to the headboard and held on for the ride, moving her hips up and down in time with his strokes, getting her own pleasure. She knew when he was on the edge and she had perfected the art of keeping him there until she caught up.

When she looked at John's wedding ring, bright gold against her pale thigh, she came with a scream.

As he lay in bed and talked about mundane things, Lisa's mind was a million miles away. She kept seeing that ring, replaying the moment of orgasm in her mind. It wasn't John who had got her off, not really. It was that ring, the proof of the forbidden, that sparked her fire. John was just the hard dick that happened to be in her cunt at the time of ignition.

When he started talking about his wife, she took the opportunity. 'Do you think she knows?'

John ran his fingertips around Lisa's nipple, watching it pucker. 'What if she does?'

'You think?'

'She might suspect, but she would never say a word. I suspect the massage therapist isn't giving her shoulder rubs, but I keep my mouth shut.'

Lisa rolled her eyes. 'The massage therapist thing is always too cliché to be true.'

'Really?'

'Men are always accused of sleeping with the secretary. For women, it's the massage therapist. Or the pool boy.'

'I'm the pool boy, and she's sure not sleeping with me.'

Lisa suddenly smiled, the question forgotten. 'Well, we had better get back to it, don't you think?'

This time she climbed on top. She rode him while he grew harder, filling her up. He grabbed her ass and she grabbed his shoulders, rocking into each other, sweat making their bodies slide with a delicious whisper. He spurted hard inside her. She watched his face as the pleasure took over, smiling at him as he came back down to earth.

He flipped her onto her back and slipped his fingers into her pussy. She spread her legs and closed her eyes, giving herself over, letting him do all the good things that always got her off. He teased her clit, pushed his fingers deeper, whispered in her ear how hot she was, how wet with his own come, and how he wanted to feel her come for him, again and again and again.

When it was over and John had made himself presentable again, she kissed him at the door. 'Want to go to a movie this weekend?' John asked. 'She's out of town with her sister on Friday.'

37

'Why don't you come over instead, and we'll watch a movie here.'

John smiled against her lips and walked to his car. She watched him go, thinking about normal dates with married men, about movies and dinners and shopping trips out of town, and realised she would much rather spend that time naked.

God, she was such a whore.

When Adam showed up at her doorstep on Wednesday afternoon, she pouted at him from the balcony. She had been thinking far too much about too many things, and the fact that he was taking his sweet time in getting there had been all over her last nerve. 'You're late.'

He climbed from the Harley and took off his helmet, shaking out his blond hair and smiling up at her while he took off the gloves. 'Traffic.'

'Why don't we ever go anywhere?' she asked him as he came up the stairs. He stared at her pretty little nightgown and the matching robe, the earrings that highlighted her long neck, the red lipstick. He gave her a raunchy grin.

'Wanna go around the world?'

'I'm serious.'

'So am I. You're not exactly dressed for Harley riding, honey.'

Lisa looked own at the nightgown and robe. She rolled her eyes at him. 'OK, I didn't mean today. I meant, whenever. Why don't we go anywhere?'

He came up the stairs towards her. 'Where do you want to go?'

'Dinner.'

He nodded and smiled. 'Dinner. How about next week?'

'How can you get away?'

'Do you want to go or not?'

Lisa walked into her apartment, Adam right on her heels. 'Does your wife know about us?'

Adam stopped, hovering in her doorway. 'No. Why?'

'Somebody left a note on my car the other day. Told me to stay away from her husband.'

'What day?'

'Monday.'

Adam's shoulders relaxed. 'It wasn't my wife. Have you asked the other guys?'

'What other guys?'

'For God's sake, Lisa, are you serious?' Adam closed the door behind him and set the helmet on the kitchen counter. 'I'm not foolish enough to think you're sleeping with only me.'

Lisa said nothing.

'In fact,' Adam went on, 'it kinda turns me on.'

'Does it?'

'I like wondering what guys you've been with on the days you haven't been with me. I wonder how long it's been since you were fucked, and how long after I leave before somebody else gets a go at you.'

Lisa slipped off her robe. 'Yesterday. I'll have another man here tomorrow night. Probably about the time you're having dinner with your wife, I'll be sucking him off. He loves blow jobs.'

Adam grabbed her as she turned to head for the bedroom. It took all of a minute to get to the bed and get his clothes off. When he thrust into her, she could have sworn he was bigger than he had ever been. He fucked her hard, her legs over his shoulders, while she told him about the third guy, the one she only saw on Thursdays, the one whose wife was a hotshot banker in the next town over. By the time he was behind her, his hands in her hair while he rode her like a pony, she was telling him about how different his come tasted from that of the others. 'You're not a smoker,' she panted. 'Your come is sweeter. I just swallow what the others give me, but I like to taste yours, roll it around in my mouth for a while.'

He gave it to her not once, but twice.

When it was over they lay on the bed, propped up on their elbows, facing each other. 'So you fuck three men,' Adam said, 'and you don't have any problems with this?'

'Why would I have a problem with it?'

Adam held up a hand. 'Whoa, now. Don't get defensive. I'm not judging.'

'Aren't you?'

'Hey, I don't even bother to take off my ring when we fuck. It's not my place to judge, believe me.'

Lisa studied his face, found honesty, and nodded. 'I'm having a problem with it since that damn note.'

'What bothers you about it?'

She flopped back on the bed and let out a frustrated sigh. 'I have no idea.'

'The wife? You feel guilty about her?'

Lisa bit her lip and thought about that. She had never felt guilty about a wife. She had always thought that if a wife was giving her husband what he wanted, he wouldn't have to go elsewhere to find it. She never went trolling for men. They always seemed to find her and, to Lisa's reasoning, that spoke volumes.

'I feel guilty about myself,' she said. 'I guess I've been thinking about how I deserve more.'

Adam shrugged. 'Of course you do.'

Lisa listened to him as he dressed, and a plan began to form in the back of her mind.

On Thursday, Ron came over. She met him with a glass of wine. The music was soft, the lights were low, and she was wearing something a bit more conservative – a velvet blouse and matching lounge pants. They clinked glasses and toasted each other before he went down on her, his lips still wet from the wine, his hands dark on her smooth thighs. She closed her eyes and let him do whatever he wanted, let him do the one thing his wife never let him try, and she came for him while he murmured with pleasure.

When she was on her knees in front of him, alternating sucks of his dick with sips of her wine, she thought again about the thing that had been taking shape in her head. She envisioned it, tried to imagine it, and reached down between her legs to touch herself while she did it. When Ron flooded her mouth, she came too, crying out around his dick.

Later, she asked him about the note. 'Do you think she did it?'

Ron slowly nodded, his eyes on the floor. 'Probably. It sounds like something she would do.'

'Passive-aggressive, is she?'

Ron smiled. 'She's a pit bull at work, but when it comes to her personal life, she's meek as a mouse.'

'So she would put a note on my car instead of confronting me.'

'Yes, definitely.'

Lisa mulled this over. Ron was probably right, which was a sad thing, because that meant the thrill was gone, and of course that meant she would have to break it off with him. But maybe she could do one more thing first . . .

She asked him before he left. His eyes widened, then he burst into laughter.

'Oh, yes,' he said. 'Yes, yes, yes.'

She lay on the bed with John on Friday, neither of them watching the movie on the television. She was on her belly and he was behind her, his hands on her hips, easing his lubed cock into her ass. She lifted her hips a bit. When the angle started to hurt, she whispered and he eased off, letting her move into the position that felt best. He was a kind and considerate fuck.

When he was buried to the hilt in her ass, they both moaned. When he started to move, she told him what she had been thinking, told him about the one thing she wanted, and asked him what he thought. In response, he fucked her harder. When he was fucking her a little too hard, far beyond stopping, she clenched the sheets and closed her eyes and yelled with each thrust. When he came, it burned like fire.

She watched him walk to the bathroom to clean up. John was the one who would take some serious convincing. He was the kind of man who expected both his wife and his mistress to be faithful to him, as if the world revolved around his huge dick and awesome personality. Once he knew Lisa had been fucking around, he would put on the puppy-dog eyes and pout for a while, then he would get mad, then he would settle down to listen, all the while acting like his feelings were devastated. She knew him so well, there wasn't much point in having an affair with him any more. Where was the excitement?

When he came out of the bathroom, she told him.

He reacted just as she had expected, but with a small twist – along with the puppy-dog eyes and the pout, he also shed a few tears, an act that freaked the fuck out of Lisa. She had seen tears during break-ups, and she made a point of being an absolute bitch, just to soften the blow and make the guy think she wasn't worth crying over. But even though she was going to break up with John, had made her mind up to do it, she wanted one last thing from him.

It took an hour of tears and yelling and pouting to get to

the discussion she really wanted to have. When she suggested what she wanted to do, John's eyes were wide with equal parts hurt and intrigue.

'You want to fuck all of us? All at once?'

Lisa smiled gently. 'I can't keep on fucking married men, John. I just can't. It's not good for them and it's definitely not good for me. I need to start thinking long-term, and start being open to somebody who might be able to give me that. But there's nothing wrong with one last fling, is there? One last fantasy?'

John shook his head. 'I thought I was enough for you,' he said, and she knew by the way his chin quivered that he was on the verge of wailing again. Her patience finally broke.

'No one man is enough for me,' she said. 'I'm never satisfied with one.'

He glared at her. 'Then what makes you think you can settle down with somebody?'

'I don't know. But I'm going to try.'

John shook his head again, as if he had just heard the most pitiful thing in the world. Lisa stared absently at him, wondering what she had seen in him in the first place. By the time he was ready to leave, he hadn't said yes or no to her proposal, so she threw her trump card.

'I'm going to do this,' she said to him. 'The other two are in. You're the only one who hasn't made up his mind. And, regardless, I'm doing it – so you can join in or you can stay at home with the little wifey.'

She smiled, kissed him on the cheek, and closed the door in his face. She waited until she heard him walking away before she pressed her forehead to the wall and cursed him.

It was a week later, on an unusually cool Friday night, when Adam's motorcycle pulled up next to Ron's BMW. Adam looked the car over as he removed his helmet and set it on the bike. He came up the steps and banged on the door.

Ron nodded at him as he walked into the room. 'Which one are you?'

'Adam.'

'Adam. I'm Ron.'

'Just you and me?'

'So far.'

Lisa appeared from the bedroom, more gorgeous than ever in a golden babydoll and matching panties. She sauntered to the kitchen in high heels, ignoring the stares of the two men. She wanted them primed and ready for the moment she climbed into bed with them, and the best way to get a man to want her was to ignore him. That's how she knew John would be there tonight. She had ignored his calls, refused his visit on Tuesday, and only spoken to him once to remind him that, on Friday night, her door was open.

Oh, yes. He would be there.

She poured the drinks. Wine for Ron, scotch for Adam, and John's beer was chilling in the fridge. She carried the drinks out to the men, gave them a smile, and headed back to the bathroom. There she sat on the side of the tub and painted her toenails while she let them wonder what the hell she was doing in there.

Sure enough, the talk soon turned to their wives. She listened, bored, having heard all of it before. She was listening to Ron bitch about his wife's job when the door opened, stopping Ron in mid-sentence.

'Where's Lisa?' John sniffed, and in the bathroom, Lisa popped up. She smoothed her babydoll, smiled at herself in the mirror, and opened the door. Showtime.

'Right here,' she purred. 'And now that all the boys are here, are we ready to play?'

John scowled at her. Adam took the last sip of his scotch and ambled to the kitchen to set his glass in the sink. Ron swirled his wine as he rose from the chair and made his way towards the bedroom. John stood in the doorway, watching them as they moved around the apartment, so familiar with the space he had considered his domain.

'You really were fucking two other guys!' he accused, glaring at her.

'I've never lied to you,' she answered. 'I'm going to the bedroom. Are you coming?'

'No!'

'Not even to watch?'

He took a step towards her, fury written all over his face. Adam stepped out of the kitchen and the two men looked at each other. John backed down, just as Lisa had known he would, and put on that pouty face as Adam followed Lisa to the bedroom.

'Come with us,' she purred to John. 'Maybe you can teach these boys how to properly ass-fuck a woman.'

The bedroom looked exactly the same as it always had. She wondered what the men were seeing, now that they knew all about each other. Were they imagining how it was done? How the other guy looked when he was fucking Lisa? Or were they thinking about the here and now, and which one would get a go at her first?

Lisa climbed onto the bed. She settled on her knees, her ass up in the air, her panties already wet. She looked over her shoulder. 'You boys work it out for yourselves, I don't care which one goes first, but I want a cock up one of my holes, and I want it right now.'

She closed her eyes, lowered her head onto her arms, and waited.

There was rustling behind her, the sound of clothes

coming off. There were low murmurs of discussion. The bed shifted with weight, and then a cool hand touched her hip. A hot, hard dick poked against her panties, and fingers pulled them aside. With one smooth thrust, that cock went all the way in. She knew immediately which one it was, and swayed back against Ron as he started to fuck her.

The bed shifted again. She didn't open her eyes, but she felt the heat of another cock pressing against her cheek, imploring her to turn her head and invite it inside. She opened her mouth and Adam slid his dick into it, smooth and easy, just like the hundreds of times she had done it before. This time he felt different, tasted different, smelled different even, and she knew it was because of the dick ramming her from behind, pushing her onto Adam with every thrust.

She opened her eyes to see Adam looking down at her, his eyes glazed with a pleasure she hadn't seen before, no matter how many times they had fucked. She watched his face as she sucked him, turning her head a bit to see him better. A shadow fell across the wall behind him, the shadow of John as he moved to the other side of the bed. She blindly reached out a hand and John took it in his own, guided it down a little, and put it on her third dick of the night.

She stroked. She sucked. She fucked. She went at all three men until the rhythm was the same, until they were all swaying to the same motion. Just when she was beginning to think it wouldn't happen for her, that she would teeter on the edge of an orgasm for the rest of her life, one of them – probably John, he of the nimble fingers – reached underneath her and touched her clit. She came like a rocket, her whole body on overdrive. She came so hard she screamed around Adam's dick. She clenched John hard, not realising what her fingers were doing, and was dimly aware of his groan. Ron didn't stop moving but instead picked up the pace, fucking her right through the orgasm until he reached one of his own.

The whole room seemed to hold its breath as Ron came, his cock buried inside her, his hands hard on her hips. He hollered and she sighed and the other two men were silent, listening and watching. When Ron pulled out, Adam yanked his cock free of her mouth and moved to the back of the bed. With one thrust he sank hard into where Ron had just been. The sound of fucking filled the room as Lisa turned her head and took John's dick into her mouth. His hands tangled in her hair.

She took all of them that way, servicing them first with her mouth or her hand, then bracing herself on sore knees while they took turns running their dicks into her pussy. When it was John's turn, he fucked through what the other two men had left, and used it to ease the way when he slid his dick up her ass. The other two watched, mesmerised, until Lisa demanded one of them in her mouth.

The most sordid names went through her head, and she came when Adam bent low to her ear and whispered them to her. 'You're a cock-sucking slut,' he said. 'Only a fucking whore would have three men at once. Isn't that right? If you had the time to fuck more of us, it would have been four. Or five. Or one for every day of the fucking week. Isn't that right?'

'Yes,' she moaned. 'Fuck, yes.'

John rammed her, an exclamation point on the end of a sentence.

It didn't last as long as she wanted. They had wives, after all. They had a few hours to spare for her, never anything more. Lisa wanted a whole night, a finale with all of them coming at once, the filling of all her holes. She settled for sucking them all off one last time, on her knees on the living room floor, her goodbye present. John was the first to leave, his face ashamed, unable to look in her direction. Ron was next, the one who kissed her so tenderly before he turned to walk out the door. Adam was the last, the one who held her head while he fucked her mouth, the one who shoved his whole dick into her throat. When he came, he shouted, his hands clenching hard in her hair.

Then he lifted her into his arms and took her back to the bedroom, where he tucked her into the soiled bed. 'Are you OK?' he asked as he zipped up his pants.

She nodded, utterly exhausted. Had she really hoped for a whole night?

'Sleep,' he murmured as he kissed her cheek. 'I'll check on you tomorrow.'

'I'm through with married men,' she said.

'I'll check on you.'

She was asleep before the door locked behind him.

'So, how are you, really?'

Adam was watching her through dark sunglasses. They sat at an outdoor café, where anybody could see them and somebody might recognise them. They weren't fucking any more, so they didn't give a damn. They had sandwiches for lunch and even shared a milkshake, sipping through twin straws. Small talk had been easy to come by, and they had gone through an hour's time without looking at a watch.

She sighed and reached for a pack of cigarettes. Her new habit. It kept her from eating while she watched too much television.

'Bloody bored,' she admitted.

It had been a month since the rendezvous with her three men. She hadn't heard from John, not a single word, and she wasn't surprised. She had heard from Ron once, by delivery of a bouquet of flowers and a sweet card, saying he would miss her. It made her smile. She had tucked it into a desk drawer and still looked at it from time to time.

Adam had called on her once a week, but never acted as more than a friend. He was trying to make things easy on her, to help her keep her resolution, but she couldn't take one look at him without the fire starting up between her thighs.

Some things would simply never change, she had decided.

'You'll find someone soon,' he encouraged her. 'You'll settle down. You're the kind of woman who always gets what she wants. Some lucky guy isn't going to know what hit him when Hurricane Lisa comes crashing into his life.'

She smiled. Only Adam could go from a fuck to a friend with such seamless ease.

He took the cigarette from her fingers, sucked a long drag, and kissed her on the cheek. 'See you soon.'

She finished the cigarette as he climbed on his bike and drove away. She opened her purse, pulled out her phone and looked at the screen. No calls. She nodded at the waiter as he refilled her water glass, then lit up another stick, watching the people pass by.

'Hello,' the voice said, and she turned to see a tall, handsome man standing behind her. Blue eyes. Impossibly blond hair, probably kept that way by a very expensive salon. Tailored suit, cut just right across the breast, the kind of detail that made the difference between a few hundred and a few grand. His tie was a bit loose, a bit too casual to be unplanned. He wore a gold wedding band.

Lisa looked at it for a long moment. She took her time studying the rest of him. She put one high-heeled shoe on the chair opposite her, pushed it away from the table and pointed to it with her cigarette. The man sat down as Lisa thought about all her promises to herself, all the bravado with which she had conducted the last lonely month, and suddenly she wondered why the fuck she had bothered.

'I'm Lisa,' she said.

Gwen Masters is the author of the Black Lace novel *One Breath at a Time*. Her short fiction appears in numerous Black Lace anthologies.

Torment So Refined
ADR Forte

He's busy, but she visits him at work on his birthday. It's a Tuesday.

The petite secretary with the very stylish, carefully messy haircut and the very high heels ushers her into the conference room, smiles, backs out and closes the door.

He stands up on the far side of the room, a frown drawing familiar lines out on his brow.

'Is everything OK?'

'Everything's fine, Bill.'

She feels the space between them. It's as if some invisible substance fills it, like styrofoam peanuts that shift and move and sometimes throw her off balance, but always keep them both neatly spaced, each at their own safe distance.

Sometimes it simply keeps her immobile: on mornings when she wakes up to his alarm but lies with her nose in the pillow, listening to the shower run, thinking about the hot water streaming down his body. Just thinking, not moving. Or when he passes her on his way through the kitchen and she merely nods over her coffee, and he nods back.

Nothing to complain about, nothing hurt, no bad behaviour. Only a whole lot of shifting, opaque Nothing.

It's been like that a long time. She's lost track of just *how* long, but that's why she knows something has to change. Something has to shift for good. Even if it means . . . well she's not thinking about what it means. Not right now.

She moves across the room with a purpose.

Two months ago she decided. Two months ago on a very hot afternoon when the house sat still and empty, so quiet she could hear the creak of wooden beams settling, the drone of a leaf blower far down the street. She'd been cleaning out the attic, dressed in some old cotton shirt and a stretched-out pair of jeans. As she pushed straggling hair from her face and shook the sweat-sticky front of the shirt with her other hand, she glanced down.

The faded blue flowers on the worn fabric jogged her memory.

She remembered the shirt brand new, tighter before the cotton went soft with washing. He'd unlaced the front and played with her tits until she went down and lay back, laughing. In the mud, because mud was no deterrent.

That was when she made up her mind to find her way back to the place when mud didn't matter, because her tits still looked just as they had then. Only for some reason it seemed easier now to not bother about things like shirts. And that was unacceptable. The heat that had soaked into her blood and beat with her pulse under her skin told her so.

But retracing steps through time is harder than it sounds. Sometimes you just have to find new ways to get there.

She comes to stand right before him and he takes a half step back, almost running into the beige wall with the lime-green stripe behind him. Who the hell picks colours like these? If she had to spend every day with walls like these to stare at, she'd lose her mind. They're worse than yellow wallpaper.

She looks at the frown lines above those dark dark-blue eyes and dark charcoal-pencil eyebrows and gets an inkling of understanding. Of sympathy, perhaps. But she isn't here to think; she's here to act.

'I have a present for you,' she says.

He stares at her. The frown changes to surprise, to confusion, as she puts one finger with one long, painted fingernail against his blue and red tie. Pushes him up against the wall with no effort, with barely a quantum disturbance of atoms, with barely a touch at all.

He says her name – just a breath of air, not really a word. With some tiny part of him it might be a protest, because she knows he would feel the need to at least try and resist.

'Yes?' She purrs it, proud of how well she *can* purr a word. Surprising herself really with just how good she is at it. She wants to laugh at that, wants to giggle madly because her head is light and giddy.

Probably that glass of wine while she put on her make-up didn't help, but, God, it tasted better than any glass she'd ever had before. The tartness in her mouth, the sweet, berry smell of the lip-gloss. The taste and the scent still linger, enticing her down this path, helping her find her next step because really . . . she doesn't *know* what she's doing.

She finds her way by touch, like a blind woman. His belt buckle first, then his zipper. She looks down to find her hands being restrained, but she doesn't relinquish her hold on the zip. Between finger and thumb she grips it tightly, refusing to surrender. Without words they struggle for supremacy, and what she ought to do is give in. She's in the wrong, by any standards of prudence or decency.

She fights him.

And finally his hands slip from her wrists. The sound of the zipper, pulled down in one swift movement is loud in this room. The walls, besides their garishness, offer little in the way of soundproofing, but that isn't her problem.

It's not so much surrender – him letting her hands go – as his challenge to her, to continue with this if she dares. A smile curves her glossy lips because of what she knows, what's in her head that he doesn't guess and wouldn't even begin to imagine.

Because she *does* dare.

It amazed her how little she knew of his tastes. Or her own.

She had to start somewhere and where better than what he liked: the collection of .avi's hoarded discreetly in a nondescript folder. Not so hard to find, but not so easy to stumble across either. She didn't ask herself how she knew what to look for. Or why she'd looked at the rocking, thrusting bodies and limbs and parts brazenly displayed across the screen without so much as a shiver, her lack of amazement far more disturbing than the porn.

Until she kept clicking. Finding the things she hadn't ever dreamed of, or thought he would save. Things painful and dangerous, appalling to the decent mind. Things that made her blush and shiver, but not with shame.

She wondered if . . . if she'd known of this years before . . . ? But she didn't think so. The girl in the blue-flowered shirt had different ideas about what Liberty meant, stricter rules for what she could accept in her freedom. That girl didn't know those same rules could end up binding more tightly than any leather.

Or that maybe, just maybe, freedom could mean seeking whatever bonds you wanted, whenever you wanted, however you wanted.

She doesn't pull his pants down. Besides being practical in case, God forbid, they get interrupted, it feels more forbidden. It's erotic to kneel in front of him, both of them fully dressed except for his naked hard-on in full view of anyone walking through that door. He shakes his head and she notices the frown lines are gone, replaced by the disbelieving, half-daring smile.

What's truly priceless is the shock on his face when she swirls her tongue around his erection. He starts, seriousness in its turn usurping his smile. She's been dreaming of this moment for weeks now.

No. For longer. She's been dreaming of it for years without knowing. Without understanding the longing. Not just for the taste and the smell of him, male and sharp – how can she have forgotten his taste? – but for *this*. The terrible, claustrophobic office with its leering walls under the fluorescent light, for the prickle of fear at the base of her spine, the fear she swallows with each drop of saliva.

Sucking him in little by little, she watches him writhe against the wall as if he would become part of it, a human figure trapped in plaster and paint. Except for the part of him surrounded by her warm, wet mouth. The part of him so driven with desire he can't stop, can't pull away, even if he wanted to. She doesn't think he wants to.

Daring a glance upwards she meets his gaze and her heart skips an extra beat in its already-frantic rhythm. Intense, like it used to be, like he used to watch her once. She sees his fear that they'll be caught, that his reputation will be ruined. But underneath it, she sees that he doesn't give a damn.

All this in the flash of one single look, while his cock presses against the back of her throat and she's forced to swallow hard. He takes a sharp breath, closes his eyes and presses his head back against the wall. She feels the space between her legs tighten with longing, responding to his pleasure as she sucks him hard and fast. His fist closes on the hair at the crown of her head. Saliva runs sticky down her chin as he pulls her hair and pants silently, desperately. As his come fills her throat and, in the sudden silence, she realises that she's done this. Really done this.

The carpet scratching her knees, the tang of his come in her mouth, it's real. Not just another fantasy about what-if?

'Jesus,' he breathes.

He smoothes her hair and she wipes her chin with the back of her hand. Moving in slow motion in her mind. Watching him button his pants, rising to her feet, it feels like time itself has slowed down. Like she's made it pause in its tracks and rethink things.

He stares at her, framed by the beige paint and the pale-blue stripes of his shirt – nondescript colours, colours that cloy and trap and negate. But the blue of his eyes is alive and bright. The bitten red of his lips is shameless rebellion.

Long and slow, so he tastes himself in her mouth, she kisses him goodbye. And he grabs her ass. His hands thrust under her skirt, dislodging her panties so that his fingers rub her bare buttocks while his mouth and his tongue press hot against hers. He only lets her go when she's gasping for air, when her cheeks are flushed and her nipples hard.

'Thanks,' he says. He runs one finger along her cheek and lets her go. 'I'll see you tonight.'

She nods, because her heartbeat hasn't slowed yet, because of the look in his eyes. She smoothes her skirt and smiles at him, flips her hair back over her shoulders.

He catches the end of one strand before she can brush it back and twirls it around the tip of his finger, lets it go to lie against the lapel of her jacket. Then he smiles. She hasn't seen that smile in ... in ...

She realises she's never seen quite *that* smile before.

She fell for his voice long before she ever even saw his smile. He used to pick up a guitar and play on the spur of the moment.

He didn't need a jam session or even an audience; he'd play and sing just for the hell of it. Just for the love of it.

He'd smile when he saw her come to sit nearby and listen. Not too close, far enough to give him his space, but near enough she could hear every breath he took between lines. She could close her eyes. She didn't have to look at him to know the way his fingers moved over the strings or the way he sat, his lanky frame relaxed, long legs stretched out on the ground before him.

He'd been so free, so beautiful with nothing but grass and stars and night behind him. He didn't have walls, no concept of them. Just that sweet voice and his blue eyes. That was all she'd wanted from him, all she'd ever wanted from him: daydreams and beauty.

Well, that and his body.

As she leaves the room behind her, walking through carpeted hallways filled with busy, industrious, well-behaved people, she can still feel the pressure of his fingers on her ass. She runs her tongue over her lower lip where she can still taste the bruise of their last kiss.

She glances up to see a young man facing her. He's coming in the doors, she's going out, and he's seen her licking her lips. He stares, and she stares right back as she brushes past him. Even though her face is on fire.

She grins as she walks down broad concrete steps to the sidewalk, leaving the overbearing, disapproving stuffy hulk of the building behind her. Thinking of the tiny little rip she's made in its proper façade, her own small victory over those greedy, soulless walls.

She hasn't felt this almighty. Ever.

Hours she'd spent, entire afternoons, looking through the catalogues of online stores, itching to buy. But she didn't know how to use any of those kinds of 'toys'. They weren't vibrators and dildos, comprehensible and normal and safe.

For that matter, how the hell did one learn to use things designed to cause pain? How did one use them to create pleasure?

She hadn't bought any, only daydreamed. Replaying movies in her imagination while she sat in rush-hour traffic or stood in the shower. Adding to them, changing them, building the frenzy in her mind until she was desperate with need.

Fantasising with all the obsession of a teenager in the grip of a crush, willing it to come true. Willing it to happen so that her body could finally experience what her brain failed to conjure, because try as she would, as she punished her clit while she drove her body to orgasm, disappointment lingered afterwards.

Because she needed him.

Naked, she stands before the open closet, pondering her clothing and swallowing regret. She could have bought a leather miniskirt, or at least the leather thong panties. Could have, should have. It doesn't help now, but neither does she want to meet him in the ubiquitous jeans and sweater, like always.

Not after today.

A door bangs somewhere downstairs, echoing faintly, and a chill runs over her skin. She needs to make a decision *now*. She knows he's going to come up to the bedroom once he realises she's not in the kitchen or the den or in her office. He'll come to find her because that was the promise in his eyes this afternoon.

That's what she's wanted all along. She doesn't move to find anything to wear.

*   *   *

The bathroom door opens. Cold air rushes in, turning each lingering droplet of water on her arms and her legs and her back to ice. His shoes click across the floor and she catches a whiff of cologne and cold. She tightens her stomach, each and every nerve in her bare ass and thighs suddenly awake and alert.

Heat from his body reaches her. He's standing right behind her, so close the static from his clothes tickles gently at the hair on her arms. She breathes out, half turning her head to the side. Something clinks, and she turns all the way around.

The dark sharp lines of his jacket outline his shoulders, his arms like a shadow shape from a paper cutout. Light catches the object in his hands and she looks down. Her heart starts racing again.

'Where . . . ?' She lets the question hang, unfinished, but he answers.

'After work.' He smiles.

She looks up. 'What . . . ?'

He might be telling her about the drive home, or what he did at work, or how the stock market fared today. His tone is non-committal, the pastel-paper tone he uses every day.

'I want to watch us fuck. Right here.' He tilts his head over his shoulder at the vanity. 'In front of the mirror. And I want you handcuffed.'

She can't find an answer, so she finds a question instead.

'And why?'

Inane, she thinks as soon as she's said it, but he grins. He dangles the handcuffs from one finger and tilts his head to look at her slantways.

'After that little stunt you pulled today, you need to be tied up and fucked.' He shakes his head. 'Such an incredibly dirty, shameless little slut.'

She throws her head back and she laughs. She laughs like

she hasn't for a long time, all the way down to her belly. A real, full laugh. And she doesn't worry about how, once upon a time, if he'd said those words to her, she'd have been speechless with anger and disgust. That's not the woman she is now, not the woman she's been, deep down, for a very long time now.

He slides one arm around her waist and pulls her close to him. Her nipples brush his clothing and she feels her clit thrill with expectation. Metal dangles cold against her ass as he puts his other arm around her hips. Nose to nose, they stumble for balance on the tiles while he jimmies the handcuffs into place.

She thinks about taking his pants down today, anticipating the pleasure in his eyes, knowing what she planned to do. She wonders what he's thinking now, what lies behind the brightness of his eyes, and the playful, distracted smile as he clicks the cuffs tight enough that she can't slip her hands free.

Curious, she tests her bonds anyway, trying to wriggle first one hand, then the other out of their shiny new metal prisons. The cuffs hold tight, slowly warming up with the heat of her body, still not warm enough that little shivers don't pass through her every time they brush against her ass.

'You're not getting away,' he says.

She tosses her head at him.

'I'm not worried about that. I was making sure *you* knew what you were doing.'

She puts as much disdain as she can into the words and she's rewarded with a flush of red across his cheeks. Jerking her arm, he turns her and delivers a single, stinging slap to her backside. Her eyes water and her nose tingles. She sniffs, looks back over her shoulder at him.

'Is that the best you can do?'

He gives her a look that would melt iron if it could and

proceeds to slap her ass again. Several times, in rapid succession. When he stops, the insides of her thighs are wet and tingles of vibration still thrum between her legs, making her clit pulse with need. She's breathless. She cannot think.

'Mm. Better. Slightly,' she says between breaths.

He makes a sound somewhere between a growl and a moan, and his hand thrusts between her legs. His watch scrapes her sore ass cheek and she gasps, rocks her hips backwards into his touch – into his fingers rolling and pinching her clit. He knows how to touch her. He always has.

The first time, she claimed him without a second thought, knowing she wanted him, dragging him through a curtain of coloured glass beads that tangled in her hair. He'd tried to help her untangle them, but fine strands had caught and pulled, and she'd vented a few choice cuss words. He'd laughed.

Then he'd stood still, one hand on the curve of her hip, warmth radiating from his touch through her jeans into her skin.

'What?' she'd asked, still pulling at a stubborn hair strand wrapped around an equally stubborn strand of curtain.

'You. Like that.'

'Like how?'

She'd looked up at him, at the play of light from the room behind her filtered through the swaying curtain, a dancing kaleidoscope of colour across his face, softening the sharp masculine angles. Just like the fall of his hair over his shoulders promised softness, at odds with the set of his mouth, the narrow line of his lips. She wanted him because he was a contradiction, unpredictable, fuel to her own restlessness.

They'd kissed, with the strands of swinging beads tinkling around them, gently striking them on face, hands, head, ass. Caught in that shifting, magical wall between rooms, he'd lifted her shirt and caressed her nipples, tweaked them to perfect points, made her squirm against him with lust. He'd taken off her shirt, pressed her against the narrow strip of concrete doorway and teased her bare flesh with his mouth.

Kissed his way down her naked torso to her hips, taken off her jeans and murmured approval when he found her naked underneath them. His fingers had been relentless, teasing her slippery clit between catlike strokes of his tongue while the beads of the curtain slid across her naked writhing body, caught in his hair and hung in shimmering trembling loops as his head moved between her legs.

It had been magic that made her come and come again. He'd been tireless, merciless, and, God, oh so good.

Without walls. With only light and colour surrounding them. Sparkles in her vision and in her head when she came.

Why oh why had they ever started to behave so depressingly well to each other?

Not now. Now there's nothing decent or nondescript at all in the bright burning red cheeks of her ass that she can't help peeking at as he wrangles her over to the vanity. She stares at herself and blushes. He cups her shoulders and bends to kiss her neck under the damp tangle of her hair. He's solid behind her. Tall and dark and handsome, she thinks. Ever more so with each piece of clothing he sheds.

Dark hair curling on his tanned chest, on his arms as his hands caress her arms. He murmurs about her softness, how much he's been thinking about her hot little mouth all day. His hard-on presses between her aching thighs.

'Hmm? So what are you gonna do about it?' She purrs it, not meaning to this time, but it seems it's starting to come naturally now. This way of talking to each other, by turns insolent and indecent and fearless.

She stretches her fingers out blind and feels the taut muscles of his stomach, the curls of his hair. The soft tip of his cock brushes her fingertips, wet from rubbing against her slit, sticky on her fingers. His breath is hot on her neck, and for a moment she thinks he's forgotten her question, too distracted by her touch, but he hasn't. He closes his eyes for a heartbeat, then opens them and looks at her in the mirror. The room behind them fades and blurs; she sees only their faces side by side.

'First, I'm going to silence that mouth.' He moves out of her vision and she blinks. 'It's only good for one thing.'

She takes an expectant, satisfied breath as he brings the tie over her shoulder, takes it in both hands and gags her with red and blue-patterned imported silk. He reaches past her, towards the basket of her paraphernalia: clips and combs and *hairbrushes*, and her stomach trembles, knowing what comes next. But he picks up a round hairbrush, the big one she uses to blow-dry her hair, and she frowns.

She looks up and he meets her reflected gaze. He gives her a wicked promising smile that she recognises now: the smile he gave her when she left his office. Now she *can't* breathe.

She sucks her stomach in as tight as it can go in the instant before the bristles touch her nipple, but it doesn't help. She moans and twists, but there's nowhere to twist away, not when he stands behind her. He draws the brush down so, so slowly and she feels every prick, every pull of every last bristle against the soft flesh of her breast, the sensitive peak of her nipple. Like a magician with a coin, he rolls the brush's handle between deft fingers, down over the swell of her breast, up to pull at her nipple for an excruciating instant before he moves it away. She gasps around the gag. It's already wet from where she's been biting it in exquisite torment.

He moves the brush to her other breast, short light strokes this time that send flashes of heat racing to her clit and her cunt. She tosses her head back and forth, frustrated that she can't curse him or stop him, that all she can do is endure the unbearable: the teasing, maddening prickle of the brush, the burn as her skin begins to bruise.

Sensation fills her clit and overflows, unsated. She wants to scream, kick, tear, anything for release. Anything to stop this delicate agony. She would beg him if she could. She does beg, with her eyes and her body, desperately pressing her ass into his cock. Fumbling to touch him and draw him to her dripping slit, but he evades her. He smiles that wicked smile and lets the brush rest for a blissful instant. Just long enough for him to reach around with his free hand, slide his fingers between her legs.

He fingers the entrance to her cunt, spreads the wet folds to expose her clit and stroke it with one skilful finger. She stands like a statue, muscles taut, hovering on the edge of release he doesn't give her. Laughing, he brings his fingers to his lips, licks them clean, and she cries out in frustration.

She's never imagined him capable of such cruelty.

He rolls the hairbrush down her belly, across the inner folds of her thighs. Over her arms, her chest, pulling back to trace the shape of shoulder blades, her back, her waist. From knees to neck she is tickling, fiery arousal. He leans her forwards, pressing her down on the counter, and the cool granite soothes her aching tits for another sweet moment of respite before he takes the brush to her sore ass, to the backs of her thighs and her knees. She whimpers and arches her ass upwards: submissive, sensual, pleading for release.

She's never imagined torture could be this refined.

Trembling, she doesn't dare move as he lays the brush on the floor with a soft click. His hands part her legs, and she shuffles her feet wider, trying to close her mind to all expectation, but her body is unrelenting, demanding satisfaction. She quivers at the feel of his lips, at the tip of his tongue flicking back and forth over just the right place. Over the very centre of her desire, the exact square millimetre of her clit where she needs it, where it sends her lurching forwards, her head hitting the mirror as she comes, but she doesn't, cannot care.

She squeezes her eyes shut, wringing every ounce of pleasure, every last spasm from the flood of her release. He doesn't stop licking and another orgasm makes her lightheaded, makes her gag and arch and sob. But she comes, God yes, she comes.

In the stillness while she listens to the harsh sound of her own breathing, he kisses the sensitive inner curves of her ass.

'I still haven't fucked you,' he reminds her, and she takes a deep breath. She twists her head to look daggers at him, daring him to do it now. In case he doesn't understand, she spreads her legs just a little more, as far as they can go without her losing her balance, offering herself to him and goading him on.

He makes a low sound in his throat, an aggressive, territorial sound, before he stands again and puts one hand on the small of her back. She turns her head and braces her chin on the counter, ready and waiting. He doesn't hurry and she savours it, every thrust in and out until he's cock-deep in her. Hips to her ass, grinding slowly inside her, making her pussy cream. He's too damn good at this. Too goddamned fucking good.

Then pain jolts her out of hazy lust. He pulls her upright by her hair and her back screams protest as she scrambles to keep her balance. He pulls her against his chest, one steadying hand across her hips. The other hand cups her breasts, strokes her skin that's painfully tender to the touch. Keeping her aroused, keeping her nipples erect, his cock moves in her cunt. And he watches her in the mirror.

The half-open closet door behind them catches their reflection, throws back the sight of his ass cheeks as he fucks her. She sees every thrust as she feels it. Sees the endless reflections of their bodies moving together, caught between the mirrors. Fucking into infinity.

No. This isn't *just* a fuck. It's a goddamned porno.

She closes her eyes for a second and he pinches a nipple as punishment.

'Keep watching us, gorgeous.'

With a squeak she looks back, and he lifts his hand to cup her chin while he kisses her cheek, nibbles the tip of her ear. Disobeying him, she turns her head and her mouth brushes his. It's like a spark to gasoline.

His slow, grinding rhythm changes, his fingers tighten on her jaw. He drags the soaked gag down, over her lower lip. His mouth clamps over hers and they struggle to breathe, to kiss while *he* fucks *her* hard and fast. Repayment for this morning. She can't think about anything but his kiss and his cock. That's all that exists.

The first time, she remembered the bead curtain and the light. Now there's nothing but hands and tongues, his breath hot on her face, skin and heat and motion. And pleasure. Nothing but them.

They lie in bed, forehead to forehead, their bodies not touching, but the space between them might as well not exist. He laces his fingers over hers on the bed between them, and she longs to hear his voice, but she doesn't want to interrupt this picture-perfect stillness.

'What is it?' he asks.

'What's what?'

'You're fidgety. I can feel it.'

She hasn't moved, but he's right of course. She looks at him and smiles.

'I was thinking I miss hearing you sing.'

He laughs. 'Sing? I haven't . . .'

'You haven't sung in years. I know.'

He looks at her.

'It's like riding a bike,' she says.

He thinks about that for a minute, then concedes half a smile. 'Maybe.' He goes on, 'Do you know what I was thinking about?'

'What?' she asks.

'I was thinking I can't wait for the weekend.' His gaze travels down her body and then back to her face. He lets go of her hand and strokes a finger along her lower lip. She's going to have to wear dark lipstick tomorrow to cover the bruising.

'When we have *time*,' he adds.

She shivers. 'Tomorrow's only Wednesday.'

'I know. But we can practise until then.'

She smiles. It's going to be a hell of a week.

The short fiction of ADR Forte appears in numerous Black Lace anthologies.

The Student
Alegra Verde

Leonard looked like money, like a slightly updated version of what his father must look like on a day off. Polo shirt, expensive khakis and deck shoes with no socks. Sometimes he wore a sports coat over the polo, but his thick dark hair always looked casual. It was slightly tousled, just short of falling over his left eye, and always a breath away from touching his collar, like magic.

I was taking Small Group Interaction, a class at the midtown campus. When he strolled in he seemed so confident, I thought he was the instructor. When he sat in the back, I figured he was a business major. I'm a film major and this class is required, but it attracts business and finance majors. It's all about observing patterns of behaviour, understanding group dynamics, learning when to claim dominance and when to listen. Good skills when you have to co-ordinate a film crew, and apparently useful in the boardroom too.

Leonard always ended up in my circle when we broke into small groups. Unless he was asked a direct question, he'd just sit there and watch. Even though he was cute with all that dark hair and those eyes, he was weird and made me uncomfortable. Early on, I'd catch him staring at my breasts or my crotch, his eyelids heavy and his lips pressed together. It bothered me so much that I stopped wearing the low-waist jeans and midriff T-shirts I favoured. On class days, I began wearing button-down blouses and loose-fitting pants or skirts. I needed this class and wasn't going to let some pervert intimidate me into dropping it.

About three weeks into class, Leonard caught up with me as I headed back to the high rise that is designated graduate student housing. I shared a studio there with a girlfriend. He was charming, even funny, as he made clever observations about our fellow students. We stopped at Starbucks on campus. I figured it was a public place and he was paying. I had a brownie and a cappuccino. He had a regular coffee, cream, no sugar.

We found a seat and he sipped his coffee in silence, reminding me of how he'd been acting in class. I decided to be straight with him.

'So Leonard,' I said pinching off a piece of brownie and popping it into my mouth, 'why are you always staring at me in class?'

'I like the way you look,' he said and took another sip.

'Thanks, but sometimes it makes me uncomfortable.'

He sat up straighter and looked a little contrite. 'I'm sorry.' He put his cup down and away. 'It's that I like girls with a little flesh. You look so warm, so inviting.'

'Thanks, I think,' I muttered. I was a little insulted. I have a bit extra on my bottom, maybe on my hips, but I am only a C cup and certainly not fat.

'No.' He shook his head, smiling. His whole face changed, lightened. 'You look great. You remind me of the way women looked before somebody decided that skeletal was in. You look . . . welcoming.'

I laughed. 'Thank you.' He gave me another one of those smiles. Then he blew it.

'I would like to have sex with you.'

My mouth fell open. I couldn't help it.

'I would make it worth your while.' *No, he didn't.* He reached for my hand and I jerked it away before pushing away from the table.

'Please sit down,' he whispered earnestly. 'I don't mean to offend you.'

'Well, you have,' I said, turning to leave.

He was up behind me, dogging my steps as I pushed through the scattering of customers and out of the café.

'I know you need the money, Leyda.'

I kept going, but he fell in step beside me. I quickened my pace. He simply adjusted his stride.

'You've got student loans, tuition payments, credit cards, and the part-time job at the library barely keeps you in Ramen.'

I stopped abruptly, but his momentum kept him going a few more paces.

'And how do you know this?'

'I like you. I wanted to know more about you.'

'So you investigate my financial status? How romantic!'

'I needed to know if you would be amenable to an arrangement.'

'Arrangement.' I was walking again, fast.

He nodded.

'I'm not a whore.'

'I know,' he said almost apologetically, like he knew I'd be upset by his next words. 'You've only had one boyfriend since you enrolled. He was your high school sweetheart. You broke up with him six months ago because he got a mutual friend of yours pregnant.'

I was still again. *No, he didn't.* He stood looking down at me, waiting. I just shook my head at him and started walking again, fast. I needed to get to my room, away from this nut. He grabbed my arm then, and pulled me up short. I stumbled, and he caught me, but his hand only tightened on my arm.

'I know it sounds intrusive, but I had to know. I needed to

be safe. I've been thinking about this, about you. I mean I can't seem to think about anything else since I saw you in the library. If you'll just give me a week, I think I can get it out of my system.'

I turned away, but he held on.

'Leyda?' It was a groan.

I looked down at the hand that gripped my arm. He let go. I continued on.

'No one has to know.' He was walking beside me, his long legs easily keeping up with my short quick steps.

'One week,' he said. 'Ten thousand dollars.'

My steps faltered, but I kept moving.

He noticed. 'You wouldn't have to do anything you didn't want to do. I would protect you. We would be tested.'

I kept walking.

'I'll give you half the money up front.'

I am not a mercenary person, but when you don't need to set your alarm clock because bill collectors can be counted on to wake you up, and your minimum wage, part-time job doesn't cover the finance charges on your credit cards, you start to consider every option, even the obscene one.

We were standing in front of the newly built graduate dorm.

'I need to think,' I said to Leonard as I tried to push through the heavy door at the front entrance.

He caught my arm, halting my progress. Tall and thin, Leonard was a lot stronger than he looked.

'I'll see you in class Wednesday?' he asked.

'Yeah, I'll see you in class.'

He nodded and then he let me go.

The following Wednesday, Leonard seemed almost docile. He sat a few seats over from me and listened attentively to the instructor's lecture on body language. He even took notes and

I didn't catch him looking at me once. I let him leave class first, taking my time as I gathered my books and pulled the long strap of my purse diagonally across my shoulder and chest. I laughed and talked to a few of the other students as we milled out of the classroom. He wasn't waiting in the hall as I'd expected. Strangely, I was a little disappointed and wondered if he'd changed his mind. *La vida es extraño*, I thought as I headed out into the sunshine.

'Leyda?' It was the Leonard of last week.

'What would I have to do?' I asked.

He smiled as he took my two books and added them to his.

'You would have to be exclusively mine, and do whatever I tell you to do.'

'Nothing kinky.' I watched his eyes.

They didn't shift around, just smiled down at me as he said, 'I'm not into anything kinky.'

I nodded. 'When do you want to begin?'

'You've got work tonight. Let's have a celebratory lunch and we'll begin tomorrow.'

He drove a vintage Mustang, red, drop top and in mint condition. It made me smile. It was so like him, and so not. I mean the throwback part I could get, but it was red and fun. I almost expected him to drive a luxury sedan, a daddy's car. He held the door open and I slid in.

After starting the car, he slipped a CD into the player, an obvious deviation from the otherwise strict restoration. The compelling rhythms of Middle Eastern drums and guitars filled the air. Then came the husky voice of a woman. 'I put a spell on you,' she sang. I laughed.

'Who is that?' I was intrigued. I had expected something more staid, not this Screaming Jay Hawkins à la Ofra Haza.

'Do you like it?' he asked, looking worried.

'Very much,' I nodded.

'Natacha Atlas.' He grinned over at me, a totally different Leonard, a boy really, playful and a little subversive.

Top down, we sped up 94. Leonard was smiling, looking happier than I'd ever seen him. He didn't even resemble that melancholy guy who stared at me during class.

We ate mussels and drank beer at the Cadieux Café, a time- and weather-beaten Belgian pub on the far east side. He was polite, asking about my family, even though I sensed that he knew everything I was telling him. He was too ready with a nod or a question in just the right place. When I told him that my dad had worked in the same neighbourhood garage for the last twenty years, he said that such loyalty was 'commend-able'. And he laughed when I called mami a *churchwife* who split her time between catering to the family, which included my teenaged sister, and organising fundraisers for the parish.

When I asked about his family, he was less forthcoming.

'My mom stays at home too,' he said.

'What does your father do?' I asked

'He's retired.' His laugh sounded forced. 'He plays a lot of golf.'

'Are you and he close?'

'I was a late child.'

'The youngest?'

'The only,' he answered.

'Oh.'

'But I have a cousin,' he added, his lips quirking up as though the thought wasn't a pleasant one.

'A cousin.' I laughed, and counted on my fingers. 'I've got twenty-five on my dad's side alone.'

'Prolific,' he said, exaggerating his surprise by widening his eyes.

'You might say that.' I grinned at him, sipping my beer.

'So how does this work?' I asked, having relaxed a little.

He was quiet again, sober.

'I'll pick you up at ten tomorrow and we'll begin.'

'But I have to work tomorrow night, six to ten.'

'Our arrangement won't interfere with your normal schedule. You can continue to go to work and class as you normally would. I don't want to disrupt your life. I just want to spend a little time with you.'

We finished our drinks and he dropped me off in front of the dorm, reminding me that he'd be waiting there at ten the next morning.

He was, and with the car still running.

He'd taken a suite at the St Regis, a classy older hotel done in the European style. Even so, I felt like a prostitute as he ushered me towards the elevator, his hand pressing the small of my back, firm and possessive. I couldn't look at him, and he said nothing.

The door opened into a good-sized sitting room, but the doors to the bedroom were open and a king-sized bed covered in rich burgundy seared my view. I turned my back on it, but he took my hand and led me through the doors.

There was a black garment bag draped over the bed. Without a word, his hands were at my waist and he was pulling my T-shirt over my head, slowly, as though he didn't want to startle me. His warm fingers were at my back, sliding underneath the catch. The bra fell, dipped, and he tossed it away. Slender fingers and heated palms slid hesitatingly, almost involuntarily, down the olive mounds of flesh, stroking, cupping, caressing. He leant down, tugged an elongated nipple between his lips. Sucking it into the moistness of his mouth, he licked at it, his tongue circling, savouring it as though the taste and texture were sublime.

I wasn't sure what to do with my hands so I stood there like a mannequin, arms out. His mouth was wet and hot as he pulled at the nipple. I could feel the draw down to the centre of my stomach. This man, this place, his mouth on my naked breasts made me dizzy. My hands clutched at his shoulders for support. I could feel the moisture gathering between my legs. With obvious reluctance he pulled his mouth away, undid the button and zipper of my jeans, slipped them over my hips, and reached down to pull them from beneath my feet.

Then he did the strangest thing. He left me standing there while he gathered my shirt, pants and bra, folded them with precision, and placed the neat stack of clothes on a nearby chest of drawers. It was as though he was taking time to gather himself.

I waited, unmoving.

He knelt at my feet, his hands first tugging at the straps of my thong. But then, as though compelled, they slid across my nether cheeks, warm and just a little rough, tugging and kneading. His nose and then the wet heat of his mouth penetrated the thin cloth, licking and nipping the sensitive skin with tongue and teeth. When his avid mouth moved lower and he nipped the swollen lips of my sex, I yelped like a puppy at the quick jolts of pain that caused the muscles of my channel to tighten in anticipation. My fingers found the thick silky tufts of his hair and I held on. His tongue lapped at the stinging place and the wetness between my legs grew. He slid his tongue into the crevice between my legs, teasing the sensitive skin as it darted in and out. I knew he could smell and taste the musk that gathered there. Sharp teeth gnawed the edge of the swollen flesh. My legs trembled. Pressing his face heavily against the plump mound of flesh, he captured the straps of the thong and slipped it down my legs. Thong in hand, he stood, folded it, and shoved it into his pants pocket. I would have laughed if I hadn't been so aroused.

He pulled his shirt over his head, undid the zipper and let his chinos fall to his feet. I would never have thought that Leonard was one to go commando, but there he was, no boxers, no briefs. Just a very tight rear end that looked even better when he bent to gather and fold his clothes. Leonard was slender, but well built, lean, and his broad chest was hard, muscled, as if he swam and lifted weights. When he turned back to me, my eyes were drawn to the wisps of dark hair that feathered his chest and wound down his belly in diminishing bits, renewing themselves with a flourish around his proudly jutting shaft. I wanted to touch it, but he didn't give me a chance. He took my hand and led me into the bathroom where he turned on the shower, tested it for warmth, and got in before holding his hand out to me.

I'd taken a shower earlier and had no interest in taking one now, but I figured it was Leonard's game so I'd just go along with it. Maybe he just liked it in the shower. I climbed in and he pulled me close, his hardness pressing against my buttocks, his lips pressed atop my head. After a few moments, he put me slightly away from him, reached behind me and retrieved a handful of hairpins from a shelf. Then, as though he was mami or *mi abuela* and I was ten, he began to put up my hair, pinning it high and secure.

OK, that was thoughtful, if somewhat strange, but again, this is his show. When he began to wash me, sudsing me up with a mesh sponge, I wanted to scream, 'When are we gonna fuck?' but I just stood there like a good little girl. He wielded the sponge with the reserve of a nurse, faltering only once. The sopping sponge made circles over my stomach before slipping just below to hover and wait for me to open my legs. But it was his fingers that slid through and along to work the suds over the quivering flesh. Slippery and wet and firm, they stroked and strummed the swollen tissue. His eyes were closed and his mouth open, but when I leant in hoping that the two wayward fingers would give me some relief, he pulled back and resumed his clinical task.

Turning me fully towards the spray of water, he rinsed me thoroughly before helping me from the shower and draping me in an oversized white towel. He slipped into a white terry robe, which had been conveniently hung on a peg behind the bathroom door.

'Come on. I'll get you dressed,' he said – the first words spoken since we'd entered the hotel.

Dressed! This was gonna be harder than I thought.

The garment bag held a nubby, Chanel-looking suit, waist-length jacket and straight skirt, and a set of pink lacy undies, bra and panties, no thong. After shedding his robe and dropping it onto a nearby stuffed chair, he knelt before me holding the panties out so that I could step into them. He tugged and patted them into place before standing to present me with the bra, the straps dangling from his fingers so that I could slip my arms into them easily.

Although he was fully erect, he performed the duty as impersonally as a saleswoman might. As he plumped and adjusted my breasts in the bra cups and reached behind me to fasten the catch, his very hard penis rubbed against my stomach, searing my already heated skin with every stroke. With effort, I held myself still, but I couldn't stop the hitch in my breath. I was not as schooled as he in this weird foreplay.

Silently, he helped me into the skirt, then the jacket, buttoning and adjusting it for fit as though he was a designer preparing a model for the runway. There were no hose but, after gently urging me to sit on the bed, he slipped a pair of matching pink heels onto my feet. A perfect fit and butter-soft. I crossed my legs feeling very much the lady and he smiled down at me, eyes and all, before moving to the closet and rapidly dressing himself in a black Hugo Boss that rolled onto his body like lotion. Dressed, he took my hand and we left the room. I didn't know what to think at this point.

Just as we stepped into the valet port, the red Mustang pulled up. He must have prearranged the time with the valet. Twenty minutes later, we pulled into the lot of an office building in Grosse Pointe and I turned to him, eyebrows raised.

'It's just the tests,' he said, not quite looking at me. 'Remember, I told you we'd both be tested.'

I nodded.

'He's a gynaecologist. Don't worry; I'll be there with you.'

I must have frowned because he added, 'He comes highly recommended.'

'I have my own doctor,' I said, not without anger.

'I know, but I want to be there,' he said, looking first at the steering wheel, then directly at me with a firmness, reminding me that I had agreed to this. 'It's what I want.'

I looked at him for a long time, trying to figure him out, trying to decide whether to continue this farce, trying to decide if it was safe, if Leonard was safe. He waited for me, patiently, so I nodded.

'As far as he's concerned, we're newly-weds, Mrs Loring.' He tilted his head, a question requiring further confirmation. I nodded.

The waiting room was stark, sparely furnished with touches of lavender, the circular seating arranged around a cluster of lush exotic flowers with thick glossy green leaves. A bossa nova played lightly in the background. Mr and Mrs Loring waited no more than five minutes before being ushered into a well-appointed examination room. Leonard must have taken care of all of the paperwork because the nurse asked no questions. She simply provided a cotton dressing gown and requested that Mrs Loring get completely undressed before pulling the door closed behind her.

He didn't help me undress this time. He held the dressing gown and watched as I shed each piece of clothing and hung it up on the peg behind the door. Having shed everything except the shoes, I stood there cold and naked, glaring at him. He looked unmoved; there was nothing in his eyes that linked him to this place and time. He handed me the gown and strode over to the window where he turned his back to me.

I shoved my arms into the gown and shed the shoes, thanking the gods that it was cloth and not paper, and could offer a modicum of warmth. By the time I had climbed onto the examination chair and pulled the sheet across my lap, there was a soft knock on the door, followed by a tall blond god. His brilliant smile boasted a set of straight white teeth and a dimple in his left cheek. I looked from him to Leonard who still had his back to me.

'Mr and Mrs Loring,' the god intoned, 'I'm Doctor Miller.' He held his hand out to Leonard, who offered a brief clasp, but no smile, before taking the seat nearest the examination chair. A tiny woman in lavender scrubs slipped through the door and hovered somewhere between the door and a white utility bin with drawers. Once she was in place, Doctor Miller turned his attention to me. Smiling, he shook my hand belatedly, but with enthusiasm.

'Your husband is eager to start a family and wants to make sure you're in top form little lady,' the god beamed at me.

I glared at Leonard as I scooted down and lifted my legs into the stirrups as instructed. The doctor sat on his stool and manoeuvred the examination chair to his best advantage. I grasped the sheet and pulled it more securely over my lap. The top of the god's golden head bobbed between my legs and the little nurse handed him a tray with a selection of specula. Thankfully, he selected the smallest.

Leonard looked on curiously, watching the head bob just above the white sheet. The speculum clamped into place briefly and I could hear the doctor humming something. *Vivaldi?* 'Looks good down here,' he was saying cheerily as cool rubber fingers sifted through the sparse hair and probed the lips and crevices of my sex. 'Just a little sample for the pap smear,' and there was a pinch. 'Might as well while I'm down here. Rather than waiting for old records.' Then the speculum was gone, and there was pressure on my anus as he shoved a long rubbery finger into the opening. It was sudden, and the shock caused me to bark in surprise and to lift my bottom off the table. The doctor let out a short laugh. 'It's always better if the patient doesn't know it's coming so they won't clinch the muscles,' he said by way of apology. Then he was up, pulling the gloves off and tossing them into a bin. But it wasn't over.

He stood over me drawing the gown down off my shoulders; his cool fingers pushed me back against the chair. The cold had squeezed my nipples into stiff kernels. They jutted out hard and brown as the tall god doctor pressed and squeezed the soft mounds of my breast. And Leonard, who had said nothing while I suffered the care of this veterinarian, had the audacity to glare at me.

'Young and healthy,' Doctor Miller said, his back to us, as he washed his hands in the nearby sink. 'Mrs Loring shouldn't have any problem conceiving. I've measured her for the diaphragm as you requested. You can have the blood drawn for the other tests before you leave. We'll do a complete work-up. Your results should be available tomorrow.'

Leonard nodded. 'We appreciate you taking us on such short notice.'

'Not a problem,' he said and he was gone, followed by the nurse.

'Diaphragm?' I asked, climbing off the table.

'I don't like condoms.'

'How do you know I'm not on the pill?'

'I know.' He stood there with his lips drawn in a straight line, looking through me.

'I'm not comfortable with this, Leonard. I think,' I began, but before I could finish, he was opening the door.

'I'll meet you in the waiting room. I must settle our account.'

He was gone, and I was standing in the middle of the cold examination room, my thighs smeared with a glutinous gel and my rear end poking out of a thin cotton hospital gown.

I'd worn a little plaid shirtwaist dress I'd found at a resale shop. It always made me feel like Grace Kelly with its snug bodice and matching belt. It had come with a crisp little petticoat that made it stand out, and I always wore a pair of stack-heeled sandals with it. I had brushed my hair into a bun at the top of my head. I looked smart, stylish and I felt good. I'd needed something to pick me up after yesterday. The hotel room, and then that doctor's office, it was all too uncomfortable.

I'd thought this arrangement with Leonard might be a fun way to earn some money. He was quirky, but he wasn't bad looking and I kind of liked him. But, after yesterday, I didn't know any more. He was hot one minute and cold the next, unstable. And while I wasn't quite afraid of him, I didn't like the fact that I never knew what to expect from him. I should call it off, I thought as I rolled my cart down the rows of books in the reference room. My task was to reshelve books. It was a pleasant enough job because the room was kept cool and was usually empty because only employees were allowed in.

I'd reached the end of the row and was bending over the top of the cart when I felt him behind me. I knew it was Leonard because he always wore something light and musky; maybe it was soap, because it wasn't strong like a cologne. He was fully erect as he pressed himself into my backside. I stood, somewhat abruptly, but he didn't move. His body felt hard and angular against mine. His hands cupped and stroked my breasts, his fingers toying with the nipples through the cloth. I struggled at first, incensed that he felt he had the right to approach me here; that he felt that he could approach me at all after yesterday.

'Shh, shh,' he breathed into my ear, 'it's all right. Everything is all right.'

I tried to turn around to face him, but he held me tighter, his chin tucked into my neck, his arms around my torso and hips.

'I've been thinking about you all night.' He was kissing my neck, my ear.

I tried to pull away again, but he held fast. 'I've changed my mind,' I said, gripping the handle of the cart.

I could feel him shaking his head. 'It's too late.'

That made me stand up straight. 'You're crazy.'

'Maybe,' he said, 'but I would never hurt you.' He nipped at my shoulders with sharp teeth and plucked at my nipples with his fingers, all the while pressing his growing sex into my buttocks.

'Ah, Leyda, I need to feel you,' he said as he pushed at my waist and back gently, but forcefully enough to cause me to have to catch myself with my hands as I perched over the cart.

The cart bounced a little as it hit the wall. I grabbed onto its sides to keep from sinking face down onto the pile of books. He lifted my skirt, then the petticoat. His hand grabbed and pressed my heated flesh and a finger slid between my legs to gauge my arousal. I knew it would come out slick and sticky because, even though I resented his audacity, I was excited by his initiative. There was the sound of a nip, like a scissor making a quick cut and he reached under me and pulled the severed thong away, baring me completely.

Then came the brief sound of a belt buckle, a zipper, and he was pressing himself against my opening, the head of his penis full and insistent. He gripped my hips and pushed just enough to breach my passage, then pulled back. I could hear his breath, eager and harsh in his throat. He pushed again, almost all the way in, and I remembered. 'Leonard, what about the diaphragm? I'm not on anything.'

'It's OK. Just this time,' and he was sliding in, the width of him pushing through the cream-coated walls of my sex. I wanted to push back. I wanted to press my bottom into the hairy crest of his groin, taking him all the way in. But he wasn't wearing anything and I wasn't on anything so I tried to pull away. He held on, his fingers digging into my hips as he pushed.

'No,' he said, pressing me down, his fingers slipping under the front of my dress and threading through the damp bit of hair until a sturdy one thudded and slid across that protruding bit of flesh. It was so taut; it felt full, like a tongue peeking beneath the hood of my sex. The contact jolted me, sending a flash of light through my body and making my legs tremble. Leonard held on, his slippery finger kissing my clitoris until I was pressing back, further into him, trying to take in more of him.

'You're never to worry Leyda, I'll always take care of you,' he was saying as he pressed his length home. 'Oh, fuck, Leyda, it's so good in here, so hot and tight,' and he was moving, stroking me with his hardness, rubbing and pulling and rasping against my walls, against my swollen labia as he drew me into his relentless rhythm. Then, as though he had touched a live wire, he stiffened. I could feel his sex tighten and grow within me. He began to thrust harder and faster, his hands and fingers, now damp, skidding across my hips as he tried to hold on. I held onto the cart, trying to stay steady for him, but as he grew I felt the need to push back against him as my muscles clenched around him, sucking and milking and pulling harder with each thrust. 'Oh, fuck, Leyda,' he was saying, 'I can't ...' and then there was a rush of wetness filling me. He jerked forwards, sliding into me like a rushing wave. I was dizzy with light and sensation, my chin pressed into the hardness of a large book. There was a keening, low as though from somewhere deep in Leonard's throat, and more wetness, and finally the weight of his torso heavy on my back.

After that, I was eager to meet him at the hotel the next day. He'd given me a key card and told me get dinner from room service because he wanted me there when he got there. *No problem.*

There was another garment bag draped over the bed, but I ignored it, remembering the last time. I had salmon and the house white and did homework while I waited. When he arrived, he was Brooks Brothers down to the wingtips, like he'd just come from the office. I wondered where or if he actually worked.

'Why aren't you dressed?' he asked, pulling a bottle of wine out of a bag and setting it on the bar.

I looked down at my jeans and Grateful Dead T-shirt and then back at him like I had no idea what he meant.

He gestured towards the garment bag.

I took a deep breath and pursed my lips.

'No more Chanel,' he said, smiling. 'Just something fun.'

Reluctantly, I walked over to the garment bag and unzipped it. There was a fuzzy suit, about the size of one of those Playboy bunny costumes, but it was fuzzy all over except for two circles, which appeared to be where one's boobs were supposed to go. I looked back at him and laughed.

He smiled back at me. 'It's very soft. Try it.'

I held the suit up. It had no fastenings, but the fabric seemed to have some elasticity.

He filled two wine glasses, handed me one and said, 'I'll shower. You get dressed.'

When he stepped from the bathroom, damp and wearing another white terry bathrobe, I was wearing the suit. It fitted snugly and the boob holes had bendable stays underneath that made my breasts seem extra perky. The thing was also crotchless with just enough cloth down there to frame the pertinent parts. And there was a removable round tail that covered another hole in back. I made sure the tail was attached securely. There was also a mask of sorts with rabbit ears and a furry half face that concealed the eyes and covered the top of the nose, leaving the mouth free. The furry fabric of the suit was soft inside and out. Strangely, the get-up made me feel wanton. So, when Leonard came from the shower, towelling his hair, I was posed on the bed, legs crossed, leaning back on my arms with a pair of very aroused nipples aimed at him.

He gave me one of those smiles and I slid my legs open. Accepting my invitation, he dropped the towel and the robe where he stood, strode across the room and, without a word, buried his face between my legs. His mouth was hot and unyielding. Lips and teeth tugged and teased and laved my most hidden places. Within moments, he had me writhing on the bed, my thighs cupping the sides of his head. He rose up and pressed his face into my stomach, swishing his face back and forth across the fur to rid it of my juices, while nipping at my tummy through the fabric. Reaching up, he tugged at the mask and tossed it away as his mouth covered mine.

Leonard's hot hands trailed the length of my thighs, teasing the skin behind my knees. His wicked fingers found the sensitive skin on my inner thighs, his touch urging my legs wider, making a nest for his hips. I welcomed the weight of his body as he pressed his sex to my opening, covering me. With one forceful surge, he thrust home.

His tongue teased the line of my lips; his lips brushed mine. I opened to him, licking his lips and sucking his tongue as he began a slow assault with his lower body. Drawing my legs up, I opened wider to receive him, lifting them high, and resting my feet on his lower back. He fitted, and I relished the way he held me and kissed me when he made love.

He was breathing hard now and I felt him tighten and expand within me so I flexed my inner muscles, squeezing him tight. He groaned and surged deeper. Then I bit his ear and clenched my inner muscles around him, trying to suck him in, hold him just there. I liked the feel of him tight within me like that, bucking and rocking against me. I wanted to bite into his shoulder. So I did, and he came, jerking and spewing his seed and grinding into me, the rough hair of his groin grazing the engorged lips of my sex. I lifted myself, pressing hard against him, letting the current take me as my wetness merged with his.

Once he'd recovered, he rose up on his elbows and chuckled. 'The suit looks great on you.'

I grinned. He lowered his head and nibbled at the peaks of my breast. Someone knocked at the door. 'Did you order something?' I asked, reluctant to let him go even as he was pulling away.

'Sort of,' he said mysteriously, as he retrieved his robe and slipped it on. 'Put the mask back on,' he ordered as he headed to the door.

I sat up on the bed and did as I was told.

'The shower's in there,' he told the guy he brought into the bedroom. He was a big guy, blond, the football type. The kind that lays everybody out flat then ambles off the field unfazed, helmet dangling carelessly from a mammoth hand. He looked at me and smiled a big toothy all-American grin. I scrambled under the bedspread, looking to Leonard for some explanation. He stared back at me, a strange war of doubt, curiosity and anger on his face.

Leonard took my glass from the nightstand and headed over to the bar without saying a word. He poured himself something stronger from a glass decanter and took a sip before refilling my wine glass. When he handed it to me, I asked, 'What's going on?'

He just shook his head

'Who's that guy?' I asked, taking a sip from my glass.

'Bradley, a guy I went to school with. Are you wearing the diaphragm?'

'Yeah, I put it on when I got here,' I said, climbing out of bed.

'Good,' he said, just as Brad came out of the bathroom wearing a towel wrapped around his waist and using another to towel-dry his hair. He eyed the costume, his eyes lingering on the boob holes. I took refuge behind Leonard.

'Leo, my man, you are a freak.' He laughed, a round happy laugh. 'What's that get-up?'

'Something I had made special,' he said, allowing me to use him as a shield. I peeked around him at the burly dude.

Brad smiled down at me. 'Come out and let me see you, little one,' he coaxed. 'I like little soft things.' Steinbeck's Lenny came to mind. He let the towel he'd been using for his hair fall around his neck as he reached for the hand I had resting on Leonard's hip. I moved it out of reach. 'She's a shy one,' he said to Leonard as though surprised.

'Would you hand me a robe?' I asked Brad. 'There's one behind the door.'

'You don't need a robe, babe. I like you the way you are.'

'Leonard,' I said, backing away from them, 'I didn't agree to this.'

He turned to face me, and for a minute they stood side by side, Leonard tall and lean, and Brad, not quite as tall as Leonard, but twice as muscular. His face was kind, kinder than Leonard's, but I was not a whore, somebody to be passed around. How could Leonard do this? I thought he liked me.

'Don't you like me, babe?' Brad was asking.

I looked at Leonard. I wanted to cry. Tears were gathering in my eyes, but I was sure the mask hid them.

'This is what you want, Leonard?' I asked.

He looked at me over the rim of his glass, took a sip and said, 'Yeah,' but he sounded uncommitted.

'You want me to fuck him?' I asked again.

'Yeah,' he said again.

Brad smiled, his eyes on my breasts, his hands twisting the towel around his neck.

'And what do you do when we're fucking?' I asked.

'What do you want me to do?'

'Watch,' I said.

Brad's towel tented and bobbed.

'OK,' Leonard nodded. I took his hand and led him over to the stuffed chair next to the bed. I pushed at his chest and he fell into it, his robe parting to reveal his excitement.

'Just me and Brad,' I reminded him as I backed away.

'I wouldn't have it any other way,' he said, stroking his fully aroused joint.

Brad had removed his towel so, when I turned away from Leonard, he greeted me in all his glory. His joint was thick and long and red. It bobbed a greeting at me and Brad looked on grinning. I slid my hand over his shaft, gripped it hard and pulled him towards me. He leaned down to kiss me, his lips covering mine.

'No kissing,' Leonard said. His voice sounded tight, strangled.

'It's your game, Leo,' Brad said, and bent low to fill his mouth with one of my breasts, nearly swallowing the whole thing before pulling back to suck hardily at the nipple. Meanwhile, he slipped his shaft between my legs, oiling it with a mixture of my new moisture and what was left of my bout with Leonard. He slid it back and forth, heating the flesh there and grazing my entrance. *I could'a been riding a horse.* He lifted me easily, wrapping my legs around his waist and spreading me wide. The huge head of Brad's penis nudged at my opening. I pressed myself against him, wanting it now, wanting to feel the pressure of its massive head burrowing into me.

'You have to use a condom.' Leonard's voice seemed to come from far away.

Brad's face was wet. I didn't know whether it was sweat or left over from the shower. He shook his head to keep the water out of his eyes. When Leonard spoke, he lifted me off the eager head and pressed my sex to his stomach. With one huge hand placed strategically on my buttocks, he held me as though I weighed nothing.

'What's the problem? You said she was clean,' he said, walking towards Leonard to get the condom he held out to him.

'Even so,' Leonard said from his place of exile, one leg over the arm of the chair and one hand still clutching his rigid penis. He made Brad reach for the packet.

Brad ripped the wrapper with his teeth and rolled the clear sheath onto his shaft. He nipped at the nearest breast, rolling the nipple around on his tongue and grinned up at me. Then, in deliberate defiance of Leonard, he kissed me hard, slipping his tongue into my mouth as his nose warred with the nose fur of my mask. He set me down feet first onto the carpet, and then, slipping his thumbs underneath my armpits, he pulled the furry suit down and off. Tossing it aside, he said, 'I want to feel you, babe. If he makes me wear a rubber, I want to at least feel your skin against mine.' I grinned up at him. 'He'd probably shit if I removed your mask.' I nodded.

Then he laid me on the bed and made love to my breasts and stroked my belly and my sex until I was squirming. Only then did he turn onto his back, lift me up and slide me down onto his shaft. It was shocking at first; he filled me so completely that I was afraid to move. But he was patient, thrusting upwards, slow, letting me become accustomed to his long slow drags until I couldn't stay still. Then he was grabbing my ass and squeezing the cheeks and sliding me up and down his hard heat, every inch of me trembling with each deliberate stroke. The thickness of him rasped and rubbed, igniting a series of flames with each thrust that ended with a nodding tap against the base of my womb, like it was playing a game of kissing tag. Then he would drag it back slowly and my muscles would clinch at him trying to keep him there.

'Fuck, babe, you're so hot you burn right through this fucking rubber,' he said, gritting his teeth. 'Your pussy is so tight and wet. You think Leo would let me keep you?'

I didn't want to think about Leonard, but Brad's words made me look at him. He was still hard, glaring at us and stroking himself. He seemed petulant, angry. I could imagine how I looked to him all flushed and rosy with lust, riding Brad's big cock. But, hey, Leonard had orchestrated this. I would not feel sorry for him. I could feel Brad getting harder inside me. He lifted his head to lick and suck my nipple. 'I need to ride, babe,' he said as he flipped me over without missing a beat. I had him tight between my legs now, the weight of him making him sink deeper into me every time he lunged forwards. The muscles of my womb began to spasm, squeezing him.

'Oh, fuck, babe, your pussy is sucking me off. Shit . . .' And he was pounding into me. I couldn't see any more, the lights blinded me and I know I cried out, but I don't know what I said. Brad's body stiffened and his cock jerked forwards again and again before he collapsed.

'Fuck, baby, that was good,' he said, and kissed my chin before rolling off me and falling heavily onto his back.

I fell asleep and when I woke up both Brad and Leonard were gone. Someone had covered me and there was a cheque for $5,000 on the nightstand.

It was a couple of days before I heard from Leonard. The text message on my cell said to meet him at the campus watering hole after work. He was sitting at a back booth when I got there. It was after eight on a Friday night so it was filling up. He looked like he'd been there a while. There were several watermarks on the table, like the drinks had been coming regularly, and a red plastic food basket held the remnants of whatever he'd eaten. Fried mushrooms?

'Hey,' I greeted him as I slid into the seat across from him.

'Hey yourself,' he said, and glared over at me.

I couldn't help but smile. His response was so done.

'So, why'd you fuck him?' he asked, like we'd been having this conversation all along.

'You asked me to.'

'I didn't think you would,' he said, shaking his head. 'I thought you would get angry and slam the door on your way out. Or cry. But you fucked him.'

I had nothing.

'Is he better than me? You looked as though you were enjoying it. He sure did. Wanted to stay for another round. I made him leave.' He waved a waiter over. 'What are you having? Want something to eat?'

'Pepsi,' I told the waiter.

'Another one.' He held up his glass to the waiter. 'You should eat something,' he said to me.

'So, are we done?' I asked.

'Done?'

'You gave me the balance. I thought that meant it was over.'

'I was angry.'

'Why? Because I wouldn't let you join in?'

'Because you said yes. To Bradley.'

'You told me I had to do what you said.'

'That's a fucking cop-out, Leyda. I told you you didn't have to do anything you didn't want to do. You wanted to fuck him. They all do.'

We were silent as the waiter set our drinks on the table.

'There have been others?'

'Not like this; we share women sometimes. And when we were at school we had a sort of competition with each other's girls.'

'Another game.' I sipped my drink.

'Why'd you fuck him, Leyda? Is he that fucking irresistible?'

'I was angry because you asked me to.'

'You shouldn't have done it.'

'Look, I'd only been with one guy before you. This is all too fast for me. I don't know what you want from me. I gotta go.' I grabbed my purse and scooted out of the seat.

He grabbed my arm before I could go, pulled a few bills from his pocket and threw them onto the table.

'I want you to go home with me tonight. I think there's still some time left on our contract.'

'I'm tired, Leonard.'

'You can rest at my house.'

He didn't release my arm as he pulled me along and stuffed me into the passenger seat of his car. This time it was a sedan, black.

When we got to his house, it was dark. He must have driven in through the back because I couldn't see the façade of the house, just a grey garage door as it lifted and the sound of lapping water. I wondered if it was Lake St Clair. I remember him mentioning the Pointes before. We entered through what appeared to be a games room and there was no else around.

'Sit,' he commanded.

I glared at him, walked over to a ping-pong table, and toyed with a paddle that had been discarded there.

He shed his sports coat, folded it over the top of a high-backed bar stool and flicked a light switch. A dim glow bathed the room, just enough so that we could see each other, but not clearly.

'I thought you were different, Leyda,' he said, glaring at me across the room. Then he crossed his arms, making his biceps bulge in the short sleeves of his polo.

I took one of the little plastic balls that huddled near the net and began to bounce it against the table with the paddle. He was across the floor in seconds, yanking the paddle out of my hand and pushing me back onto a large play pit that felt like a soft trampoline. I fell back, bounced and landed in an unladylike sprawl.

'You've adapted well to the role of whore.' His voice was tight as he stood over me. 'I don't like it. I was paying for innocence and what I thought was loyalty.'

'Paying and thought.' I sneered up at him from my less than elegant position. 'The operative words.' I scooted to the edge of the pit and sat up. 'Look, you can't expect me to live up to your assumptions.'

He patted the paddle against the palm of his hand. 'When you went with Brad, you made me feel . . . inadequate.'

I stood up, smoothed the skirt of my sundress down. 'Look,' I sighed, 'you and Brad have some issues you need to resolve. You don't need me. You need a counsellor or a psychiatrist.'

'You *bitch*.' The word burst from his mouth. 'I thought you . . . I wanted to . . . Fine, just give me my money's worth.'

He grabbed the front of my dress. I could hear the rip of fabric as he pulled me to him. Then a rough hand reached under my dress. 'I've always liked your ass; it's so high and round.' He was pushing me face down onto the tufted edge of the pit and shoving my dress up. A rough hand gripped the edge of my thong and began to pull it down, but it ripped. So he tore it off, causing it to chafe a bit as it was torn from between my legs.

'Leonard –' I tried to rise, but he pushed my face back down against the pit.

'There is nothing more to say. This is our last time together and you have to do as I say.'

'I don't think –' I began.

'I'm not paying you to,' he countered.

'But Leonard –'

'You've been bad, Leyda. Haven't lived up to our agreement.' As he spoke, he stroked and plucked at the bare skin of my bottom. He drew a finger down its centre and traced circles around the protruding labia just below my nether cheeks. 'I told you in the beginning that you had to be exclusively mine, but you cheated. Either I am due recompense or you endure the consequences.'

'I haven't cashed the cheque,' I offered, feeling uncertain and a little frightened.

'It's not the money,' he said, grabbing both my wrists in one of his hands just before I heard the sound of wind and felt the sting of the paddle. It fell hard against my bottom with a resounding slap.

'Fuck, Leonard,' I said, and squirmed harder, trying to free my hands and move my bottom out of range. 'That hurts.'

'It's meant to.' With another swoosh, the paddle fell again, harder this time. The rubberised facing grazed the jutting lips of my sex, causing them to tingle and swell. The paddle came down again and again, slapping and stinging, causing my bottom to redden with heat.

After twenty or so resounding smacks, his hand slowed, and there was one last half-hearted slap. He released my wrists and leaned his forehead against my head burying his face. Then his hand was smoothing over the stinging place and down, down, to the now-engorged lips where he discovered the wetness of my arousal. He probed the damp pouty flesh, penetrating me with one finger. I groaned in appreciation. Then he was behind me, the slow drag of a zipper, and he was mounting me from behind, breaching my opening with his long hard thickness. He felt so right. I slid back, rubbing my bottom against his groin in welcome. He laughed and, wrapping his fingers around my hips, he rode me until we both collapsed in oblivion.

I figured it was a good way to end it. Neither of us had much to say once he located a safety pin for my dress and dropped me off at the dorm.

I was disappointed when he didn't come back to class, but I reasoned it had all been part of the game. Life went on for me as usual. I finished the semester, enrolled in a new one, and kept working at the library. Late fall, about three months later, I was having a cappuccino and working on my script at the Starbucks on campus when he slid into the chair across from me.

I wasn't paying attention because people are always plopping themselves in any unoccupied chair because the place is so small. But he sat there waiting until I got this niggling feeling that I was being watched. He looked good in his Brooks Brothers. 'More,' he said. I looked at him. My brow must have furrowed because he shook his head and said, '*Yo quiero mas.*' I laughed, and he took my hand and kissed its palm.

Misbehaviour features the short fiction of Alegra Verde for the first time in Black Lace.

Our Scam
Eva Hore

My boyfriend Peter and I are travelling with his sister Sarah throughout Europe. We did this to save money. Triple-share accommodation is so much cheaper and, when we need some privacy, Sarah is always happy to oblige. So far it's been great.

We have the best scam ever when we're short on cash, which fortunately or unfortunately, depending on the way you look at it, has happened quite a lot.

We'd never do this back home, you never know who might know you, but halfway around the world it's as easy as anything and has brought out a new side to our sexual escapades I can tell you.

At first I was apprehensive but once we began it was easy. I focused on Peter and nothing else, blocked everyone else out and did what I had to. It's been amazing and I absolutely love it.

This is our scam.

Peter goes to a bar an hour or so before we do. He usually hangs out with as many single guys as he can. Tells them what a great time he's had travelling and how he can get almost any girl he desires with his pick-up lines. Naturally he brags about the fact that he has a great cock, that women fall all over him when they see it and, by that time, we've walked in.

Naturally we pretend we don't know each other. We usually

flirt with the most unattractive singles there to begin with so the guys that Peter's with don't get suspicious. We deliberately dance near them, give them the eye if they glance our way, and then he suggests he could get one of us and makes his move.

He naturally picks me – couldn't have him do this type of thing with Sarah. He makes a big play for me, always checking to see that the guys are watching. At first I pretend I'm not interested. He plies me with what the guys think are very strong alcoholic drinks and then gets me up dancing.

While we're dancing he grabs at my arse. I always attempt to push him away but before the dance is over I'm putty in his hands. He kisses my neck, touches me where I'd never let a stranger go and then, while the guys are still watching intently, he gives them the nod.

They're so predictable, eager to believe in the power one of their own has over women. So far not one has doubted Peter's ability to pull it off, which amazes me. I'd like to think us females would be more sceptical.

Anyway, once a few of them have disappeared into the men's toilet, Peter and I wait a few moments before making our move. I could go on about all the different locations but the best encounter we had was in Germany.

When we entered the toilets I saw two men at the urinals. They turned, open-mouthed, and watched us enter a stall. I thought these guys were the ones that Peter had set up to come in and watch, but they weren't. They were just two guys taking a leak; as we were acting out this scam we couldn't say anything, so they got a free show.

Peter pushed me towards the toilet and turned me around but didn't close the door.

'Step out of your skirt and panties and straddle the toilet bowl,' he demanded.

'What?' I feigned outrage.

'I said straddle the bowl.'

Giggling girlishly, I did as he asked.

'Piss,' he said.

I did.

He ran his fingers through my hot stream, knocking my legs further apart so he could watch. I saw one of the guys peering hard at the mirror from the other side of the room. He must have been unable to believe his eyes. He would have been able to see only from the waist up but I didn't care.

I knew there would be guys watching from the top of their own stalls, next to the one we were in; that was the usual plan. They'd watch from above and I'd pretend I didn't know they were there.

With these two guys watching I thought Peter had changed the scenario, that perhaps they'd paid more to be closer to the action. As I said before, I usually block everything else out and just concentrate on Peter and what we're doing.

When I'd finished he turned me around and pushed me up against the cubicle wall. My hands shot out to support myself and he knocked my legs apart, pushed down on my back and slapped my arse.

'You have a great arse,' he said.

In this position the guys up top would see most of Peter not me. The fact that the other two guys were still there watching had me a bit nervous but also very excited. Knowing they could see my arse and even my pussy if they came closer had me throbbing with excitement.

'Come here,' Peter said to one of the men. 'Would you like to watch?'

'Hey,' I said. 'What do you think you're doing? You didn't say anything about a gang-bang and that's something I'm definitely not into.'

I attempted to move but Peter had one hand on my back and the other between my thighs.

'I didn't say there would be. Now do you want me to fuck you or not?'

'I don't know. I still haven't seen this fantastic cock of yours that you've been raving about.'

'Oh, you will, little lady,' he said, and then to the guys, 'Well, do you want to see what a pretty pussy she's got or not?'

Over my shoulder I could see one guy nodding stupidly and my pussy contracted in expectation while my face flushed scarlet. The other guy scurried out of there as quick as he could.

The word 'slut' burned into my brain but I didn't care.

Fiddling with his trousers, Peter pulled out his cock. I licked my lips, desperate to feel him inside me. I didn't have long to wait. With a few slaps on my arse cheeks he pulled me into his pelvis and his cock slipped straight in. Like a steel rod, he dived in, pumping hard while slapping at my thighs.

'Oh, my God,' I screamed. 'Fuck, that's so big it's hurting.'

'I told you it was a monster,' he chuckled. 'You,' he said to the guy who stayed, 'you like watching?'

'You bet,' the guy said.

'See her cunt wrapped around my cock?'

'Yeah,' he said, coming in closer.

I peered over my shoulder, watching this guy eyeing our fucking. It was such a turn-on. As I said, I usually don't see the guys. Peter and I just fuck and then I leave. He's already worked out a price and they've usually paid him before we begin but tonight it was different and of course I couldn't ask; having this guy so close to me had me on the verge of coming.

I pushed back eagerly, encouraging Peter to fuck me harder, faster.

'You see how much she likes it? Probably likes having an audience too, don't you?'

I didn't say anything; I couldn't tear my eyes away from the guy. His hand was stroking his cock and Peter was withdrawing his own out a fraction so the guys could see my juices over it before he slammed back into me.

'Don't you? You like having an audience, don't you? I can see just how wet your cunt is, and the more I talk about it the wetter you're becoming.'

It was true. I wasn't acting. I was so enjoying this guy watching us up close.

'Oh, fuck, yeah, it's fantastic,' I said.

'Then why don't we come out of here so the guys can watch properly?'

'What? What guys?' I could barely talk I was so turned on.

I could hear their voices, indicating that's exactly what they wanted, and then he was pulling out of me. He grabbed me by the arm and dragged me out of the cubicle. There were probably five men in total all milling about.

'Hey, wait just a minute,' I said, showing some outrage.

'Come on, you love it,' Peter said.

'I told you I'm not into group sex and, if they don't leave, I'll start screaming.'

'Listen, none of them will touch you, I swear,' Peter said convincingly.

I was standing there half naked with five strangers. Peter's eyes were shining with excitement. Having sex with him in the cubicle was one thing but out in front of all these guys who we didn't even know was downright dangerous. Well, that's what I thought at first.

'I don't think I want to do this,' I said half-heartedly, trying to cover myself up.

'Come on, don't be a prude. No one is going to hurt you and you don't want to see this cock go to waste do you?'

I knew I had to do it and I really did want to, I just wasn't sure how much longer to play this game. Peter ran his hand down my mound and over my slit.

'Beautiful, just like I knew it would be.'

I had the grace to blush.

'You've got a great cunt and you know it,' he said.

'And you've got a great cock there,' I said, lunging for him.

'Then what are we waiting for?'

'Well, come on then. You promised me a fuck I'd never forget and it looks like that's exactly what's going to happen.'

'Lock the door,' he said to one of the men.

I was wild with carnal lust. I ripped my shirt off as Peter hoisted me up on the dirty basin. Unclasping my bra, he demanded I open my legs and show the men my pussy.

I've never felt so fucking horny in my life. I did what he asked. Lifting my soles onto the bench, I lay back against the wall and allowed them all a good look.

The men stood back, uncertain what to do. Peter lowered his head and licked my cunt, his tongue probing around my flaps in between the folds.

'Oh, God,' I moaned.

'Your cunt is delicious,' he said.

I rubbed my clit, arching my back as a spasm overtook me. I grabbed a breast and squeezed the nipple until it hurt.

'Fuck, that's good,' I said, barely able to talk, still rubbing while another orgasm gushed from me.

Why Peter had organised this I didn't know, but I was so grateful. I didn't know if he was enjoying it as much as me and even if I found out later that we hadn't been paid for it I couldn't have cared less. It was the most amazing sex I've ever experienced.

A couple of the guys took their cocks out and were pulling them openly. I've never felt so fucking alive; all my senses were in tune with what I was doing.

It was exhilarating to be stark naked, to be lusted over by these strangers, and as they came closer I felt another orgasm erupting. Peter pulled back, his knob now probing me as my orgasm gushed out to pool on the bench.

He began to fuck me, his huge cock filling me completely. I wrapped my legs around his back, kicking my heels into his arse, urging him to fuck harder, faster, and he was happy to comply.

I could feel someone's breath on my back, knew at least one guy was so close he could have touched me. My body screamed out for him to but my voice stayed silent. I wanted nothing more than to feel their hands on me, touching and exploring my fevered flesh.

They too were turned on. Two of the guys spurted their spunk over the toilet wall. All I could think about was how turned on they must have been to do this in front of me, and that made me even hornier.

'Get off me,' I screamed at Peter.

The look on his face was priceless.

'What?' he asked as I jumped down.

'Fuck me from behind,' I ordered.

I made sure I wiggled my arse at all of them. With my legs wide open I leaned forwards, stretching my back out so my arse was up high and my pussy would be totally open for them. Wet and hungry. Just how I liked it to be.

Peter, who had only dropped his trousers, now took them off and stripped out of his shirt. His face was wild with adrenalin. With the two of us naked, we fucked our brains out. Sweat was pouring off us as he pummelled me with such force I almost sprained my wrist trying to hang on.

I could feel he was about to come but didn't want him to stop.

'No,' I said, pulling away.

'What?' He was clearly dumbfounded by this change in me.

'Get on the toilet,' I demanded, grabbing him by the arm and running naked into the disabled cubicle.

I knew there was more room in there and I wanted them all to watch me humping Peter. With him sitting on the toilet I hoisted myself up, straddling the edges of the bowl. I stood high, allowing them all a good look at me, and watched Peter's eyes as I lowered myself, opening my legs, squatting over him, my pussy gaping, the guys all only inches away from us before I slammed down, impaling myself on his monstrous cock.

I slammed up and down, grinding my pussy into his groin. Hands now did touch my arse. I didn't care, I was loving it. When a finger gently probed my puckered hole, I pushed back, hoping he'd continue, fingering my hole while I fucked my boyfriend.

Unfortunately he didn't.

A banging on the toilet door and a voice indicating it was security had us all frantic. I jumped off Peter and scurried about for my clothes while he too quickly dressed. I hid in the cubicle while they opened the door, assuring the security guard that all was well.

They eventually left one by one and as I waited I rubbed my clit, imagining the gang-bang of a lifetime. I couldn't get enough, didn't want them to leave, wanted Peter back in here with me again so we could give another show.

'Hey,' Peter said, knocking softly on the door. 'Are you OK?'

'Are they gone?'

'Yeah,' he said as I opened the door.

I pulled him in and we finished what we'd begun.

Later, back on the dance floor and looking for Sarah so we could leave I asked Peter why he'd changed our routine.

'They said they'd double the money if they could get a closer look and I thought why not?'

'What about the two guys who were at the urinal when we came in?'

'The one who stayed got a free show.'

'You're kidding,' I laughed.

'Imagine him telling his mates. They'd never believe him.'

'Why didn't you tell me?'

'I thought it would be more exciting if I didn't and it was, wasn't it?'

'Well, yes, but you should have told me,' I pouted.

'You might not have agreed and then we never would have known how fucking turned on you'd get having all those guys watching up close.'

I giggled. 'You enjoyed it too, didn't you?'

'You bet. You were wild. I've never seen you like that before and your cunt was so fucking wet.'

'Don't talk about it. I want you again,' I laughed.

'So, do you want to stick to the old routine or the new one?'

'Definitely the new one,' I said, hugging him.

In the back of my mind though I was doing some other thinking. That guy who'd been touching my hole. I'd give anything to have someone do that while we were fucking and I thought after today that I might be able to get Peter to agree; once he'd agree to that, maybe, just maybe, he'd let a guy fuck me in the arse.

The thought of it had me creaming my panties so I told Peter we should go to another pub and do it again.

'What, tomorrow?' he asked.

'No, now,' I said.

We left Sarah there. We couldn't find her and I didn't want to wait any longer. We made an absolute fortune that night and I was still working on getting that fuck in the arse.

Our scam has turned our relationship and prospects of future travel into something really special.

Misbehaviour **features the short fiction of Eva Hore for the first time in Black Lace.**

Concerning Etiquette
Rhiannon Leith

It began as a private game for one, or perhaps a dare with just herself. Eliza had never been one for following the letter of the law. She'd never actually been caught speeding. And no one knew when she wore scarlet suspenders under that pristine finishing-school uniform.

She'd graduated ten years ago, left home, started her own business and turned down a proposal of marriage her mother would have killed to see her accept. She'd made it quite clear to her whole family that her life was her own, but Aunt Augusta still tried on a regular basis to treat her as if she was still some sort of 'silly gel needing some sense knocked into her'. And who better to do so, in Aunt Augusta's opinion, than that self-same elderly busybody.

Eliza glanced at the invitation again. Well, dinner wouldn't be too bad, even a formal dinner. There would be the usual crowd of guests. Her aunt's oldest friends, an artist or actor whom she was patronising – in both senses of the word – and of course the man Aunt Augusta had earmarked for Eliza.

There was always a man. A suitable match. Rich, well-bred and dull as yesterday's dishwater. The old dear meant well. She claimed she saw in her niece a lot of herself at the same age. And while there were the usual jokes about keeping the elderly spinster aunt happy, Eliza actually liked the woman.

Apart from the busybody end of things.

Independent, self-possessed, a shrewd businesswoman, Augusta had travelled the world more times than Eliza could say.

'And lonely, m'dear,' Augusta would say, if it came up. 'Don't leave that out. Good breeding can close as many doors as it opens. And etiquette can only take you so far. Sometimes you have to rebel a little. Sometimes you have to pay the price. Punishment and reward.'

Eliza rolled her eyes and put the invitation on the mantelpiece where it glared at her. It was only a dinner party after all. And Augusta had sent over an ancient fur coat, a beautiful enticement that Eliza could not wear anywhere else. There was a note with the invitation – Augusta had also invited an etiquette coach. Obviously some word of Eliza's small rebellions had reached her elderly relative and were frowned upon.

If anyone else had suggested it, Eliza's blood would have boiled. That it was Aunt Augusta's idea merely brought it up to scalding point. A plan began to form, not shocking, but one that left a smile on Eliza's face for the rest of the day.

The grandfather clock had already chimed eight as Eliza stepped into the extravagantly discreet restaurant. Not quite on time, nor yet fashionably late, which in Augusta's terms, and presumably those of her future etiquette coach, translated as 'late because she couldn't be bothered', which was even worse than merely running behind schedule. Eliza handed her clutch bag to the maitre d' and shrugged off the fur coat. She had the pleasure of watching his face in the mirror as her dress – or rather the full length of her legs – was revealed. The hem skimmed her upper thighs. Bend over in the wrong company and there could be an international incident. God, she hoped Augusta had invited an ambassador or two this evening. The beaded lengths of shimmering thread hugging the sheer fabric glittered when she took a step forwards. With a vinegar expression the maitre d' passed her belongings to a nearby waiter and led her to Augusta's private room.

At a guess, three men nearly swallowed their tongues, or at least choked on their drinks as she approached. Eliza graced each one with her most languid smile, wondering which one *he* was.

Bald, rotund, face shining with sweat? No. Not possible. Too bad a joke on the world of etiquette.

Well-groomed, Oxford-educated and propped up by Daddy's money? Unlikely.

Most probably *this* was her 'date' for the evening, she thought, suppressing a resigned sigh.

Ancient, almost bent in two, regarding her with a disapproving glare from Augusta's side. Bingo!

She discounted the fourth man in the group, partly because she didn't see him until after merrily knocking back two glasses of very fine Sancerre and partly because, when she did lay eyes on him, something inside her liquefied.

The first things she noticed were his eyes: bright, alert with intelligence and interest. They were such a deep grey that she couldn't entirely be certain of the colour at all. His face was sculpted, high cheekboned, strong-jawed. His sensuous mouth parted in a smile when their eyes finally met. No. Not a smile. A grin. Wolfish. Knowing.

As Eliza watched him over the rim of her glass, he took out a BlackBerry, checked some messages and tucked it away again. Businessman? Perhaps. Successful, by the look of him, but of course looks could be deceptive. That air of calm self-assurance seldom was, however. She was captivated. Instantly.

His eyes trailed down the long line of her neck, across the sweep of her bosom, and it felt as if his fingertips followed.

Her body reacted at once, and deep inside her something clenched around the sensation as if to hold it within her forever. A small breath escaped. Quickly she drew it back in and dipped her gaze.

When she looked up, he was smiling still. He knew, she realised. The bastard knew what he was doing to her with only a look, how her body was reacting to so simple a thing. She would have said innocent. But there was nothing innocent about it.

He stepped closer, offered his hand. 'Henry,' he said by way of introduction.

'Eliza,' she replied with her blandest smile. She almost hesitated to touch his proffered hand, fearful for a moment of what actual physical contact might do.

Standing on the far side of Aunt Augusta, Mr Etiquette sniffed and murmured something to her aunt. Apparently Augusta laughed off whatever was said, but the ghost of a frown skirted her brow as she looked towards Eliza and Henry.

'Time to take our seats,' she said, in her clear voice. 'Now everyone is here.'

Henry offered Eliza his arm in a fluid and decisive move. She hid her surprise and twined her arm with his.

And suddenly Eliza knew why she had hesitated to touch him.

He exuded control. And with her hand on his arm, she found herself swept up in that aura. Her heart hammered against her ribs and in her core, beating wildly, though in protest or joy she could not tell. How could anyone tell when faced with such an overwhelming physical desire as this?

Henry pulled out her chair and leaned over her as she sat. She inhaled his scent. Oh, God, too much. She was almost glad when he left. Her eyes followed him as he circled the table and took his own seat opposite her. And part of her mourned.

The meal was torture. There was the usual small talk. The only thing that made it halfway bearable was stealing glances at the seemingly oblivious Henry and tormenting Mr Etiquette by such small distractions as drinking from the wrong glass, swiping her 'date's' side plate and using her dessert fork to eat her salad.

Normally she would have laughed away to herself, but this time it didn't amuse her as much. She swallowed hard and, feeling the old grouch still glaring at her, felt anger rise in her instead. She reached out over the table for the salt cellar, only to meet Henry's amused eyes as he passed it to her. The grey had deepened with his obvious mirth. As she took the salt, her fingers brushed his and came away tingling. Her lips parted on a surprised breath and drew up, sharing his conspiratorial smile.

Just before dessert, she excused herself, deliberately casting a glance over her shoulder. A special glance to him. One she hoped had the right amount of come-hither without too much naive hope or blatant desperation. And if he didn't follow, she would just slip out early, without a word to any of them.

Her heels clicked as she walked down the tiled hallway to the alcove cloakroom. It was late in the evening now, and most of the staff had gone. Only her aunt's party remained in the restaurant, contained in their private dining room. With the tables set for another day, the place had an eerie, almost forlorn quality. She stepped into the shelter of the cloakroom and reached up for the fur coat. Hesitating, her hands brushed the soft fur. Her dress rose up against the curves of her bottom. Cutting out early, despite the hour, was her last dig at both her aunt and Mr Etiquette, but for once she didn't find the joke so funny. Not when she was leaving on her own.

'Going so soon?' Henry's rich voice made her start and turn.

He moved so quietly, like a cat stalking his prey, powerful and exotic. More than a little dangerous.

'I've an early start,' she replied, just managing to keep her cool. She clasped both hands behind her back to hide the trembling that seemed to have possessed them. 'Besides, I don't think I'm flavour of the month in there.' She threw him a daring smile.

But this time he didn't smile back. 'Yes. You seemed to manage that effortlessly. Do you go out of your way to misbehave on a regular basis? Or is this a special occasion?' His eyes trailed down her figure again, like fingertips, or a warm tongue sliding across her skin. Between her legs, her body melted to liquid honey.

'If the time seems right.'

Henry stepped into the alcove, his presence forcing her to take a step back. Her fur pressed against her bare shoulders and the back of her neck, the soft texture both comforting and stimulating against her shivering skin.

His fingers touched her cheek, traced down the line of her cheekbone. Then he brushed the pad of his thumb across her lower lip, drawing it down. His thumb carried moistness over it on the return path. Then he pressed gently against her teeth, which parted to let him slip inside her.

Eliza stared into his liquid grey eyes, and closed her mouth around him. For a moment she just held him there. Then she sucked, rolling her tongue around his thumb, teasing the sensitive pad.

When she released him, his knowing smile had returned. He brought the same thumb to rest on her chin and then drew a wet line down her throat and cleavage, to the valley between her breasts.

From back in the private room, she heard a burst of laughter. And from somewhere far off in the kitchens, plates clacked together and soft voices murmured of tomorrow and the events of the day. Eliza jerked, but didn't push him away. He was like a rock before her. How could she escape, even if she had wanted to? Really, there was nowhere to go, but she knew instinctively that, if she said the words now, this would never have happened. She would be free. Etiquette would be appeased. No one would catch them, or hear a gasp of pleasure they were not meant to hear. She could walk out of the door right now, his eyes told her.

God, she didn't want that.

She tilted her hips towards his and felt the force of his erection through their clothes. Lifting her face, she met his lips and the world changed, becoming hands and flesh and mouth; becoming the fur against her bare skin as the dress fell away in a sequinned puddle beneath her stilettos. Henry's hands moulded her breasts through the filmy lace of her bra, teasing the nipples to straining points with his skilful fingers before he finally pushed the fabric aside and took one, then the other into his mouth, swapping between them as if he couldn't decide which he liked best. He sucked hard, forcing gasp after gasp from her. She threw back her head, nuzzling the fur coat, burying her face in it for fear she would cry out in her lust.

He knelt, lifting her, his hands so strong, so certain. He slid her legs over his shoulders and pushed aside her panties. His mouth descended mercilessly on her cunt. Knowing that at any moment anyone at all could happen upon them, from a waiter, to her aunt, to the sneering maitre d', just made it worse. His tongue pushed its way inside her, fucking her like a cock for a moment, curling up until she wasn't sure any more that it was not, before withdrawing to her clit, the burning point of need that longed for just this kind of attention.

She must have pleaded. She knew the words consumed her mind and she must have at least whispered them. A finger entered her, then two, curving as his tongue had done, but deeper, so much deeper, turning in a way no cock could. His tongue curled too, encircling her clit, and then he sucked while deep inside her, and his questing fingers found their Holy Grail.

Eliza bucked against him as he stroked her G-spot, transforming her need to cry out into a physical rapture. She pulled the fur around her, muffling her whimpers in its folds, and came more furiously than she had ever done before.

Henry's hands soothed her gently to the ground. He helped her slip the dress back on, and wrapped the fur around her.

'Yes, misbehaviour is certainly your element,' he said. 'It becomes you. But if you'd like to explore such behaviour and its consequences a little more deeply with me . . .' With a flourish, he produced his card: a slip of ivory, with gold and black lettering. She took it without a rational thought.

'But you –' She couldn't finish the sentence. He silenced her with a kiss.

'Consider this round one, Eliza,' he said. 'The opening act. Come to my office tomorrow evening. Seven, say? Promptly, though, if you please.'

He left her standing there by the door. She turned the card over in her hands and read the words under his name. ETIQUETTE LESSONS.

Eliza's first instinct was 'no way in hell'. She'd been angry by the time she got home, too wound up to sleep. Yet she had to admit that she was intrigued. Her hands wandered across her naked skin as she lay in bed, trying to recreate the extraordinary sensation of his touch, so knowing, so sure of his abilities and of her reactions. She'd had other lovers, skilled and determined, lovers who had pleasured her as well as themselves, but she couldn't recall anyone taking her as high as Henry had done.

And then he'd walked away.

He'd made her come with hands and mouth that seemed to know her body better than she did.

And then, without a backwards glance, left her.

Anger gave way to the heat that stirred within her at the memory of the encounter. The fur moving against her skin, his fingers within her unfurling like flowers, and his mouth, his glorious devouring mouth. Her own hands acted as a poor substitute, but as she circled her clit and forced her fingers deep inside her, the silken flesh turned harder with need. She came with a cry, arching up on the bed and the name she shouted was 'Henry'.

Eliza had promised herself she wouldn't go, and normally she was very good at keeping promises. But the day dragged along and all she could think about was the previous night.

And that was why she found herself standing in the corridor outside his office, wearing loose jeans and a light cotton shirt. Knowing all the time she wore nothing underneath.

Evening had drawn in around her as she walked there. She took a steadying breath, knowing that she shouldn't have come. Henry was too much for her. A trembling stirred in the pit of her stomach whenever she thought of him. Whatever he wanted from her, it wasn't a new student of etiquette. Just because she loved to flout it didn't mean she didn't know what she was turning her back on.

And yet the image of a master and a student wouldn't leave her mind. Henry definitely had much to teach her. Problem was, did she want to learn?

No. She wanted to learn. But did she dare?

Eliza shook her long hair back from her face, steeling herself with inner resolve. She had left it unbound, as last night, though she had no idea why. Same reason she wore the coat, perhaps? The blind fear that he might not recognise her?

Her hand shook so hard she had to curl it into a fist in an effort to regain control. Then, before she realised what she was doing, she knocked on the office door.

The urge to bolt seized her. But her legs froze.

Henry opened the door himself, which surprised her until she realised that 7 p.m. was late for a receptionist to still be working. Did he have a receptionist? She had no idea what to expect from an etiquette coach.

Henry smiled. 'Good. I'm so glad you came,' and she was certain she saw genuine pleasure in the expression. 'You're early.'

Was she? Eliza had no idea how long she had dithered over coming here, circled the building, waited in the elevator or paced the corridor outside. But she hadn't expected to be early.

'Well, I came,' she replied, lamely.

Henry offered her his hand, to welcome her or usher her inside she presumed and, without thinking, she took it.

Alarm bells rang in her head. At his touch, so simple and formal, so innocent, her stomach jolted and her head swam. She must have paled.

His eyes glistened with gentle amusement and his hold on her turned a little more supportive.

'There's nothing to be afraid of Eliza,' he told her. 'We won't do anything you wouldn't ask for if you could, nor go any further than you might wish. If you want to stop, just say "etiquette" to remind me. Do you understand?'

Perfectly. That was the problem. She stepped over the threshold and heard the door close decisively behind her. Her wishes, when it came to Henry, were becoming pretty extreme.

She'd never been afraid of a lover before. She'd never been so afraid of herself. And she trusted Henry to give her exactly what she wanted, even with the casual placement of a safe word. That was the problem.

Henry stood behind her now, so close she could feel the warmth emanating from his skin through coat and clothes, so near that his scent – an expensive aftershave and beneath that a bewitching, masculine musk – wrapped its spell around her. Henry's hands closed on her shoulders. He buried his fingers in the fur for a moment, caressing it and, through it, her body.

'I'm glad you brought this.' His breath tickled the back of her neck.

'My aunt's. She gave it to me. A bribe to turn up last night, I think.'

'Well, I'm relieved you took it.'

'I can't wear it often. Fur doesn't go down well these days. Meat is murder and all that.'

'I expect it would have been long dead by now, anyway.'

'Probably.' A laugh hitched in her throat, unexpected given the circumstances.

He removed the coat, as if he was stripping her barriers away with it.

'So why did you come, Eliza?'

To fuck you. Oh God, she longed to say it. But the words stuck.

Henry folded the coat and laid it across an armchair in the corner of his office.

This was his domain, she realised as she took in her surroundings. Polished mahogany, understated wealth, an antique desk, the deep-pile carpet in rich shades of green, the gold of the upholstery studs gleaming against the aged brown leather of the chairs. Thin Venetian blinds, made of wood, covered the windows. They were half closed against the glare of the early evening sun and sent lines of light and shade across the room. Dividing everything.

'Do you know why?' she asked at length.

'I think it's a question of etiquette,' he replied, stepping back towards her. He circled her, examining her as one might a skittish colt. The comparison made her somewhat uncomfortable. 'You're sick of it. So you want to break some rules. And you need a safe place to do that. Because I don't just mean switching cutlery or outrageous evening wear, Eliza. I can guide you into much more interesting ways of fulfilling your desires. If you want. Only if you want.'

Eliza closed her eyes, listening to the spellbinding tones of his voice, the lilt and cadence that were almost songlike in combination. Her breath deepened as he spoke and she felt the coiled spring inside her begin to unwind.

'Yes,' she replied on a breath, and looked up.

Henry smiled down at her. 'Then the first thing we need to do is curb those wild tendencies, don't you agree?'

He unbuttoned his cuffs and rolled up the sleeves to reveal statuesque arms, lightly tanned, the muscles beneath toned to perfection, betraying the hidden strength she had only guessed at before. His fingers, as she recalled from last night – as they furled and unfurled within her, as they drove her higher and higher – were long and elegant, aristocratic. He had the hands of an artist.

Eliza's teeth worried her lower lip. She'd just agreed to put herself in his power, hadn't she? To let him instruct her? To be her master?

Henry stepped closer still, smoothing his palm across the silk of her hair. His hand folded around her skull, cupping the back of her head. She leant back slightly, just to feel him take her weight, support her.

'We moved very fast last night,' he told her. 'But we can make up for that now.'

Confident, wasn't he? If she was honest – and it did appear she was finally prepared to be honest with herself – that was an important part of the attraction.

His hands slipped down her neck to her shoulders. He cupped her breasts, lifting them until the light cotton of her shirt tugged free of her waistband. His thumbs ran over the nipples which stood instantly to attention. She couldn't suppress the groan. It came from deep inside her and rumbled through her throat to break like a wave on the air.

'You're so responsive,' he murmured, and leaned in to kiss her.

He started slowly, a light feathering touch of lips to lips, lips that parted willingly. His tongue teased, drawing out her promised response effortlessly.

'You've never really let go, have you?' he asked, pressing his forehead against her and gazing deep into her eyes.

She shook her head, unable to find the words because his clever fingers roamed beneath her shirt.

Fingertips skirted her skin, heightening her sensitivity with a gossamer touch. Within seconds he had slipped free the buttons and allowed the shirt to whisper down her arms and fall to the ground. It took a moment longer to realise the pounding she was hearing was her own heart.

'So beautiful,' he whispered so that the breath and the words trembled across her breast a moment before his mouth claimed her nipple. Eliza glowed from within as he circled his tongue. Then he sucked hard and her legs almost gave out. She stumbled against him. Never releasing her, Henry chuckled and caught her, holding her still so he could continue his ministrations. By the time he switched breasts she was repeating his name on each breath, her own personal mantra. She felt his mouth smile against her nipple, just before he started all over again.

Henry unbuttoned her jeans and pulled them down. She stepped dutifully out of them, unable to remember exactly when she had kicked off her shoes. Her body pulsed with desire. And vulnerability, she realised, standing there naked before a fully clothed man who studied her intently as he got to his feet.

'The thing many people forget, Eliza,' he said, taking her trembling hands in his, comforting her as his fingertips soothed her frazzled nerves, 'is that etiquette is about poise and dignity. You have that in almost every area of your life. Always have. And no one ever reprimands you when you choose to cast it aside.'

'Will you?' she asked.

Henry smiled, drawing her after him, like a dancer leading his partner to the floor. 'It would be an honour.'

He stopped at the far side of the antique desk and pulled out the chair. 'First you need to make amends for your shocking behaviour of yesterday, and for arriving here as you did.'

He sat down, waiting. This was the moment, Eliza realised. She could say no and turn away. She could go back to her own petty rebellions and never have to face the consequences. She could forget this had ever happened.

Liar, her inner voice chided. Nothing could ever make you forget this moment.

Her hands rose like those of Venus, one to shield her sex, the other to cover her breasts. Henry just watched her, his face grim and yet still expectant. He would carry this game through to the end. There would be no going back if she truly placed herself in his power. He wouldn't stop until he felt she had learnt what he wanted to teach. Not even if she begged.

Unless she said the word and broke the spell.

'You can stop it if you need to,' he reminded her, his expression never changing. 'I won't think worse of you for it.'

Ah, but *she* would. She would regret it forever. She bowed her head.

'I've behaved shamefully, Henry.'

'Then come here.'

He laid her across his lap as if it were an executioner's block. He adjusted her position with practiced ease and, like the condemned, she complied. Her hair trailed down over her head, brushing against the floor. Her hips balanced against his. Through his trousers she could feel the stirring of his cock against her sex. He took her hands and placed them together against the small of her back, fingers clasped together.

And still he made her wait.

The first slap took her by surprise. Her breath escaped in a great whoosh of air and the cheeks of her arse flared with tingling heat in its wake. Another followed quickly, just as hard, just as unexpected. She cried out, unable to help herself. That was when he found his rhythm. Just when she thought she could handle it, another slap landed, stinging her skin, jolting through her like an electric shock, bringing tears and cries and the most cathartic release imaginable. He varied his strokes, some heavy, some penetrating, followed by a series of light slaps, like rain which almost soothed her burning skin until the intensity of blow after blow built up unbearably.

Finally he stopped, leaving her sobbing, panting for breath. Draped across him, her body slick with sweat, she felt his hard-on pressing against her, as intimately as if they were already having sex. But she didn't have the strength to react.

Henry's hands closed on the globes of her arse, cool and smooth against the heat they had left there and she sobbed again at the gently punishing caress.

'Do you have something to say?' he asked in his unruffled voice.

'I'm sorry,' she whispered, hardly daring to speak, her throat hoarse from her wild cries.

'And?'

'And . . . and I won't do it again?'

A laugh tangled with his voice and he moved his hands, brushing them up and down, working the skin so the pain sent a deep ache right through her. Her clit throbbed in answer.

'Oh, I think you will. I'm kind of counting on it.'

He had that right, she thought, and finally found the strength to thrust her aching clit against the bulge in his lap. Especially if this was the result.

But she didn't say anything. That was part of the game.

She heard him open a drawer and remove something. Moments later his hands were back on her martyred flesh, spreading a cool and soothing ointment or oil over it. She groaned as he worked, his touch like that of a practised masseur. Every caress ground her against his cock. His clever fingers were at it again, she thought, as he skirted the edges of her labia, mixing the oil with the copious juices welling up there. As his fingers traced whorls and spirals back, teasing the sensitive line between vagina and anus, her whole sex began, slowly and unbearably, to throb. Whatever that dangerous substance with which he was coating her was, her body reacted with blind and painful need.

'Oh God, Henry.' She ground herself against him now, her action a plea for release from this torment. 'Oh God, what is that?'

'Shh, just a few specialist herbs in an oil base. Just relax and enjoy it.'

His fingers darted into the cleft of her bottom, trailing

around the puckered rose of her anus. The ointment followed, slick and warm, setting nerve endings tingling in a mixture of alarm and lust. Her blood pounded against her temples and she fought for breath after breath. He must have applied more as he pressed at her anus. It opened for him and the oil trickled inside her.

Groaning out loud now, her hips bucking, Eliza felt something enter her. Not his fingers. They still played around the opening. This was cold and hard. Unyielding. It too was coated with the oil. Her breath dammed up as he edged it in with a maddening, twisting motion. He took his time, letting her initial resistance die, letting her body re-form around it, before beginning again, twisting this way and that, working this strange dildo inside her. When she clenched against it, he tutted and his other hand found her clit. She leapt at his touch and, unable to help herself, she cried out his name, opened to him and was filled with the cold, solid length.

'Now I need you to hold still a moment,' he murmured. Hold still? She shivered against him, ready to come at any moment. And yet she obeyed, quelling her urge to thrust herself against him, to bring herself off here and now without any further regard to his wishes. Tears stung in her eyes and she struggled to control her breath. 'I had this made specially,' he said, and gently twisted the dildo again. 'It's not as solid as it seems. Clever little thing also acts as a funnel.'

She heard a small clink of glass against glass and a few moments later the oil flooded deep inside her, working her with its insidious touch. Like the liquid form of Henry's fingers, deep, so impossibly deep inside her, teasing and caressing her, stimulating her beyond endurance. Her muscles clenched, though whether to expel the invader or keep it inside her she couldn't say. Quite honestly, if anyone had asked her name at that moment, she would have struggled to remember. Only one name mattered, the only one she could recall.

'Henry! Henry!'

He lifted her, running his oily hands up and down her front, clutching her breasts and working oil and sweat together until they glistened. He placed her standing, her upper body on his perfectly neat desk. Her breasts rubbed against the inlay, the combination of oil and leather nearly sending her out of her mind at last. He forced her legs apart, planting them firmly on either side of the chair, her bottom high in the air. The glass dildo he left in place. Eliza closed her eyes, sliding back and forth across the desk, unable to formulate what she expected next. She could feel him watching her and her whole body flushed with embarrassment.

And desire.

She didn't feel him move. He didn't brush against her, or make a sound. The first thing she knew was the touch of his tongue on her clit, just the tip. It rested there for a moment and then withdrew. She sighed his name, a plea she couldn't fully articulate, and heard his deep chuckle. It ran right through her, as deep as the dildo, as deep as his precious oil.

'Don't worry, love,' he told her, his voice a little hoarse too, as if the word had slipped by unbidden. 'After punishment always comes reward.'

Relief made her desire pump even faster through her veins. But did reward have to take so long? She wanted him with every atom in her. She needed to feel the cock that so far she had only brushed against, that long thick cock, pounding into her, filling her. Her cunt, her mouth, she didn't care. The thought of it almost made her come then and there. She arched her back, pushing herself down towards him. The dildo stretched her anus and she clenched around it, wishing it filled her everywhere, wishing it was him.

Henry's hands on her hips stopped her. He wasn't underneath her any more, but behind.

Slowly, with all the care and reverence she was coming to expect from him, he drew out the glass and understanding washed over her at last, in a dizzying wave.

She wanted him to lick her to orgasm, to bury his tongue in her and suck her clit until she screamed. She wanted to sit astride him and sink onto his full length until they were one. She wanted to ride him. She wanted him to fuck her hard and fast, and then long and slow and start all over again and never stop. And all of that would come in the future. Each and every fevered desire.

But now, her mind tuned entirely to his. She wanted him to bury himself in her arse, to take that last virginity and possess her completely. It had all led to this, right from the moment she laid eyes on him last night. Her body pulsed with need as his clothes rustled to the ground, as his fingers – his clever, wicked, knowing fingers – opened her, so much more easily than before.

The sweetest punishment, she thought, for any transgression, before coherent thought tumbled away in bodies moving in unison, in mouths straining to reach each other, and fingers twining together, in her pounding clit and his artful touch which both soothed and intensified everything. In the madness of all this, and the sheer wonder of her release. The sweetest punishment and the greatest reward.

In that final moment before she came, everything knitted together in crystalline clarity. Henry pushed deeper and deeper. One hand steadied her bucking hips while the other cradled her vagina, two fingers inside, the thumb pressed to her clit, soothing away any last traces of pain. Her arms lashed out and sent the papers on the far side of the sweat- and oil-slicked desk flying, like so many demented butterflies. She found purchase, digging her nails into the leather and pushed back, forcing him fully inside, and they cried out together, voices harmonising in hunger and need.

His lazy rhythm sharpened, the movement of his fingers a counterpoint to his thrusts. The world fragmented, re-formed. Eliza threw back her head and gave voice to her joy, her new freedom and the glorious knowledge that from now on no misdeed, however petty, would go unpunished.

Two days later, while dining with friends, Eliza deliberately and with full understanding of cause and effect, used her salad fork for her seafood starter. She looked up to catch Henry's eye and smiled. Inside, that wanton, honeyed feeling melted between her legs.

The Black Lace anthologies *Lust at First Bite* and *Seduction* feature the short stories of Rhiannon Leith.

The Distraction
Portia Da Costa

He's back again. Distracting me. He's not doing anything he shouldn't be doing. Not at the moment. But just his presence in the room makes me flaky and unable to concentrate.

Why, oh why, does he have to work in *our* office? Surely there's a place for him elsewhere?

But it seems not. Apparently there isn't a spare desk in the entire building other than one alongside mine here in Personnel.

So I've got the freelance IT guy who's installing the company's new computer system loitering in my personal space for the next six weeks. And it's going to be a long six weeks if he insists on hanging around, flexing his muscles, and God knows what else, right under my nose.

It's a conservative firm and a conservative office. Suits and ties for the guys, and smart skirts and blouses for us women. A good thing really for a forty-year-old bird like me. I'd look stupid in skimpy tops and jeans with a chunky figure like mine. OK, women my age do wear those kinds of outfits, but I like to preserve a sense of decorum, you know?

Not much decorum in me when I steal a glance at 'him', though. It's hot today, muggy as hell, and he's in a tight black T-shirt that clings to his pecs and abs and the muscles of his arms. I'm not a techie, so I've no idea what he's doing, but whatever it is it looks suspiciously as if he's posing at the same time.

Lounging back in his chair, he flaunts himself at me, sitting in a way that automatically draws attention to his crotch. Or is that just me who's unable *not* to look at it? To add insult to injury, or just an additional, slavering layer to temptation, he's a biker too. Which means tight leather bike jeans and heavy menacing boots with zips and buckles.

Oh, God.

Why am I letting these things get to me? He's just not my type, on top of the fact that he appears to be nearly twenty years younger than me too. I just don't do the cougar thing, but even so, I can't stop imagining him taking off his clothes. Imagining it again.

He's gym-toned and tight and he's got gilded-satin skin. In my mind that extends to every bit of him. With the magnificent exception of his cock. My picture of that is of a ruddy monster, thick and veined and hot, hot, hot.

Pretending to focus on the top of a heap of personnel files – old ones, on paper, that are going to have to be manually inputted into the new system – I picture Edward, my lust object, getting naked.

Slowly, in an insultingly leisurely tease, he stands up, turns towards me, and starts tugging the hem of his dark T-shirt out of his waistband. Tug, tug, tug, he tweaks at it until finally it's loose, and then in a smooth animal action, he peels it off.

Oh, his body is just beautiful. It's a dream but I know it's real too. Like heather honey his torso gleams and my fingers slide over the manila surface of the files, experiencing the mundane stuff as firm flesh and silky skin.

He stares at me, forcing me to look at him. But not just his body, his handsome face too. And handsome he is, with dark-blue eyes, a tender but masculine mouth and a rakish little goatee beard that matches thick brown hair brushed straight back from his brow.

Very deliberately, he touches his own nipple, drawing attention to the single piercing there, and immediately I wonder if he's pierced anywhere else. His ocean-blue eyes glitter mischievously, as if he's heard me.

'Do you want me to show you it?'

His hands are on his heavy belt buckle, fingers tapping.

'Jane, do you want me to show you it? The new login procedure?'

I blink like a fool. He's actually leaning across in his seat, reaching to twist my keyboard towards him.

'Um . . . yes . . . please. Is it sorted now?'

A waft of some deliciously unctuous male cologne floats my way, tickling my nostrils, filling my head. And that's not all that floats. He's been sweating, but it's not bad. It's raw. It makes my mouth water, and not *just* that. A million hormones fire and it's not just the humidity that makes this place a jungle. We're like beasts responding to ancient primitive signals.

Mate. Mate. Mate.

He gives me a slick little smile, the bastard, because he knows.

For five minutes or so, we do some kind of computer dance. I barely pay any attention. I suppose my subconscious is resisting the information – in order to provide me with reasons to seek him out again.

As he pushes his chair back on his castors, and says, 'Now you do it', he's fingering his belt just the way he did in my daydream.

Oh, God!

That belt conjures all sorts of fantasies. Ones I'm not quite sure I understand. He might as well show me the computer manual. It's all arcane mystery, but I know it makes sense to him, that it's powerful.

I muck it up. I make a mess of the login and the damn thing locks me out again.

'Naughty, naughty, Jane. You weren't paying attention. I ought to smack your bottom for wasting my time.'

He laughs, every bit as naughty as he accuses me of being. But in those blue eyes, there's a deadly serious threat.

I ought to tell him not to be so cheeky. That we don't make jokes like that in this office. But I can't. I'm paralysed. Rapt. Frozen, yet burning in a column of heat, seeing myself across those leather-clad knees, my bum bare.

'Come on, Jane, let's try it again,' he says softly.

Perspiration slides between my breasts as I apply my fingers to the keyboard.

After lunch, it's even hotter.

I managed to get logged in earlier and, satisfied, Edward moved on to another terminal. I felt bereft, abandoned, insulted. Then I remembered that all the sexy stuff was purely in my mind and he probably thinks I'm just a silly old uptight middle-aged bitch.

He's back now, though, working at the desk next to mine. Not looking my way, his face placid and calm and untroubled, while I'm going crazy inside, my body wanting . . . wanting something.

Do I want him to fuck me?

Christ almighty, I shock myself even thinking the word, but I'm not quite sure that's exactly what I want.

Edward does his clever things with his keyboard and mouse. He talks on his mobile to people in other parts of the building. He hooks up a drive of some kind, loads more software.

He has absolutely no interest in me, and I'm just being stupid thinking he might ever have had any.

Boink!

I get an email.

Not so unusual, but the back of my neck prickles for some reason. It has an attachment. Again, not usual. People send me documents and forms all the time, and everything's scanned and safe, thanks to Edward having beefed up the system's security.

Still prickling, I open the mail . . . and nearly knock my bottle of water off the end of the desk.

It's an image. Made of pixels this time, not a pattern created by the deluded neurones of my sex-addled brain.

Just what I've been imagining since this morning though.

In a softly lit room, a nude woman is sprawled across the knee of a man in leather jeans. She's face down and, even though it's all in sepia, you can see that the bare rounded moons of her bottom are reddened. His face is in shadow, and his hand's on her back, fingers curved, as if he's stroking and calming her.

The buckle on his belt is an exact match for the one holding up Edward's jeans.

I glance to one side.

No response. Not a twitch. Not a smirk. Total calm and serenity. His finger curves on the dome of the mouse, as if he's stroking and calming it.

I wish someone would calm me!

I snap the email closed but its contents are seared on my brain. I have to get out of here, away from him. He's the devil.

There's a small office at the far end of the main room. It's for interviews, privacy. Sometimes, when one of us is doing a detailed job of some kind, we go in there and work alone, in peace and silence.

'I need to go through these,' I announce to the room in general and nobody in particular. 'It's cooler in the little room . . . I think I'll go through them in there.'

After sweeping up my water bottle, my pen and a random selection of files that I've already processed, I stride up to the end of the room, heading for sanctuary.

In the little office, the air conditioning hums loudly, but works a treat. It *is* cool. I switch on the terminal there, one that Edward has already hooked up, but I don't login. I'm not here to work.

How in God's name did he know what buttons to press with me? I don't even know myself . . .

Who was the woman?

When did he spank her? Where? For how long?

Did they fuck afterwards? Did he touch her? Did she suck him, caress his cock with her lips and tongue?

I wish I could open my email from here. I want to see that image again, assure myself it's him.

But of course I can.

Making no errors this time, I key in my password and finesse on into the system.

I open the file again and the sight that greets my eyes again makes my sex ripple.

God, that's never happened before.

Spontaneous desire.

Physical response with no stimuli but vision and imagination. I clench the muscles of my pussy and my anus, imagining them exposed to him, across his knee, my bottom cheeks jumping from the spasm.

I slump back in my chair, my fingers tingling with energy. They want to stray to my crotch, but I'm trying to retain some semblance of control. I don't do things like this! I'm a grown-up, in command of myself. Responsible and all that.

Yet here I am, horny as a teenager, desperate to play with myself because a hot young man sent me a picture just as hot.

I spread my legs, but I'm not going to touch myself.

I shuffle down, pressing myself against the chair, but I'm not going to touch myself.

I place my hand on the stretched fabric of my skirt, over my thigh. But I'm not going to touch myself.

Feeling my heart turn over strangely, I cup my crotch . . . and the door to the little room swings slowly open.

Every muscle in my body leaps, including the ones that are connected to my clit, but as Edward slides into the room, through the narrow gap of the partially open door, he presses his fingers to his lips in a 'shush', and I subside back into the chair, completely stilled by him.

The door snicks shut, then snicks again as he turns the lock. There's only one window, but it's obscured by a flipped-down blind.

We're alone, enclosed, locked in, wrapped in silence but for the hum of the air conditioning.

Edward glances at my crotch where, I realise to my astonishment, my hand still rests. I should snatch it away, but I can't. It's as if his eyes have the power to paralyse me . . . or compel movement. Slowly, slowly, he licks his firm, sculpted lips.

'So this is what people do in this little room. I've been wondering about it since I arrived here.'

I open my mouth, but I can't speak. Instead, to my horror, my fingers start to grip, move, clasping my pussy through my skirt.

He laughs, and it's a quiet, sweet, strangely wise sound. I count the years again, those twenty or so between me and him, but he seems ancient in wisdom and experience. Like a young god, tall and strong and beautiful, and imbued with esoteric knowledge and exotic preferences.

'I would say you surprise me, Jane. But somehow, you don't.

I knew immediately you were a wicked woman beneath that straight, businesslike surface.'

Glancing at the screen, he raises his dark eyebrows.

'Do you like that? I suspect you do.' In a swift, darting movement, he pulls a straight-backed chair from the corner of the room and sets it opposite to me, with the desk and the computer to one side of us. He sinks onto it, all grace, setting his booted feet four-square on the carpet, his thighs slightly parted, gleaming in their leather.

The question loosens my tongue, gives me permission to speak.

'I don't know. It's like nothing I've ever seen.'

Which is a lie, I now realise. I've seen films with hints of this in them. Documentaries. I've watched them, thinking What's wrong with these people!, and all the while I've been ignoring what's going on in my pussy.

Those beautiful midnight-blue eyes darken.

'I think you're fibbing to me, Jane. Why do you do that? Don't you realise that dishonesty is wicked?' His chin comes up, as if in triumph. He's brought the conversation around to exactly the place he wants it to be. With me cast as the wicked, misbehaving bad girl. Or bad woman, more like.

How can I let this happen?

How can I not?

'Do you want me to help you understand?' His voice is low, mellow as honey. It's as if he's controlling me – completely – with dulcet kindness.

I nod my head, unable to speak again. All of a sudden I want to weep. It's a kind of relief. An acceptance.

'Touch yourself, Jane. Through your skirt. Just squeeze a bit.'

I obey him, burning up, gasping aloud as my clasping fingers knock my clit. It's like a kind of sweet electricity stimulating a naked bundle of pleasure receptors. The tiny organ jumps, almost the way it does when I come. But it's not that yet, not quite. I'm very close though.

Just from his voice, and a squeeze, and a lot of thoughts.

'How does that feel? Are you ready to come?'

'Yes.'

I flex my fingers to grab again, work my clit, force the issue.

'Uh oh . . . no, not yet. Not until I say so.' He rises from his chair and looms over me. I wish he'd give me permission to grovel at his feet and kiss his boots. Either that or just to keep working myself until I have an orgasm. 'We've a way to go yet, Jane. A long, long way.'

Somewhere in the corner of my mind, I wonder what my colleagues outside must be thinking. Me, in the little room, with the technical whizz-kid who wears leather and has the body of a film star. I'm supposed to have authority, keep people in order, but I'm the one who's being kept in order now.

The air in the room is cool, because of the conditioning, but it feels as thick as pudding on my skin. It presses down, like a blanket of sex, moist and hot. Or is that just me?

I'm moist and hot between my legs. I'm like a pond. My panties are saturated.

As I shift in my chair, imagining I can hear myself squelch, Edward looks down on me, reaches out and touches my hot cheek. His fingers feel cool, gentle yet unyielding. Just like the rest of him, I suppose, feeling dreamy yet wildly, distractedly excited.

'Are you wet, Jane? Is that why you're wriggling?'

My heart thuds, my knickers get wetter. My face burns hotter, so hot I'm surprised he doesn't flinch, singed. But he just slides his fingertips under my chin, making me face him, forbidding me to hide my embarrassment. My mouth is so dry that my tongue cleaves to the roof of it.

But still those blue eyes command me. And his voice too.

'Jane, don't be stubborn. Are you wet?' His voice is still low and mild. He doesn't need to shout. He just has to *be*.

'Yes,' I admit, wondering how all this can have happened. Not half an hour ago, I was annoyed with him. Wishing him out of our office and my life. Yes, I thought he was attractive in his blatant, aggravating way, but in the grand scheme of things, that didn't seem important.

But now . . . now . . . I adore him.

It doesn't make sense.

'There, was that so hard to admit?'

What, the fact that I'm wet, or the fact that I've gradually, without my really knowing, become obsessed with this confident, beautiful man?

'Not really.'

'So what shall we do about it?' He's still touching me, the tips of his fingers against my face. I lean in to the contact and it's as if it's a signal. His hand slides down my face, my jaw, my throat . . . and dips to cup my breast through the fabric of my blouse.

'Ah!'

I can't contain myself when he strums my nipple as if it's his sovereign property.

'You're a horny, beautiful woman, Jane. You make me want to do things to you, you really do.'

He strokes and strokes, then closes his thumb and finger over the tip of my breasts and squeezes quite hard.

I groan aloud, wriggle again in my seat, pressing on my clit with my clenched hand. When my pussy flutters, I toss my head, almost beside myself on a high wave of mixed sensations. Pleasure, pain, frustration, confusion . . . sweet longing.

But what do I want? The same thing as him? As he twists my nipple lightly in his fingers, I gasp, panting in time to the delicate little tweaks. My face turns from his, and my eyes light upon the image still burning on the computer screen. The woman's naked bottom cheeks seem to pulsate, even though the picture is static. I feel her heart beating with excitement in my own chest.

'Yes, that,' confirms Edward. 'That's what I want. How about you?'

I nod. Because I do want it. Here and now. Even with a dozen folk in the room beyond wondering what the hell we're doing. Even though I scarcely know this man from Adam, and he's not my type, and he's far too young, and I don't like arrogant, domineering males . . . and a score of other reasons.

I think I'll die if I don't show him my bare bottom and he doesn't spank it.

The moment seems frozen. My gaze skitters around his face. That neat little beard of his looks masculine, yet soft. Would it tickle my thighs if he was giving me oral sex? Would I still laugh, even if he was lapping at my clit?

His slight smile widens. His blue eyes dance.

'What are you thinking about, Jane? Something naughty?' His brows are dark, lifted in amusement. I want to bite his lower lip it looks so sinful.

'Er . . . nothing. Not really.'

'Liar. Tell me. Don't keep things from me.'

Roaring blood colours my face even redder. 'I was just . . . just wondering about something.'

He makes a little 'tsk' sort of sound, impatient with me.

'I was wondering if your beard would tickle if you went down on me.'

He laughs, and it sounds so happy. As if he's pleased with me. That makes my heart lift in my chest like a bird, and it's more than sex.

'Maybe you'll find out,' he says, with a smile in his voice. 'But you'll have to earn it. You'll have to please me, in my particular way, before we get around to pleasing you.' He gives another little twist to the tip of my breast and this time it really hurts.

I bite my lip, knowing that, even though this room is partially soundproofed, if I scream with thwarted lust and desire, someone might hear it. My clit flutters again. I'm lost . . . lost.

He releases me.

'Undress, Jane. I want you naked. Just like her.'

I know he's talking about the girl in the picture, and suddenly I'm jealous. Not only because he shared a moment like this with her first, but also because she's slim and young and beautiful, and I'm not particularly any of those.

Don't get me wrong. I like myself. I'm happy with my shape and my face and I can't do anything about my age. But, right now, I'd love to be perfect and young, for him.

His hands fall away from me, and so does mine. I start unbuttoning my blouse, reluctantly aware that I've been sweating and I smell a little less than fresh. In these close quarters, he'll smell that, not to mention the pungent aromas of my sex, when I take my knickers off.

But he's commanded me to strip, and strip I will. As he returns to his seat, and sits down, crossing his long, leather-encased legs, the blouse comes off, and I lay it across the back of my chair. My white bra gleams almost fluorescent in the artificial lighting. My nipples poke through the thin cotton, dark smudges beneath it. Being shy at this stage of our journey is ridiculous, but I can't help myself. Instead of exposing my breasts to him, I reach for the zip of my skirt and whir it down. I'm awkward as I step out of my skirt and I have to hold on to the chair. My heels aren't high, but I'm not used to undressing in front of a man. It's a long, long time since I did it, and then never for a man who disturbs me and distracts me the way Edward does.

But I manage to get the skirt off and toss it on top of my blouse. I'm still dithering. I'm still embarrassed. I'm in my shoes, pants and bra in front of a man I barely know and, the worst of it, I know those pants are damp. They're cotton too, finer weave than my bra, and there's a visible dark stain at the gusset, spreading and revealing, where I've seeped for him. There's even moisture gleaming on my thighs.

I start to kick off my court shoes, and he says 'No!' quite sharply, so I leave them as they were. Lounging back in his chair, he uncrosses his legs and exposes a startling erection pushing at the leather fly of his jeans. It's phenomenal and I feel a sudden huge rush of confidence. All that? For me? I find myself standing straighter, standing prouder, almost flaunting myself. I have everything that younger woman he was with in the picture has. My body is ripe, his for the picking, and mine to enjoy and to exhibit.

Daringly, I touch my breast through my bra, and catch my breath as a dart of pleasure spears my pussy.

'Yes!' hisses Edward, through his teeth.

I stare back at him, both challenging and questioning. What do you want, my beautiful leather-trousered boy? Do your worst . . . command anything. I can take it.

I fucking well relish it!

'Turn round. Show me your arse.'

I relish the crude word too. It makes me melt inside, more juice trickling down inside my panties. I never knew I was like this, but I'm glad I've finally found out.

I turn, managing a passable dancerlike spin. Not quite sure what to do, I extemporise, teasing the elastic of my knickers down, a very little way.

'Good. Very good, Jane . . . but leave them like that. Just rolled down a little bit. Just to the crease.' I comply and he praises, 'That's beautiful!'

I can't see him now, apart from a vague, slanted reflection in the computer screen. But the creak of leather tells me he's not quite as still and calm as before.

Are you adjusting yourself inside those skin-tight jeans? Nudging that monster a bit to one side, to get some ease?

I hope so.

'Bend over. Rest your arms on the seat of the chair. Part your legs a bit. I want to see the crotch of your panties.'

Feeling the heavy stickiness between my thighs squelch, almost hearing it, in fact, I obey his wishes. I've never felt so rude and exposed and vulnerable, and I've still got my pants mostly on. He can see how saturated I am, though. He can see how much I want him. Or even just want *something* from him, perhaps barely a touch.

Or a spank. Yes, that. Definitely that. I want to prove I can take anything *she* can.

He gets up and moves behind me, and I feel his fingertips on my lower back, drifting down to the elastic of my knickers. They hook beneath it, edging it down until it's stretched tighter across the roundest, plumpest portion of my bottom and the cleft is exposed, almost to my anus.

My breath stills in my throat when a hot fingertip slides down there, finds the little vent, and begins to stroke it. Up and down, up and down. Shame, heartbreakingly delicious, bubbles in my chest like effervescent wine and I make a weird animal noise I've never made before, all the time pushing my bottom against his finger, increasing the contact.

The torment goes on for what seems like an age, and I continue to perform for him, waving my arse around because I can't *not* wave it.

'You're a dirty, sexy woman, Jane. You must be or you wouldn't like me fingering you there so much. Admit it!'

I nod, beside myself.

'No, admit it in words.'

'I like you touching me there.'

'Where?'

'My bottom . . . the . . . the hole.'

I feel as if I'm going to faint right here, right now, but I can't stop wriggling like some kind of horny cat on heat. Lubrication is streaming out of me.

'Good girl, good girl,' he murmurs, doing it more. 'But also . . .' He pauses, finger stilling, resting, right there. '. . . naughty, so naughty, liking something so dirty.'

I'm beside myself, dying of shame and at the same time soaring on a wave of dark exultation. I feel as if I've found something I've being looking for all my life. And it's taken this wicked, beautiful man to light the path.

'I shall have to punish you, of course.'

The words are perfect and right. I almost sigh aloud to hear them at last, and it's so strange. Half an hour ago, I knew nothing, but now, I have wisdom and power, despite my temporarily subservient position.

His fingertip withdraws. 'Now then, Jane, undress for me. Bra and panties off, but leave on the shoes.'

I obey, for once not bothered too much about the minor imperfections of my body. A little roll of extra padding here, a hint of a droop there. I sense that he's more than satisfied with me.

When my sticky knickers and my bra, also damp with nervous sweat, are dropped to one side, he takes hold of my forearms and positions me. I'm to pose across the table, arms among a muddle of files and keyboard and mouse and writing implements. He pushes down on the middle of my back, making me dish, making my bare bottom pop up, perfectly proffered for his hand. With a booted foot he nudges apart my feet, making my wet thighs separate and provide a lewder view.

My heart leaps in my chest when the door handle rattles. I tense and hold my breath, waiting for a voice to call out from beyond the door, but Edward massages my back, and then my bottom in slow, sure circles with the flat of his warm hand and I calm again.

After one experimental twist, the handle remains still. There's no more rattling. God alone knows what they're thinking out there, knowing we are in here together with the door locked. But I don't care. I don't care. I've never cared about anything less in my life.

In these strange, stolen, out-of-time moments, nothing matters on this earth but him and me.

He continues to massage for about a minute. Then he gives me a hard pat on each cheek.

Then a harder one, and a harder one, gentling me into it.

My bottom starts to sting a little, and the next few pats aren't pats but light, lazy slaps, stirring that sting.

Then he smacks me, good and proper, instigating fire.

Oh, God, it really hurts! Oh, God, it's dreadful!

But also not dreadful at all. I don't quite know what I was expecting, but this isn't it. An almost indescribable amalgam of pain to be cringed and shrunk away from, and pleasure, evanescent pleasure, sinking like hot warm honey, into my sex.

My clit throbs like a tiny star, pulsing with each slap. It's almost as if he's hitting me there, knocking the sensitive nerve bundle, even though he's nowhere near it. The impact of his hand, and of his presence, goes right through my muscle and sinew and bone.

I bite my lip, quashing my cries of pain, my moans of delight.

I wiggle and weave, and he pauses in his sequence of strikes, and stills me again.

'Behave!' he purrs, then, to my astonishment, he dips down and kisses the reddened crown of each buttock.

Surely the stern master or whatever he is shouldn't do that?

But it seems he's a rule-breaker in this as everything, as badly behaved – when it comes to conformity – as I've become.

I shiver at the utterly delicious outrageousness of him when he laves his cool tongue over the heat that he's created.

How can anything so wrong feel so right?

And then he's spanking again and it seems to hurt more because of the little gentling that went before. I rock and hitch about, my pussy dripping, and aching as much as the cheeks of my bottom do, but he never misses the target, or a beat in the relentless punishment.

When my behind feels as if it's been turned into Steak Tartare, he finally halts, his hand stilling on the heat.

'Had enough, Jane?' he whispers, inclining over me, his flanks alongside mine, leather against skin. I hiss through my teeth as the smooth hide rubs my flaming haunch.

'No!'

The catch in his breath shows I've surprised him, even though it's not more spanking I want, but something else entirely. I swivel sideways and cram my burning buttocks against him, rubbing them, hoping he'll get the message.

He does, pressing his big, beautiful, randy young man's bulge into the cleft between my buttocks. He's hard, and rude, and it bloody hurts where he presses against the spanked zones, but all the same I want to sing at feeling him there.

'So, you expect me to fuck you?' he demands archly, pressing harder.

For a moment my world falls away and I feel intense sadness.

Doesn't he want me after all? Is he just playing some cruel and capricious game?

But no, even though he might be playing the arrogant bastard just a bit, his body is totally honest. It doesn't lie.

'Yes, I do actually. Is that OK with you?' I nearly add a snarl when he drags his nails across the crown of my bum.

'Completely, my lovely wicked Jane. Completely.'

All business now, he positions me yet again, kicking my legs really wide now and getting in between them, right behind me.

I hear the chink of his belt, the purr of his zip, then tiny sounds of rummaging.

A second later he presses his cock against what feels like the reddest spot on my sizzling bottom.

'Oh yeah,' he sighs, as if the heat in my flesh is exquisite pleasure to him. Maybe it is? He rubs his cock around the war zone, going 'mm . . . mm . . .' and leaving a trail of silky pre-come on my skin. I look over my shoulder, craning hard to see the size and shape of him and the sticky marker he's leaving on me. Leaning a little to one side, he catches my eye and gives me a wink.

'Ready, babe?'

Babe? That makes me laugh, and he laughs too, chuckling to himself while he whips a suspiciously convenient condom out of his pocket and enrobes himself in it. Twisted to one side, I observe the process, loving the expression on his face as he rolls and rolls.

If I was expecting measured finesse I was sadly mistaken. With no further ado, he positions himself with his fingers and then pushes on in. I go 'Oof!' as he shoves me hard against the table and stirs the fire in my abused and reddened bottom.

But the joining is everything I'd hoped for. He powers into

me, hard and hot, and slightly ruthless. Thump, thump, thump he knocks me against the hard surface beneath my belly, every impact juddering my clit and stretching me inside.

Within moments, I'm coming hard, seeing stars as I bite my own knuckle to stop me screaming. He's not far behind me, and he hisses a curse as he pumps into me.

Afterwards, there's not much to say.

Well, no, that's wrong. I have a thousand things to say to him but they'll all be stupid when they come out. This was just a game, a one-off, a bit of naughty behaviour to tell in my dotage as one of those mad office stories that nobody really believes. And even if there is a stupid, misguided, lonely middle-aged bit of me that wants it to be more, I know such thoughts are pointless. Edward's a stud, with notches aplenty, I'll be bound, on that leather belt of his.

Probably much better and less pathetic for all concerned if I laugh off what's just happened and chalk it down to wild experience.

When I do risk a peek at Edward his face is unreadable, but at least I'm warmed a little bit by the lack of any gloating, macho smugness. If anything, he looks thoughtful. Slightly puzzled.

As I put my fingers on the door handle, ready to brave the no doubt intensely speculating denizens of the office beyond, he opens his mouth to speak. But I forestall him.

'Look, don't say anything, will you? It was just one of those things ... Like the song says, you know? I won't say that I'm going to forget it, but it was a one-off. A distraction. That's all.'

It all comes out in a bit of a gabble and with far too much vehemence, and Edward looks at me, his mouth compressed and rather hard.

'OK, Jane. Whatever you want. I'm not a guy to kiss and

tell, so you've no need to worry.' He slides into a chair in front of the computer. 'I'll just work on this a bit. It'll look better. Less . . .' His smooth brow puckers a moment, but it's not in irritation or displeasure. I don't quite know what it is. '. . . suspicious.'

Then I can't look at him any more, and I grab the handle and dive outside.

But later, back at home, I can't stop thinking about the odd look on his face.

Did I miss an unmissable chance there? I'll never know. It's too late. I've burnt my boats. All the upgrades will be done in a few weeks, and I think I can manage to do the cordial, civil, it-never-happened dance until he's gone. Our extended sojourn in the little office might never have happened as far as everyone else is concerned. Not a single colleague seemed to have noticed. Or at least, if they did, they weren't letting on or smirking.

And now I'm here, in my robe, looking over my shoulder at my bottom. Which sadly also shows little evidence of this afternoon.

No redness. No soreness even. Just a pair of pristine rounds of slightly too plumply rounded flesh. I press with my fingers, imagining his. I give it a little slap, imagining the impact of his hand. I touch myself between my legs, imagining him touching me, then gracing me with his cock.

At least our little escapade has given me plenty of masturbation material for the months to come. Although maybe not right now. I think I need a glass of wine.

But as I'm reaching into the fridge, the doorbell rings.

And I don't know why, but my heart goes pit-a-pat.

I open the door and my jaw drops and my heart sings, both at the same time.

'Look,' he says without preamble, almost pushing me back into the hall by stepping straight over the threshold, 'I don't kiss and tell . . . but I don't do one-offs either! And if you think that's the kind of man I am, you deserve to be punished again.'

Before I can protest, he kisses me hard, his tongue in my mouth while his hand slides over my bottom, through my robe.

But who am I to argue? I don't do one-offs either, and as for the future, I'm far too distracted to give a damn!

Portia Da Costa is the author of the Black Lace novels *Continuum*, *Entertaining Mr Stone*, *Gemini Heat*, *Gothic Heat*, *Gothic Blue*, *Hotbed*, *Shadowplay*, *Suite Seventeen*, *The Devil Inside*, *The Stranger*, *The Tutor*, *In Too Deep* and *Kiss It Better*. Her paranormal novellas are included in the Black Lace collections *Lust Bites* and *Magic and Desire*. Her short stories appear in numerous Black Lace anthologies.

Alley Cats
Jennie Treverton

This is a midnight café in the middle of the city. Hiding among high street retail outlets and pubs that used to be theatres, it's been run by the same Italian family for three generations. The tablecloths are yellow gingham PVC and each table carries a fake cyclamen in a plastic pot. At a certain time of afternoon someone takes all the pots away and replaces them with Chianti bottles-cum-candleholders with wide mantles of wax trickles. At ten-thirty or so someone takes the bottles away and the tables are left bare until the last drunk has gone home, whereupon the cyclamens come out again.

I'm what you might call a regular. A few weeks ago, I was in here when I met the most astonishing man.

The interior walls of this café have a colour and texture like skin on a bowl of cold porridge. There are framed faded landscapes of windmills and haymaking peasants, and behind the counter is a black and white photo of the family patriarch, Matteo Nerone, clinking wine glasses with a British film star who came here once. The wall around it is bare, anticipating further photographs of celebrity clientele, but so far nobody else has come in.

You can come here after clubbing at five in the morning, bang down an espresso doppio or two, then stroll to the office while eating a sugar-dusted croissant to soak up your excesses. Not that I've done that for a while. At thirty-two I don't have that kind of stamina any more. I'll come at other times of day, such as Saturday afternoons, when I sit and read a novel, legs crowded by shopping bags, or after an evening out with friends, as a final, selfish, solitary treat before I go back to my flat, a fifteen-minute walk from here.

This place hasn't changed much since I first discovered it. The coffee machine is new, the ashtrays have disappeared since the ban, but everything else is exactly the same. These days, whichever Nerone happens to be working when I visit will show me to my favourite table and pull the chair out for me, and if it's Matteo he'll use his towel to beat any crumbs off the seat with a flourish and a wink. I sit facing the window, taking velvety sips of the best hot chocolate I've ever tasted, made with grated dark chocolate from Italy. No gritty powders here, not at Matteo's. In the grand old days I'd smoke a cigarette too, but these days I hold on to my craving until I leave.

So I sit here and I watch the people outside, the hardcore drinkers, the tarts and the lovers, the wandering innocents, the perverts, the pugilists looking for an excuse to throw a punch, the desperadoes looking for true love in the wrong place, wrong time; I see them all. And they always see me, because this window is warm and bright at night and because I am an unusual-looking woman who stands out in any situation.

Two weeks ago, I walked in here a little after midnight and about a minute later it began to rain heavily. I ordered my hot chocolate and settled in my seat to wait for the weather to pass, thinking that I could be there a while since I didn't have an umbrella. I'd come from The Royal, where a friend and ex of mine, Robert Checkman, had just made his stand-up comedy debut. He'd been a brilliant parody of himself, the shuffling, mumbling pessimist too tired to be truly hostile – 'My New Year's resolution, to give up' – and the audience had tittered doubtfully, but by the end was in stitches. He and I met at college in London and were an item briefly. My best memory of that time is my joy at discovering how skilfully he gave head, a talent that really came into its own on those occasions when his cock was disabled by antidepressants. He had quite a following back then, when he'd burst into spontaneous knife-sharp tirades aimed at whatever had got under his skin that day, making everyone around him roar and get hard or wet.

But, as with many of his ilk, the nearer you got to him the less amusing he was. Up close, there's nothing funny about an outlook like Robert's. We split up one night on Waterloo Bridge and he threatened to throw himself into the Thames, vainly, because I knew he wouldn't do it. He loved the melodrama far more than he loved me. Anyway, we remained good friends and I found that I could enjoy his black jokes again, and only occasionally did I miss his flickering tongue.

I thought I'd never find a man with a tongue like his. How wrong I was.

A few years ago Robert came out as bisexual and has hardly had a girlfriend since. On the pavement outside The Royal he gave me a hug and went off to celebrate at home with Aris, his new Macedonian shag. I crossed the road and came here for my hot chocolate and my view, which on that night was all broken up by spattering raindrops. The looming edifice of the Millennium Plaza, which contained The Royal among other bars and clubs and eateries, was already showing signs of age. Its once-white prefabricated panels were streaked with the grey of exhaust fumes and were awash with waterfalls from breaks in the guttering. Through my wet window pane the neon of the eye-shaped Millennium Plaza sign seemed to bleed away. The people in the queue for the cashpoint were all huddled together with coats over their heads. And all this was overlaid with my own reflection, pale and quite solid in comparison with the disintegrating outside world.

Yes, I am an unusual-looking woman, and not only because I am considerably larger than the average. I have a certain look which I've cultivated for a long time and that is inspired by a time long dead. I have Rita Hayworth pin curls, Lana Turner eyes, porcelain skin, rouged cheeks, Chinese Red lips. I have a heart-shaped face framed with black waves that sometimes I pin up elaborately but on that night I'd left loose round my shoulders. My eyelids are haughtily dark, my eyebrows thin, sceptical slivers.

I'm not obsessive about historical accuracy. Generally I'll wear a blend of modern and wartime styles. And nothing I wear is really vintage, because during the war women didn't have forty-two-inch hips and a forty-inch, DD-cup bust. So I buy reproduction clothes or make my own, and I eschew such details as miniature veiled tilt hats which, though authentic, just don't do anything for me. Thank goodness, we live in a time when you don't have to wear a hat to be a lady.

On that night, I was wearing a knee-length pencil skirt and a short-sleeved blouse that I'd created by upsizing a vintage pattern in black lacework with a flared peplum that flattered the swell of my bottom. I wore seamed stockings and kitten heels, and my faux astrakhan swing coat hung on the back of my chair. Fake fur, another gift of the modern world for which I'm very grateful.

I'm happy to be voluptuous and I think the look works for me. The style is supposed to be about wartime austerity but on my extravagant body it becomes something quite different. I love wearing boned underwear that squeezes my waist and allows my hips and breasts to spill out to their true fullness. I have a whole wardrobe of girdles and waist-cinchers made to vintage patterns in fabrics far more luxuriant than the times would have allowed. I don't wear them tightly enough to be really uncomfortable. I have no interest in achieving an extreme silhouette, only a curvaceous form that exhibits some of the sensuality I feel inside. I am equally at home in loose camisoles and silky French knickers. I hear they're coming into fashion again. I can recommend them highly.

On that night I was wearing a black satin bullet bra and a matching girdlette, which is a useful item halfway between a girdle and a suspender belt. I'd teamed them with modern skimpy satin knickers, not wanting a visible pantyline and because sometimes you just want drawers that slip off without a fuss. I find that part of me is always conscious of what I have on underneath, especially in the most public of places, like Matteo's, when I see people glance at me, look away, then look back for a longer appraisal as they so often do. I like to stare right back at them to see how they react. Call it a psychological test. Most people, being terribly British, will look away again immediately, but occasionally someone will surprise me. I love doing this. I feel as if I'm flirting with the whole world.

Anyway, here I was, imprinting an ever deeper Chinese Red crescent on the lip of my cup. I reached into my bag for my brass powder compact, the only genuine vintage item I own, checked my lipstick and brushed some specks of eyeshadow from my cheekbones. I snapped it shut and looked up to see a man in a hat walking along the pavement outside my window. His head was turned towards the Plaza so I couldn't see his face. But what struck me as unusual was that he was wearing a fedora.

A fedora. If he'd been wearing a trilby I wouldn't have looked twice. Even teenagers wear trilbies these days. But a real, wide-brimmed, Humphrey Bogart fedora, mid-grey and immaculate with an ivory band. Then I noticed that he was holding a black umbrella, and this also seemed strange. British men, on the whole, don't carry umbrellas because of a misplaced idea about masculine indifference to bad weather. That is, until they reach a certain age and masculine indifference becomes less of a worry to them than personal comfort. But this man wasn't old, I could tell that from the jaunty, speedy lope of his walk. He passed close to my window and just before he went out of view his head turned towards me. I saw that he was Asian and young – twenty-five, twenty-six at most – and he had strong features, a square jaw, straight nose, narrow eyes. He had such a generous mouth, slightly open as if he was drawing in air through his teeth, the middle of his lower lip jutting fatly. Illuminated by the café window his skin tone had delicious warmth. His colour reminded me of Dulce de Leche, the thick, buttery caramel sauce from Argentina that I first tried last Christmas when my friend Cassandra gave me a jar, knowing I'd die with delight, each spoonful taking me as close as humanly possible to oral orgasm.

He was wearing a great suit, charcoal grey, single-breasted, and like any great suit it transmitted a wealth of information about the body enclosed within, slim and lithe, long-limbed, tall but in proportion, not spindly or overgrown like some young men who haven't quite reached their mature form. With his decadent, pursed mouth and his half-closed eyes, he looked deep in thought. As his eyes met mine it was as if I'd startled him. His face opened up and he looked as though he was about to smile at me, and then he was gone. All this happened in two seconds, no more.

I adore a man in a fedora, any man, but that man was something else entirely. A young, thoughtful, intensely sexy Asian man with sinful lips and exquisite dress sense. I almost sprang to my feet there and then to chase after him but common sense stopped me. I wondered whether he was a forties aficionado like myself, or whether the hat was part of some uniform, some costume. Or whether I'd missed something and fedoras were having a long-overdue fashion renaissance.

I wondered what he'd thought when he'd looked at me. Did he see my style, my hair, my breasts? Or did he just see a big woman in a lot of black? There's no accounting for taste, after all, and there's no denying the attraction of men, especially younger men, to waifish women.

At this point I began to feel the futility in my state of excitement, because the man in the hat was long gone, and whatever impression I'd made was evidently too fleeting to persuade him to come back. It was time to go home and have Dulce de Leche dreams. But the rain was falling quite heavily and I didn't want to get wet. Still, I had the strongest urge to get out on the street.

A cigarette would be my solution. I would stand on the café steps and hide under the awning while I smoked a cigarette and waited for the rain to stop. And who knows, maybe I'd catch a glimpse of him at the bottom of the street, if I was quick enough.

I gathered my things, putting my coat and gloves on, leaving a two-pound coin on the table for Matteo. As I opened the door, two girls in denim shorts and opaque tights raced in to claim my table.

Outside the cold air was full of voices and the pulse of distant dance music. The rain seemed a little lighter. Opening my brushed-steel cigarette case I looked down the street and saw a mass of party people, some beanies and baseball caps, a pink cowboy hat or two, but no fedora.

It's inevitable, I suppose, if you play this game, if you flirt with the world, that this behaviour will lead on to proper contact, to talking and touching and finally to bed. My last boyfriend, Lucas, was an unapologetic starer. His mother was French which would go some way towards explaining his lack of embarrassment. He worked out when I'd be likely to visit this place and began to turn up whenever I was here. He'd lean on the counter, gossiping with Matteo or whoever was on, looking over at me so often and so lecherously that it was painfully obvious what they were talking about, and he'd send Matteo over with amaretti biscuits, begging for my phone number, and I refused for ages because I just didn't find him attractive. By the time he'd got me into bed, in a five-star hotel near the coast, and made me come three times and taken my anal cherry, all in one night, I thought I was in love. Things happen, personalities emerge and change, all the time, it seems to me. Lucas and I broke up after a series of heated arguments about politics. When it emerged that he was pro-vivisection in cosmetics, in psychological research and practically as a leisure pursuit, he lost the power to bring me to orgasm. Nothing is fixed. My love life, least of all.

So when I saw the black umbrella bobbing over the crowd, getting closer and closer, there was a small, vain part of me that understood what was happening. And he understood too, because when our eyes met again we shared a smile of recognition, a soft, almost sheepish smile that confirmed everything.

'Got a light, lady?' he said, his accent local, the unlit cigarette in his mouth wagging as he spoke.

And really, he needn't have said anything. He could have taken my hand and led me anywhere, willingly, wordlessly. But because we were strangers and terribly British, we had to strike up a conversation.

'Of course,' I said.

I lit a match and, cradling it in my palm, held it towards his face. There was a certain dignity in the line of his brow and his long straight nose. His eyes were two dashes of acute cleverness.

'What's your name?' I asked.

'Syed. Yours?'

'Claire.'

'I've seen you,' he said. 'Here, in the window. Why are you always on your own?'

I could smell that he'd been drinking whisky. One of my favourite aromas, whisky on a man's breath.

'I like my own company,' I said. 'And I like having no distractions.'

'Distractions from what?'

'From my view, of course. My view of the world.'

'I see,' he said, nodding.

He blew smoke upwards, showing me his throat, his Adam's apple, the underside of his barely stubbled jaw. I noticed that he was wearing a navy silk tie handpainted with a night view of Paris, all white and yellow and red. It was undoubtedly a vintage piece.

'I must be in your way,' he said. 'You'd rather I retreated back into the street scene.'

'You don't have to go just yet. I don't mind you being up close.'

He took this as permission to move in a little closer, bringing with him a stronger smell of whisky as he looked into my eyes. I found myself wanting nothing more than to taste his whisky lips.

'Sure I'm not in your way?' he said.

'Well, perhaps you should retreat,' I said, fighting back a smile. 'And I'll come along too.'

He was too cool, too self-possessed to show surprise at my boldness.

'Let's retreat,' he said, holding out his elbow.

I slipped from the protection of the café awning to that of his umbrella, sliding my arm into his, fingers brushing the swell of biceps. The sudden nearness of him made my head swim as we began to walk along the pavement.

'Your name's Claire. That kind of fits with the image I'd built up in my mind.'

'Do I look like a Claire?'

'You do.'

'Gosh, I'm curious about this image. What did you come up with?' I asked.

He laughed. 'Oh, I've given you quite an elaborate back story.'

'You must tell me.'

'You'd be offended.'

'I doubt it,' I said. 'I'm very broad-minded.'

'Yes, I thought you would be,' he said with the merest hint of irony.

'Oh, come on,' I said, tugging his arm. 'I want to know what impression I give out.'

'The impression you give,' he said, 'is that of a sultry, worldly, deeply sexy woman. As I'm sure you're well aware.'

The back of my neck began to tingle.

'Go on,' I said.

'You've lived in different places, different countries, but you've come home, to live near where you were brought up,' he said.

'True,' I said. 'Well done.'

'Recently divorced.'

I shook my head.

'Afraid not. Never married, in fact.'

'You like to draw,' he continued, unfazed. 'You design rococo furniture for a living. You hate giving blow jobs and you always drink champagne cocktails on your birthdays.'

All this imaginative nonsense made me smile, and I decided to reward him with the reaction he was hoping for.

'Hang on, what makes you think that?' I said in mock outrage. 'I happen to adore giving blow jobs.'

'You haven't given one in a long while,' he said.

I opened my mouth to speak but nothing came out. Did I give the impression that I was a desperado? But to deny his claim, which happened to be true, might make me seem a little too worldly.

Then again, he wanted to see me as worldly, didn't he?

'That's untrue,' I said. 'I sucked a cock last week, in fact, and it was heaven. So there you are.'

'Oh yes? And whose was this cock?'

'Just a man who came on to me in Matteo's. Some stranger in a hat, with nice eyes. I took him home and I sucked him and fucked him, and I didn't even catch his name.'

'A lot of men would be too wary to approach a woman like you. Most men don't have the balls.'

'You don't believe me?' I said, wishing that I'd come up with some more convincing attributes for my fabricated lover.

'Not at all,' he said, quick as a flash. 'I'd say it's been months since a man gave you a proper, screaming-out orgasm.'

'Look, you,' I said with something approaching annoyance. 'That's just not true. You might think you've got me all worked out but, let me tell you, my boy, I am far from straightforward.'

'If you'd been fucked really well, I could tell. I'd have seen it on your face.'

'How long have you been watching me?' I said, feeling a slight uneasiness and wanting the feeling to go away because it was a dreadful distraction from his body's warmth which was triggering, in my sex, such a pleasant tension and a tickle of gathering moisture.

'I haven't been watching you, as such,' he said. 'But, you must admit, you're pretty impossible to ignore. Sitting there in your window, all wrapped up in your glamour and mystery. I want to see what's underneath. Here, come with me,' he said, grabbing my hand.

He pulled me away from the main street into an unlit lane too narrow for cars, with tall brick buildings on both sides. Our surroundings were partially visible in the slanting yellow light from the main street. The ground was strewn with sodden sheets of newspaper and takeaway detritus. There was another main street at the far end of the alley, the route blocked by a row of bins. A cascade of rainwater was falling from a roof, landing on a pile of dismantled cardboard boxes with a loud, continuous blatting sound. Thankfully we were sheltered by a wide overhang. It was the kind of alley that would smell, on dry days, of stale urine.

At this point my brain was on red alert. I felt distinctly unsafe with this amorous stranger, who might possibly be some kind of stalker, in a dark place away from the safety of the crowd. He closed his umbrella and leaned it against the wall with the easy air of a man entering his own home. Then, facing me, he gripped me by the shoulders. My chest was thudding and I was aware of the determination in his hands and his heavy, slow breathing. He swallowed and I saw a knot rise on his cheek as he clenched his teeth. It occurred to me that this would be the appropriate moment to knee him in his balls and run.

But I didn't do that. Of course I didn't. Instead, I kissed him.

And, oh, it was such soft, whisky-laced heaven. You know how a kiss can be a signature gesture, telling you the essence of a person in an instant? I had such a powerful impression of this man, in the melt of his mouth, this man who was strong and serious and subtle. His hat brim was against my cheek, hiding everything so that there was no city, no Saturday night, only our faces and our private atmosphere. After who knows how long, I broke away and laughed to see him entirely smeared with Chinese Red. He smiled and held my face round my chin, making my head tilt back.

'I knew you'd look good with your lipstick all messed up,' he said and kissed me some more.

I loved the way he held me by the chin as his tongue lapped mine, making my throat stretch and my whole body open up. We grew hungrier, bodies pressing, his thigh between mine, his chest crushing mine as we moaned into each other's mouths and ate each other's ragged breaths. He had me up against the wall so hard I could feel my lungs restricted by my flattened ribcage. I anchored my heel on the brickwork so that I could raise my knee and rub my sex on his thigh, my skirt scrunched high, his hand running up and down my leg, fingers slipping under my suspender. He had me so aroused I couldn't think. I had become feral, running on instinct, grinding against his thigh muscle. My sex was sobbing for direct touch, and digging into my hip was the solid proof that he was as lost as I was.

My hands delved under his jacket and I felt, through his shirt, a hard lean body, a flat stomach, sleek pectorals. I love this about men's shirts. The cotton is so thin, such an insubstantial nod to civility, and all you need to do is run your hand across it to feel his nakedness. I would have given anything to remove his shirt for him. Instead I loosened his tie and undid the top few buttons, breathing in his escaping body heat.

We heard voices and two girls appeared at the top of the alleyway, one very drunk with the randomly lurching gait of someone about to pass out or throw up. The other, who was keeping her friend upright, propped the drunk against the wall and let out an irritated sigh.

'Not down there,' slurred the drunk. 'My bed . . . Justin . . .'

'Oh, for Christ's sake,' said the other.

'Will you kindly fuck off,' said Syed loudly.

The more sober girl looked at us, eyed my exposed suspenders, and with a disdainful sniff she dragged her incapable friend away.

'It's not very private here,' I said, knowing full well that I'd let him screw me here anyway.

'Your coat hides a lot,' he said with a grin, his hands diving inside my astrakhan.

Through my clothes his fingertips traced the lines of my girdlette and bra. He looked at me with curiosity.

'Your tits are incredible. It's a bullet bra, isn't it?'

I nodded and flinched as he pinched my nipples.

'They go all the way to the tips of the cones. I did wonder.'

'They're very sensitive,' I said. 'More than most, I think.'

'Too sensitive to touch?' he asked. His hands fell away.

'Sometimes, they can be,' I said. 'But you're welcome to try.'

'OK,' he smiled.

He did something interesting then, something quite novel to me. He bent his head low and sucked my breast through the material of my bra and blouse. His lips were strong, his mouth warm, his humid breath percolating through to my skin. The fabric managed to dampen my nerve endings and I shuddered with the kind of pleasure I have only rarely enjoyed.

'Good?' he asked.

'Good?' I mumbled. 'My God. Yes.'

Still mouthing my nipple he reached under my skirt and began to explore. No doubt he was gratified to discover I was wearing uncomplicated modern knickers over my suspenders so that they were easy to pull down. They caught on my shoes and I trampled them off, ruining them and not caring, because his fingers were sliding through my sex lips and making me realise how wet I was and how full my clitoris had become. I turned my head and rested my cheek on the rough bricks while his mouth and fingers coaxed my body to points of pure arousal. I heard my own breathy groans, the gurgle of drainpipes, the blat of water on cardboard. There was bawdy male laughter on the main street and the thought crossed my mind that we were the focus, but I was utterly helpless to do anything about it.

After a while I noticed tremors in his lower body, such was the contorted position he was holding. Reluctantly I pulled at his shoulders, inviting him to stand up straight, and I noticed that I was still wearing my leather gloves. I went to take them off but he grasped my wrist and guided my hand down to his crotch.

'I'd like to know what it feels like,' he said with a smile.

I wasn't sure if my gloved hand would have enough sensitivity to handle his erection so I was careful at first, undoing his fly, reaching inside and exposing it with care, feeling as if I were handling a museum piece. It was strange not to be able to feel any of the detail but to have only a vague sense of something hard and upright and thick. It became obvious that he didn't want such tenderness, though, as his fist enveloped mine and he showed me how roughly he wanted me to masturbate him. I picked up this new rhythm and soon he was fingering me with equal vigour. I looked down and saw the underside of his wrist at my hem, the tendons shifting like threads on a loom. I saw the head of his blood-filled cock, nearly black in the streetlight, and the thin skin of his shaft appearing and disappearing amid a flurry of soft dark leather. Our eyes met as we worked each other, shoulders shaking, and we laughed and grunted and thrust our groins onto each other's hands. I felt that familiar quickening in my lower body. I was grateful that I had the support of the wall.

Then he took his hand away. I was about to protest but I saw in his face that he knew what he was doing. His fist curled around my hand, halting it.

'OK,' he said, looking into my eyes. 'Where do you want it?'

I wasn't expecting him to be so coarse. He took me completely by surprise. Well, I hardly knew what I was saying, but I opened my mouth and out it came.

'In my arse,' I said.

He didn't betray an iota of shock.

'Not here, though. Come further back,' he said, leading me by the hand deeper down the lane.

We stopped next to what looked like a bricked-up window, although it was so dark I couldn't see anything properly. We'd lost our overhang so I could feel the rain but by now it had become an easily ignorable light drizzle. We were roughly equidistant from each main road, as private as was realistically possible.

'Lean here,' he said, patting the ledge of the bricked-up window.

I did as he said. Scrolls of peeling paint crunched under my elbows. He came behind me and rumpled my skirt up to my waist.

'You've got a heart-shaped arse,' he said. 'A heart-shaped face and a heart-shaped arse.' He laughed, stroking my buttocks. 'Two moons, and this pointed pouch down here.' His hand cupped my vulva. 'It's beautiful.'

'Thank you.'

'You're welcome.'

By now my confidence was faltering and I wondered why I was trusting this man to penetrate my anus. I heard the rip of a foil packet and the quiet slither of a condom and I was rigid, my body perfectly still, my sex awash with apprehension. Would he be too rough? Would he understand how to make it pleasurable for me? Or would he just fuck away and hurt me? I couldn't bring myself to turn and look at him. And then I felt his tongue, on my poor tense anus, lapping softly. He understood, of course. I was so relieved, so gratified, even more so when his hand came up and continued rubbing my clitoris.

'I need your wetness,' he said and some fingers entered my vagina, I couldn't tell you how many, more than one, and they pumped me a few times and withdrew.

I felt a fingertip at my rear, pushing, sliding in, and soon another joined it, making circling movements.

'Relax,' he said.

I began to breathe deeply, in through my nose, out through my mouth, willing myself to let go. It felt good and I found that if I concentrated on the sensations themselves I was able to leave my fear behind to an extent. He scissored his fingers apart and I let out a groan.

'Nearly,' he said, digits closing and opening.

His other hand was still on my clitoris, not rubbing now but keeping up a steady pressure. It was as though he had done this hundreds of times. His fingers withdrew from my arse, gradually, in stages.

I knew what was coming next and there it was, the round, pushing head of his cock. I tried hard not to squirm. He was on the edge of me for so long I began to think he wasn't going to make it. He was grunting with the effort, until finally his cock slid past the barrier and suddenly it was so easy. He screwed my arse with a light, quick rhythm and it was gorgeous, so filling, so slippery. He had one hand on my buttock, the other between my lips, tapping my clitoris. I backed on to him, my legs locked stiff, my forearms braced on the window ledge, head spinning, sex clenching, and it was gloriously wrong.

Noises were escaping from his mouth, groans and grunts and heavy exhalations, and he said, 'You're so tight,' his voice sounding constricted.

Then from far away, on the main street, I heard a man shout, 'Slut!'

A moment of perspective. I saw myself, knickers off, bent over in a seedy alley with a stranger's cock in my arse, and loving it.

I still don't know if it was directed at me. I couldn't see anyone watching. But in that moment I was convinced someone had seen us. And, whoever it was, I couldn't disagree with them. I was a vision of sluthood.

And I was gone. My orgasm came up and shook me from front to back, inside and out, leaving me whimpering, limp, lost. Grabbing my hips Syed slammed twice, three times, and I felt his climax explode inside me.

He stayed locked in place for a few minutes while his erection subsided. Then he withdrew gently, came around and gathered me up for a long and tender kiss, something else I hadn't been expecting. He was full of surprising notions, this man Syed.

We leaned against the wall and shared a cigarette.

'Your hat didn't fall off,' I said.

'It's a good fit,' he said, his eyes contentedly half-closed.

'So why the fedora? And that tie? Was it to impress me?'

'Why, are you impressed?'

I laughed in reply.

He looked at me, waiting for my answer, and when it wasn't forthcoming he said, 'The tie was my grandfather's. And the hat I bought yesterday. I just liked it, that's all. I wasn't thinking of you. But in retrospect it was a good purchase, I think.'

At the mouth of the alley we tidied each other up, using our thumbs to wipe the lipstick off each other's smiling faces. When we left we walked in separate directions. I didn't turn back until I was sure he was a good distance away. I could just make out his umbrella.

That was two weeks ago.

This is my favourite café, my favourite window. It's a dry, sharply cold night and the city is much quieter because of it. Matteo brings my hot chocolate to me. I wait for it to cool down a little, and as I take my first sip I see Syed walk past my window again. No umbrella, no tie, a different suit, pinstriped. The hat is the same. This time he stops, smiles and beckons.

Things change all the time. Eventually, I'm sure, he'll go the same way as the others, Lucas and Robert and all the lovers I've known. But that's tomorrow. Tonight I'm going to take him home.

I gather my things and put my coat on. Matteo is going round the tables and taking away the Chianti bottle candlesticks. He picks up mine and winks at me before blowing out my flame.

Misbehaviour features the short fiction of Jennie Treverton for the first time in Black Lace.

Phone Sex
Sommer Marsden

The man on the TV talked about spicing up your love life. Keeping your partner happy, role-playing, risk taking, dressing up and the like. The man on the TV was rather enthusiastic about this topic and the man on the TV had a personal experience he simply had to share with the studio audience (and viewers at home). The man on the TV was a moron, however, and I could not help but notice the shine in Jim's eyes and the smile on his face. I could not help but notice his interest and the way he kept shifting like he was turned on. I most certainly could not help but notice his hard cock pressing up and creating a tent under our key-lime-coloured bedspread.

I slid my hand down to his boxers, wormed my hand underneath and fisted his hard length. 'That guy is an idiot.'

'You know it, baby,' he said. But then his eyes rolled back and his breath caught. I watched the bang and flutter of his pulse at his throat and smiled. Thumbing the tip of his cock, stroking that velvety skin, I kissed his throat.

'That guy is full of shit.'

Jim could only nod. Then I buried my head under the comforter and slid my lips along his hard-on. I tasted each inch of his skin and sucked lovingly until his hips did that jitterbug bang against the mattress that says he's close. Cupping his balls, I hummed so the sound travelled up through him.

But how many times had I done it this way?

A lot.

And here he would flip me . . .

He flipped me.

And fuck me from behind . . .

He grabbed my hips and slid into me. His hips banged greedily against my ass as his dick slid home and pressed my cunt in all the right places.

And his finger would find my clit . . .

He started slow circles on the hard, swollen button of flesh and my face heated with blush and my nipples went hard. It felt good. It always felt good. But how many times this way now?

And now he would say, 'I'm done for, baby . . .'

'God, I'm done for, baby.' His circles grew more harsh, his movements more frenzied until he let out a groan and I followed suit. The orgasm flickered and danced inside me. I was light and air and heat as I came, Jim's arms wrapped around me.

Now he would kiss me on the back of the neck.

His lips touched the back of my neck and I shivered. 'That was great, Lexi. I love you, baby.' And then he was pulling me in and kissing my forehead and the next thing I knew he was snoring.

How many times had it all played out this way? God, I had no fucking clue. The man on the TV was a fucking asshole. A busybody. A meddlesome twit. But I couldn't shake him and his urgency at trying new and unexpected things. I fell asleep wishing we had watched the History Channel after all.

I just couldn't shake it. I pulled into the driveway and yanked the parking brake so hard I was surprised it didn't snap off in my hand. All day long my mind had been conjuring up unusual ways of fucking my husband. Dirty, naughty, possibly illegal.

Gone were thoughts of romance that would be my norm. I had run the gamut mentally, and was so over-stimulated I was bordering on irritated.

Jim was home but I couldn't find him. And then I smelt it. The distinct scent of a cigar. Which meant he had just suffered a really hard day and was sitting on our back deck. I threw my bags down and exited through the kitchen door. The shade of our oak brought a welcome coolness in the too-sunny, too-warm day. I dropped my suit jacket on a deckchair and slid my shoes off. He was reading the paper, cigar in hand, beer by his side.

'I need something from you,' I said.

His eyebrows went up and he puffed slowly. A departure from my normal, *Hi, honey. How was your day?* 'What do you need, Lex?'

I pulled the zipper of my skirt so it hissed loud enough and slow enough for him to catch it. He cocked an eyebrow and looked amused and confused simultaneously. 'What's up, babe?'

I dropped the skirt on our deck. I was gambling and the thrill of it shot straight up through my pussy and made my heartbeat skip drunkenly in my breast. Our neighbours on the right had a fairly good view of our deck, but their routine said they wouldn't be home yet. The neighbours to the left had a restricted view of our latticework wall. So that was fine. I dropped the skirt and it hissed against my nylons.

'I need something from you,' I said again, my voice lower so he would have to strain to hear me. All day my mind had been full of erotic, bizarre, lewd, sex-filled visions. My body was beating like one big pulse. My pussy was wet, my knees weak. I wasn't sure what I wanted first. His cock, his fingers, his mouth. I just wanted. I needed. I needed him.

Jim's attention was captured. He set the cigar to smoulder

in an ashtray and he sipped his beer, an exaggerated lazy sip that made my nipples peak. He was excited already, his cock pressing the charcoal-grey fabric of his slacks. I shimmied out of the hose, a boring normal nude but somehow sexy as I peeled them off. The proper silk blouse went next, hitting the deck with a haughty sigh.

'What did you need, Lex?' His eyes were tracking me and he seemed so very, very calm against my feelings of restless insanity. I caught myself flexing and then relaxing my hands like a junkie in need of a fix.

I stooped in my pale-grey silk panties and black lace bra. I grabbed the nylons and handed them over. He took them, wrapping them once, twice, three times around his fist before unwinding them. 'I need you. I need you to do something to me. Something you normally would not do.'

'Like what?' His voice was curious, but when he looked at me, I could see it shining in his eyes. The knowledge of what he wanted to do and what he would do. He already knew the answer.

'Whatever is making you look like that. Whatever you're thinking,' I breathed, and my tongue felt too big and the air felt too heavy in my lungs. 'Please,' I said, and I sounded like I was begging.

Because I was.

His face shifted just a bit. Not the normal face that greeted me every day. Maybe there was something under there, deep inside that he always wanted to do. And I was offering to do it. He wrapped and unwrapped the nylon on his hand again and then he patted my thigh. 'Come sit with me, Lexi.'

I moved slowly. I felt like I was dreaming but I knew I wasn't. I could hear the Jack Russell terrier behind us barking its damn head off as usual. The ice cream truck making its final summer rounds through the neighbourhood. The men three doors down laying the brand new in-ground pool. My legs moved like I was walking through water and he reached out and took my hand. Tugged me to him. Before I could sit, he shook his head. 'Let's get these off first.' And then I was being fully undressed slowly. Dappled sunlight falling through the full green trees around our deck.

I sat on his lap, stark naked while he remained dressed in his work clothes. I could hardly breathe, I could see my heart beating under my skin it was going so fast. I felt light-headed and woozy and excited. And my cunt was seeping onto his nice work pants. I wiggled around to try and get some relief and couldn't. The air stirred and a warmth brushed over my skin. My nipples were teased to tight little nubs by the summer breeze. What a small and simple pleasure. Warm air on your naked skin.

'Spread your legs for me,' Jim said and I let them fall open at a whorish angle. I couldn't quite manage a deep breath, I was panting. I watched his big hand slide up my thigh, pushing it aside just a bit more until he reached the summit. He rested his hand there, at the top of my thigh, his thumb just barely grazing my pubic hair. My ears were ringing from holding my breath. I wiggled, trying to force his hand. Literally.

'Stay still, Lexi. Stay still. You never just slow down. It's always a rush. Just slow down and be calm.'

I stilled. Did I always rush? I realised that I did. I stayed perfectly still, though it was killing me. I listened to the sounds of the neighbourhood and my eye flitted to our neighbours' on the right. I didn't see anything, but the big dark windows looked like inquisitive black eyes in the side of the house. Jim's thumb brushed over me, parted my nether lips, pressed my clit. Pressed it with the pad of his thumb like he was pressing a button. Inside, I grew warmer and wetter. But I focused on not moving, even when he dipped his head and sucked my nipple into his mouth. He pressed his thumb and sucked my nipple harder. Two single points of pressure on my body and I felt like I was vibrating from the excitement and the want and the newness of this version of us. And the need. I needed it. I needed a fix of him fucking me.

'Please,' I said, barely audible. God. I was begging again.

'Patience.' His thumb pressed me again but stroked a circle, too. I bit my lip to keep from begging and watched him touch me. That was something else. I never watched. I liked the look of his hands on my pussy, his forearm bunching and moving under his rolled-up sleeves while he rubbed tight little circles on my swollen clit.

I started counting my heartbeats. It helped me not whimper and moan and plead. Five heartbeats later, he dipped a finger inside me. Pressed me here and there until my hips started to arch and the moan I had been holding back slid over my lips against my will. 'Stand up for me,' he said.

He withdrew his finger and it was all I could do not to promise him anything in the world if he would put it back. I stood.

'Now turn around.' I turned and I felt my soft nylons looping around my wrists. Felt him tug them tight and then test the bonds that now held me gripped.

I turned, testing the bonds just to see. I had never been bound before. I found it highly erotic in a bizarre kind of way. I had to trust him. I could not catch myself should I fall. I had to believe that he would keep me upright should my balance leave me, which it felt like it would do at any moment. Excitement buzzed like electricity along my skin and I fought the vertigo that swept over me. I wanted to ask Jim what he was going to do to me but I swallowed the words. I would wait and be silent and patient. I went back to counting heartbeats.

'Open for me, Lex,' he said. He pinned me with a stern gaze.

'And let me do this. You never let me do this. You never let me take my time with you. I know you think it's all perfunctory and nothing but priming the pump, so to speak, but that's wrong. I like the taste of you. And the feel of you on my tongue.' As he spoke he ran his palms up the insides of my thighs. My nerves and muscles fluttered under his touch and I felt my body sway just a little. He steadied me with a big hand on my hip. 'I like to have my mouth on you. I like that you taste different when you've eaten strawberries and smell different in the summer than the fall. So, don't say a word. And I want you to watch.'

It wasn't a request. I nodded, his confession and demands stealing my breath and my ability to argue. I watched as he lowered his mouth to me and started. His warm lips dropped kisses along the tops of my thighs. He kissed just under my belly, just above my mound. He kissed one hip and then the other. And then the sweet spots where my waist dipped. That always made me jump and it did this time, too. So he kissed me there again but steadied me so I wouldn't fall. He kissed my belly button and I felt warm fluid sliding down my inner thighs. Had I ever been this wet before he'd even started? No. Jim looked up, big brown eyes finding mine and he smiled.

My knees threatened to buckle but when he pressed his lips to my nether lips and parted me with his tongue, I really didn't care if I fell or not. I could fall and I wouldn't be upset because sweet hot pleasure was thumping through my cunt. He sucked hard and then let up. He sucked harder and then licked. Rigid tongue, flat tongue. Swirls, figure of eights, circles. I watches his dark hair, the tip of his nose, his impossibly long eyelashes. The flashes of pink that were his tongue darting and moving over my pussy lips. I closed my eyes with the pleasure but then would spring them back open to see. His fingers smoothed

173

along the tops of my thighs and a thrill rushed right up the centre of me. All the way up into my womb and then a flurry of butterfly feelings in my belly. 'I'm going to come,' I admitted.

'Then come,' he said and the vibration of his words tipped me over the edge. That final drop of water in the cup that forces it to overflow. I came, and wished I could put my hands in his hair and yank him closer to me. Not let him stop. But I didn't have to worry about that because he didn't stop. He kept right on eating me as the orgasm flashed from fast red pleasure to lazy purple. Colours swirled behind my eyelids and I was making crazy-woman sounds.

My gaze shot to the empty windows again but I really didn't care. Part of me hoped someone was watching. Seeing me like this. Bound, naked, mid-orgasm. I probably looked insane. Or fucking gorgeous. Or both.

Flickers worked through my pussy. Spasms that warmed me and made me dance in place a little. Jim cupped my hips with his hands and kissed the blonde curls of hair between my legs. I heard his zipper and peeked at him, almost blushing from our odd encounter out in the semi-private sanctuary of our own backyard. 'Come on. Get on. Now I get to fuck you. You are definitely wet, Lex.' He laughed. I let him hold my waist as he lowered me towards his lap. My legs straddled the chaise lounge and then I found a good position where I wouldn't tip over. 'Good?'

'I feel like I'm going to fall.'

'I won't let you fall.'

I believed him.

He pressed the velvety head of his cock to me. 'I'm so wet,' I said. It was unreal how wet I was. From myself. From his mouth. From my orgasm. I was slick and ready and I had to steady myself to keep from dropping onto him.

'I know. I know, baby. Go slow, OK? Slow.' He arched up under me and shoved into me slowly, stretching me. I gasped. The air was too thick and too bright and I was so sensitive. 'Shh. Go on.'

I lowered slowly when I really, really wanted to just impale myself. But he said I always hurried and I was realising now that I always did. I went as slowly as I could without going crazy. He pulled my hips and pushed up and then I was full. Stretched and full and hovering right there on the cusp of coming again. The phone rang.

I stopped with Jim's cock buried to the hilt inside me. I moved my hips this way and that and sighed, but my eyes were on the phone. 'Shit.'

'Leave it,' he said and thrust up under me. I felt my eyes roll back as my pussy, plump and stimulated from his tongue and his fingers, responded with a tightening that made me sigh.

'I'm supposed to hear from Gordon. It's important.'

'No way.' He gripped me and arched up under me. Pulling me down and fucking up into me at the same time. I gasped as my cunt grew even tighter. God. How tight could I get before I simply died?

'I have to.' The phone had not stopped.

'No fucking way, Lex.' His face was dark. From pleasure and anger and somehow that turned me on even more.

'Jim,' I hissed, but my hips were rising and falling, my body eager and needy. My body didn't care about what was going on in my head. It only cared about what was going on down below.

'Alexis,' he growled. Then he sighed, grabbed the portable, flicked a button and pointed to me.

'Hello?' my boss asked from the speakerphone.

'Gordon. Um, hi!' I said, and Jim pushed his cock deep inside me and grabbed my hips, grinding me against him. I hiccupped and squealed.

'Alexis? Are you OK?' Gordon's uptight, stuffy, know-it-all manner came through the phone line loud and clear.

'Fine,' I said on a sigh. I cleared my throat and then coughed. The cough tightened up my cunt and my whole body seemed to throb. Jim and I locked eyes and he grinned. It was an evil grin and, when he touched my clit with his thumb, I knew why he was smiling.

'I need to run these final numbers by you. Simpson called back and we have a little more in the coffers than we thought.'

Rub, rub went Jim's thumb and my pussy wound tighter and tighter until I was biting my tongue to keep from panting. 'Good, good!' I yelped. I meant both. Good to more money, good to the hard cock inside me and the thumb pressing against my already stimulated flesh.

'Yes, well, glad to hear you sound so excited about it.'

'I am, I am.'

Coming, mouthed Jim and I bit my lip on a groan. I wanted to laugh and groan and moan and come. Instead I tried to breathe deeply.

'Good, I'm excited, too. It's so hard sometimes,' he said.

I swallowed a hysterical burble of laughter and I could tell Jim was doing the same. He reached up, a devilish look on his face, and he pinched my nipples so hard I hissed. 'What's hard?' I asked. God, I was so close to cackling like a witch with laughter and screaming from an orgasm, I didn't know what to do. My insides were a chaotic mess of mixed emotions.

'The money thing. Running the numbers. Balancing the red and the black.'

'Well, I appreciate you letting me know. I knew it was iffy. I didn't know if I'd have to make some calls.' I was riding Jim faster now, and I could tell by the set of his jaw that he was really close to coming.

'Nope.' Gordon chuckled deep in his throat and I could almost see him polishing his nails on his suit jacket like the pompous jackass he is. 'I bet you thought I was calling to stick it to you.'

I dissolved in silent hopeless laughter as Jim simultaneously clutched at me and thrust up into my willing body. He was right there. I was right there. And here we were laughing help-lessly at poor, innocent Gordon. 'Yeah, I thought I was in for a reaming,' I practically wheezed.

Jim's shoulders shook but then his eyes turned serious and I shook my head.

'Well, I guess we're done then,' Gordon said. 'Are you sure you're OK? You don't sound yourself.'

'Oh, I am fine. I am wonderful. Thanks so much!' I trilled, and Jim reached out and disconnected.

'Oh, God, ream me, baby,' I snickered, but the humour was gone. Now I was ready. Ready to come with my husband.

'That's what I'm doing, baby.' His movements grew more aggressive and he smoothed his fingers over my nipples until I shivered and jumped. 'Come with me, Lexi,' he said, going rigid under me. Clutching me closer.

So I did.

I fell forwards onto him and kissed his neck. 'Well, that was different.'

'That was good,' he growled and nipped at my throat until I kissed him into stillness.

The next day my head was full of our phone sex. How I had to regulate my voice and exercise self-control. How I could feel pleasure but had to hide it. How I wanted to scream out loud and had to stifle the urge. I emailed Jim.

I want to do it again. I want to do it from the start.
On the phone. Phone $ex.
Loveyoume

He called me on the phone. 'We can do that. We can totally do that. Figure out who you want to call. And by the way . . .'

'Yes?' My heart was pounding so hard my blouse jumped under the rush of blood.

'I cannot fucking stop thinking about you.' He hung up.

'Oh,' I said to no one. Then I rushed off to the Ladies' room. The mere thought of masturbating at work was irrational at best. But there I was. Off to the private restroom. My skirt around my ankles, braced against the wall. Getting myself off at the thought of my husband across town in his office thinking of me. And fucking me. And the way I had been laughing so hard the vibration had added to our orgasms.

And I couldn't even comprehend how very bad and wrong it was, what we had done. Mischievous didn't even cover it. Dirty, naughty, filthy, nuts. And we were going to do it again. And this time – on purpose.

I came, standing there, ankles wide. My spectator pumps looking pretty damn proper for a woman finger-fucking herself to orgasms in the washroom. I sighed as another spasm worked through my pussy. Trying to keep my moans soft as I curled my fingers harder and faster, pushed the heel of my hand against my clit and came again. Thinking of sex in the sunshine and sex on the phone. Phone sex. But not the kind one imagined.

'More phone sex,' I laughed and then washed up. The day seemed to take forever but also passed in a blur of distraction and fantasising.

At home, I found him in the kitchen, making rice and rubbing seasoning on a steak. 'You're glowing. What did you do?' He grinned at me, his five o'clock shadow making him that much more sexy. I always liked it when Jim kissed me hard with a stubbly face. I liked the scrapes and redness that it left. Liked being marked. I touched it and it rasped under my fingers.

'I didn't do anything. Why?'

He caught my finger with his lips, sucked it into his mouth. He sucked hard and an invisible line of pleasure between my finger and my cunt flared to life. 'You got off at work. Or on the way home.' It wasn't a question and I felt a blush heat my face.

'How did you know?'

'I can taste you on you. Therefore, I know you've been touching yourself. I was shaving this morning when you were in the shower so it's from today. Not from yesterday. You were all clean this morning.' He turned, pulled me into his body. Flush against him. His blossoming hard-on pressed my pussy through my skirt. I wiggled against him.

'And now?'

'Now, I guess you're dirty.'

'I asked Jan to call me at home. Tonight. Soon.' I blurted it out like a confession. Because it was a confession.

His eyes were darker. He was horny. He smiled, kissed my bottom lip. Licked my neck. My nipples went taut and I shook a little in his arms. 'OK. We have dinner and then you handle your phone call.' He bent a bit, ran his hands up the insides of my thighs as he said it. His calluses hissed on the nylon and a new wetness spread in my panties.

'Can I help with dinner?'

He told me what to do and I did it.

I barely managed my dinner. My insides were humming with anticipation. When Jim looked at me (as he calmly ate his steak) it felt as if he were touching me. His gaze as intense as if his hands were stroking over my skin. I shifted in my seat, the friction pushing the crotch of my tango panties against my body. All in all, I felt pretty much unstable and high-strung. When he touched me under the table with his hands a high hysterical giggle slipped out.

'Someone's wound too tight.' He pushed his hand slowly under my skirt. His fingers moved gently along the tops of my hose. He plucked the garters like guitar strings and I realised I was holding my breath.

'A bit,' I admitted. Fuck. A bit? Try completely and thoroughly torqued up.

'What time was she to call?'

'Supposed to be after dinner.' I swallowed some water and inched around in my seat. I moved my hips a bit to the left so he could reach me better. He didn't. He simply stroked my skin gently above my stockings. He was trying to drive me insane, I was sure of it.

I twisted my napkin over and over again, willing the phone to ring. Willing it to emit its shrill call in our silent house. The air conditioning kicked on with a whir and I jumped. 'You really need to calm down a little.' He grinned.

'Touch me,' I blurted. Then I bit my tongue, embarrassed at my desperation. Even with the man I loved. The one who knew me inside and out.

Jim laughed softly and ran his fingertip over my thigh again. 'I am touching you.'

Smart ass.

'You know what I me –'

The phone rang and he touched his finger to my clitoris through my panties. I sucked in a breath, shivered. I was so wet now just from that one touch and that stupid ring. A bell. I was the Pavlov's dog of sex.

It rang again and I stared at it. Jim touched me again, pushed me harder through my lace panties. 'Aren't you going to get that?'

I wanted so much to go one step further with our phone sex. I wanted to intentionally fuck while trying to hold a rational conversation. But I was hesitant to break contact with his hand between my leg, his fingers stroking me through my panties.

He moved his hand and half stood, snagging the handset from the base. He handed it to me and I read the read-out. The number I knew by heart and the name Jan Alban, the head Administrative Assistant at work. I had asked her to call.

It rang again in my hand and I flinched at its shrill yip. Jim rose, came around behind my chair and touched my shoulders. 'Answer the phone, Lex. It's OK. Hit the speaker button. Go on.' Then he reached around my throat and started to slowly unbutton my blouse.

I couldn't breathe at all, it seemed, but I managed to hit the button and when the sound of an open line hit my ears I stammered, 'Hello?'

'Alexis! Is this a bad time?'

Jim's hands slid inside my now-open blouse. He cupped my breasts through my sheer bra, tweaked my nipples until that tickly sensation in my throat started. I cleared my throat, arching my back so that my tits filled his warm hands. 'Yes . . . it's um. It's fine. How are we doing with the mmm . . .'

His fingers were stroking an invisible line from my solar plexus down my middle. They tripped over my belly button and my stomach muscles danced under his touch.

'I'm sorry?' Jan said, sounding confused. Who could blame her?

I coughed to cover it but the vibration didn't help me between my thighs. The force of the cough made my pussy grow tight. Made me wish for something that would fill me. Like the hard-on I had had pressed against me not long ago. 'Sorry. Tickle in my throat. How are we doing with candidates for a new receptionist and office assistant?'

Jim's hands pushed at my panties and I arched up so that he could slide them down over my hips. He disengaged the garters and I worked at the hose as Jan rambled on and on about the women and men who had applied for our two open positions. I sat there in my garter belt and watched his hands come from behind. Like being fondled by the semi-invisible man. His left hand parted my nether lips, his right hand found my wet and slippery centre and stroked. 'You're so fucking wet,' he said in my ear. Right up to my ear so that my nipples grew harder and my pulse beat almost painfully hard.

'Pardon?' Jan said.

'What?' I was panicking. Had she heard him?

'Did you say something?'

'No, oh, God, no,' I said, meaning yes. Oh, God, yes, because his fingers were working me faster now, pausing here and there to slide into my slick cunt and flex against the swollen walls.

'Are you . . . are you um, certain this is an OK time?' Jan asked. 'You sound a bit distracted.'

'No. No, it's fine. No one said anything. It's probably the TV you're hearing. I'll turn it down.' I put my fingers to my lips in the universal signal to be quiet as Jim peeked over my shoulder. He bit the side of my neck after a sly smile. Then he was on his knees, his lips latching onto my nipple, his tongue making me squirm in my seat.

'Oh, OK, well as I was saying. That girl Simone looks promising . . .'

I lost her words, hearing only the monotonous drone of her voice as he kissed down my belly and then around my mound. He licked me only a few times, just enough to have me panting like a dog. His tongue hot and searing and able to go exactly where I needed it to be. I didn't rush or talk. I watched and tried to catch some of Jan's words. *Experienced, qualified, fast, friendly* and *outgoing* all penetrated the sex fog in my brain.

'Good, good,' I said to her and to him. I didn't say 'so fucking good', which is what I meant because she might be startled by such language.

'Yes, she really isn't as qualified as the other girl. Oh, what was her name? Mary . . .'

Gone again. Just the white noise of a woman talking work. He parted my legs, pushing them wide. My bare ass on our antique dining room chair. He worked his button and his zipper and then winked. He put his fingers to his lips. 'Shh.' He made the sound so softly that even I hardly heard him. I watched him jerk his hard cock with his hand. God, that turned me on. When he handled himself it made me half crazy.

'It's hard,' I whispered, licking my lips.

He nodded, laughing silently.

'I'm sorry?' Jan asked, her monologue ceasing as she heard my voice.

'It's um, hard sometimes to make these decisions. But you seem to have a good handle on it.' When I said that, Jim's shoulders started to shake with laughter, but he pushed the head of his dick to me and I pushed back against him.

Please, I mouthed.

'Oh, yes. That's true. We've had some really good candidates this time. Not like the last time. The one girl could really do a good job, even with Barbara out on maternity leave . . .'

I thrust my hips forwards, pushing him into my depths.

I watched his fingers bite into the flesh of my hips. He started to rock into me. Nice and slow. So slow I wanted to smack him, but my body responded with a warm surge of happiness. Yes, yes. He was in me, deep inside me. Fucking me and fucking me while Jan prattled on and on about office help. 'God, yes.'

'Yes, I know! Can you believe it?'

Jan thought I was talking to her. Jim hooked his arms around my waist, lowered his upper body onto mine, bit my neck right above my collar bone so that I jumped and shivered in his arms. His hips thrust over and over, driving the polished mahogany chair back over the hardwood floor. He scooted forwards on his knees to keep up and when the chair hit the wall, he was able to drive into me deeper. Harder than before. 'Oh yes!' I said.

'I thought so too!' Jan said, oblivious that she was not in on this particular conversation.

His hands wormed under my ass, cupping my bottom as he rocked against me harder. His finger worked against my ass and then the pinch of his intrusion sent a shiver of pain through me. The pain tipped the pleasure and then, when he bit me, it was all done. I came, wrapping my legs around his waist as his tempo increased. 'Fantastic,' I crowed, riding out another blissful spasm.

Jim came hard, shaking with his release and his laughter as Jan chimed in.

'I'm so glad you're excited. So it's settled then?'

Jim and I stared at each other. I was confused, he was amused. His cock, still hard, was deep inside me. I moved a little and an aftershock of orgasm stuttered in my womb.

'Absolutely!' I said, shrugging. 'Thanks so much for all your hard work on this,' I said. 'I'll see you bright and early Monday.'

'Great. See you then, Alexis, and thanks for backing up my decision.'

I disconnected, arching up again to trigger another blip of pleasure in my pussy.

'So, who did you hire, baby?' Jim asked, kissing my throat and then biting me a few times just for fun. He knew I liked a little pain with my pleasure.

'I haven't a clue. I'll find out on Monday, I guess. It will be a surprise. Like Christmas!' I laughed.

We sat on the porch as the sun went down, with cold beer and a cool breeze and of course the lovely afterglow of great sex. 'That was phenomenal,' he said, taking my hand.

And to think it all came about because of an idiot on the TV. I nodded. 'I know. I think I have a kink.' I swigged my beer.

'I think you do,' he laughed.

'Hi there, Kourys!' our neighbour Giovanni yelled.

We waved as he made his way up the walkway, holding his own beer. Ours was a neighbourhood of porch-sitters and hammock-layers. Everyone knew everyone and a spontaneous weekend block party was not unheard of. 'How's it going, G?' I asked.

'Good, good. Glad it cooled off. I wanted to ask you, we're organising a charity event at the Fraternal Order of Police and I wanted to know if your company might sponsor us. Do they do that kind of thing?'

'They do.' I nodded. 'But I'd have to ask and get particulars.'

'Do you mind?'

'Not at all.'

I saw Jim smile in the purpling light of twilight. 'Why don't you give her a call? She loves to get on the phone,' he said. He was setting us up for another rendezvous. Such a bad, bad boy. A lovely, perfect, sexy bad boy.

'Really?' Giovanni asked. 'Me, I just can't wait to get off.'

'Me, either,' Jim said, barely suppressing a laugh.

The short fiction of Sommer Marsden appears in the Black Lace collections *Lust at First Bite*, *Seduction* and *Liaisons*.

Girls' Talk
Chrissie Bentley

I guess I just wasn't thinking straight.

I was so excited when he started to come, and the thin milky liquid gently seeped across his helmet, that I was already leaning forwards, my tongue tip poised to taste him, completely forgetting there was more to come. Spurt. Instinctively I flinched back. Splash. A thick streamer lashed itself to my cheek. It was on my nose, it was on my lip, it was in my hair – and it was still pumping. Above me, Dave was groaning his ecstasy, and I wanted to feel it too. I closed my eyes, opened my mouth, and clamped down on the end of his cock, and the spurting started all over again, as his hands closed around the back of my head, and he raised his hips to meet my face, moving himself inside my mouth, fucking my lips and flooding my mouth.

I'd done it. After how many years of dreaming of this moment, after all those nights spent caressing myself to sleep while my mind conjured hot, hard cocks for me to devour, I had finally sucked and swallowed – yes, mustn't forget to swallow it all – a man. And I loved it.

It was strange. Listening to my girlfriends talk, I really wasn't sure what to expect. It's slimy, it's sticky, it tastes of salt and cheese. Maybe it is, maybe it does. I'm sure there are times when it really isn't pleasant. Like, if he hasn't bathed in a while, or he's sweating a lot, or if you simply aren't in the mood, but decide to do it anyway. But right here, right now, with my pussy screaming so loudly for attention that the juices were trickling down my leg, with one hand massaging my own breast while the other held his cock upright, and every other fibre of my being focused firmly on drawing as much of his magic as I could milk from his balls . . . fuck going for a slap-up feast at the ritziest restaurant in town, I could dine like this forever.

Dave was softening now, but I continued to suck. In fact, I was sucking harder now, as the thickness receded and my jaw could relax more, now I could really go to town. I pulled him in deep, felt my nose brush his stomach; I liked the way it felt and went down even deeper, enfolding his entire prick in my mouth, while he just lay there gasping, his hands idly stroking my hair while I ground my face into his stomach and my mouth still hung onto its prize. And that felt good as well. Next time, I resolved, I would do it while he was still hard. I didn't know how my mouth would accommodate it, but now was not the time to worry. Details. I was going to deep-throat this boy, even if it meant removing my tonsils myself.

I sat up and looked him in the eye. Dave was still lying there, exhausted, his body putty. I kissed him on the mouth, wondered if he could taste himself all over my lips, and what he was thinking as he did. His hands slipped onto my waist, tugging at me; for a moment I wasn't sure what he was doing, but I relaxed and went with the flow, as he drew me up, up, up, and then his hands were on my ass, pushing me towards his face . . . pushing my still wet, still screaming pussy closer and closer to his darling mouth. And when his tongue finally touched me, traced my folds, invaded my pink, slipped inside and began to roll, it was as though my mind completely surrendered control of my body to my instincts. For the next thing I knew, I was riding his face, not gently, not sweetly, but without an iota of tenderness. I was bucking, I was grinding, I was crying out to Dave and Jesus and the gods of Fuck-Me-With-Your-Face-Oh-Christ-I'm-Coming-Yes-Yes-YES! And I was, and I did, and my entire body was shattering into thousands of pieces, and every other orgasm I had ever had in my life felt like a mere undressed rehearsal for the real thing.

He was still licking me; I placed a hand on his forehead and shifted a little. 'No more,' I breathed. 'Let me.' The last few wriggles, the last few thrusts, I needed to be in control of them, wringing the very last drops of joy out of my pussy, as he caught his breath and I felt his wet face sticky against my inner thigh, his damp stubble adhering to my flesh. I raised myself and lay beside him, so warm, so secure, so safe. Neither of us spoke. What was there to say? *You were amazing?* We knew that already. *I've never come that hard before?* We knew that as well.

I reached down and felt his cock. Still soft, but that was OK. I didn't need it so badly now, was no longer consumed by the desperate urge to feel it driving down my throat ... in fact, now I was wondering whether that was even possible? I can set off my gag reflex when I'm cleaning my teeth. I couldn't imagine what a thick cock would do.

Back in class on Monday morning, looking around at my fellow students while Professor Glyczwycz droned on about the constitution in an accent that only thickened as the class went on, I tallied in my mind the girls who I *knew* had given their boyfriends 'good head'. Or, at least, who claimed to have.

Gloria. Yeah, well I wouldn't doubt that for a second. Five foot nothing of sheer sexual magnetism, she only had to chew her pen for every guy in the class to drop everything to watch.

Martha. She's been going steady with the same guy since High School. If she hasn't, then what on earth are they even doing together?

Lisa. I don't know. She's got a mouth on her, that's for sure. But whether she uses it for sucking cock or simply bragging about her conquests, nobody has ever been able to decide. The fact that she's been my best friend since Junior High only makes the mystery all the more intriguing.

And Jenny. An English Major, the class poet, and a girl so gifted with erotic rhyme that it's criminal that she will never get the chance to teach it in college. I've read verses she's written that could make your hair curl with excitement. She *has* to know what she's talking about; there's no way you could make that stuff up.

Anybody else? I don't know. Most of the girls here keep themselves to themselves, at least when it comes to the real nitty-gritty. Jenny did point out an intriguing stain on Sharon's blouse one morning that wasn't there before she disappeared between classes, and we spent far too much time trying to manoeuvre ourselves around, trying to catch the sunshine glistening off droplets of come on her cheeks. We didn't see any, but Jenny wrote a verse about it anyway, and how privileged did I feel, knowing that I was alongside her when she got the inspiration? I'll tell you. Very.

I made a beeline for Jenny at recess, asked about her weekend (dull, studying, and cold pizza for dinner every night), then told her about mine. In brief. Just a general, 'then Dave came over yesterday . . .'

'Your folks are out of town *again*?' Her voice was a mixture of incredulity and envy.

I nodded. 'Sick aunts can be very demanding.'

'Is she that bad?' We talked for a while about that; I can be blasé on the subject when it suits me, but in truth, I rather like

Aunt Lil, would probably even have cut class for a few days to travel up to visit her, if it hadn't been for Dave.

'Wow, he must be good,' Jenny smirked, and I really don't think she was expecting an answer, but she got one anyway.

'He's better than good. I haven't come that hard in my life.' And then it all came pouring out, what I did to him, what he did to me . . . Or was that me doing it to him again? I wasn't sure. Quite honestly, at the end, it wouldn't have mattered what his tongue and mouth were up to, just knowing he was there beneath me was all the stimulation I required. And I was about to tell her what I intended doing next when recess was over and we were hustling back to class, while Jenny smiled that secret smile that always precedes a new burst of inspiration. Jesus, was she going to write a verse about me?

Cocks followed me all over campus that day. Not literally . . . or maybe yes, literally. In maths class, it took me a good twenty minutes to confirm that Jerry Harris in the seat in front of me wasn't masturbating furiously through the lesson, but was surreptitiously playing with a calculator – banned from Mr Henderson's lessons, although Jerry wasn't the only student who disobeyed the prohibition. On the way to the cafeteria, I passed a couple of freshmen discussing a porno they'd watched over the weekend. And no sooner had I sat down with a salad and a soda than Martha slumped into the chair alongside me and announced, without a single word of warning, 'I'd kill for some cock.'

What? I turned and stared at her, certain that I'd simply misheard what she said amid the noise of the break room. 'I'm sorry?'

'I said, I'd kill for some cock right now.' She raised her Coke and took a deep draught. 'It's bizarre. I've been with Gerry so long that I don't even think about sex any more, it's just something we do. But now he's been gone three weeks, I'm dreaming about *things* every night.'

That's right. Her childhood sweetheart had deserted her briefly, while he flew home to tend to an ailing relative. What is it about family members just lately, all falling sick at the same time? I returned my attention to Martha's remark.

'Well, go out and find one,' I laughed. 'So long as that's all you're looking for, just a good hard cock to spend a night with, Gerry need never know. The things are everywhere. Come on, anyone here you fancy?' I looked around the room. In truth, there really wasn't much in the way of good pickings, a mish-mash of overbearing jocks and undersexed nerds, a handful of stoners and a few studious nobodies. I wondered where all the cool kids spent their lunch, and why I'd never tried seeking them out? Because I had Dave, of course. But maybe Martha wouldn't be so choosy. 'So?'

She shook her head. 'I couldn't. Not with a stranger. Not that.'

'Not what?' I love Martha dearly, we've been friends for ages and have seen one another through many a break-up. But she does talk in riddles sometimes, and today, lucky me, looked like being one of those occasions.

'OK,' she ventured tentatively, 'I had this dream. I don't know what caused it, because it's not something I've ever wanted to do before, but I can't get it out of my mind. Just the picture of it, and imagining . . .'

'Tell.'

'All right. He's come, OK? I don't know how, probably a hand job. Anyway, I'm looking down and there's come all over his cock, just streaks of it. And, in my dream, I lean down and I just lick it off, really slowly, like I don't want to miss a drop of it.'

Oh my God! Word for almost word, she was repeating the exact same confidence I'd been sharing with Jenny. I looked around to see if she was anywhere in sight, chuckling quietly to herself as I was set up for one of her little jokes. I looked again at Martha and I realised the girl was deadly serious. Even with my heart no longer pounding betrayal in my chest, I wasn't sure how to respond.

'Well, like I said, I've never done that. Never even thought about it. And now it's all I can think about', she said.

'What do you usually do when he comes?'

She laughed. 'Duck.'

'So you do . . .'

'Blow him? Of course. But, you know . . . only for a while. He's usually more interested in fucking, anyway. That's why this dream's so freaky. I don't even know if he'd like it.'

I thought about Dave, how he responded when I did that. How he bucked and fucked even as his dick softened, and how the come just kept on pumping out, as though the very force of suction was drawing it out. 'I think he will. And, if he doesn't, well, like I said, there's plenty more guys around who would love it.'

She smiled. 'Yeah, well. We'll see. Anyway, what I wanted to ask was, Jenny and I are going to the mall this evening, some late night shopping, a few drinks. Are you up for that?'

'Yeah, why not?'

Hmmm. I'll tell you why not. Because, if there's one thing I should have learnt a long time ago, it is that Jenny does not like leaving questions unanswered. And the question was, as she explained while we were waiting for Martha to decide between the pink dress or the blue one, how were we going to find her a fat throbbing cock, with two balls' worth of hot come dripping down the helmet? Oh God, when she puts it like that it sounds positively revolting!

I suppressed a shudder. 'I don't know. She'll just have to wait for Gerry to get back.'

Jenny laughed scornfully. 'Gerry's no good. He's strictly a pussy man. He's never even wanted to come on her tits. And Martha's such a prude, she'll never do it with a stranger. Hey, how about this Dave guy you've been seeing?'

'Hands off! He's mine. Besides, he's a stranger as well.'

'Actually, I was wondering whether he had any cute friends? We could all go out together and just see if Martha's interested in any of them?'

I thought about that for a moment. There'd be no harm in asking, would there? I doubted whether Martha would go for it, of course, but . . .

'*Or*,' said Jenny slowly, 'we could get her really drunk, and then the three of us could go over to his place right now and give him the treat of his life. Three girls, one cock, and Martha gagging to clean him up afterwards? He'd adore you forever.'

And, I had to admit, she had a point.

OK, confession time. I fancy Jenny. Always have. There's something about her, about the way she walks and talks, but most of all, the way she looks at you, that makes me so horny I can hardly stand it. Some nights, before I met Dave (but once or twice afterwards, if truth be told), I'd fall asleep thinking about how much I'd like to . . . what? Touch her? Kiss her? Caress her? Yes, all of those things. But, most of all, I'd like to be beneath her, like Dave was beneath me this weekend, feeling and tasting and glorying in her pussy while she ground herself to orgasm on my face.

It is only a dream. I've never said anything to her, and would probably die if she ever found out. And I've never felt this way about any other woman. But after I went to bed that evening, when the light was out and the house was silent, I had barely closed my eyes before the image started to unfurl before my eyes, of me sucking Dave's cock until he was so close to coming, then leaning back while Martha took over, and Jenny stepped forwards to sit on my face. The last thing I'd see before her pussy enveloped my face, the last sound I'd hear before her soft thighs covered my ears, would be Dave in the throes of the wildest orgasm, while Martha's pink tongue darted back and forth, slurping up the flying seed before her mouth closed tightly over the tip, and he filled her mouth with his come just as Jenny filled mine with hers.

If you'd pulled back my bedclothes and looked at the puddle, you'd think I'd just pissed the bed.

But then morning arrived and a calmer head prevailed. If you'll excuse the pun. Not Dave. Dave was mine, Dave was special. If he's going to adore me forever, it'll be because of what I do, not my friends. And I have plenty of ideas in that direction.

The thought of Jenny, though . . . that was a harder one to shake, especially when I saw her that morning, and saw how short her skirt was that day.

Did she know the effect she had on me? No, of course not. Did she know the effect she had on other women, though? I think so. Her verses made no secret of the fact that she'd at least thought about going with other girls, and there were at least a couple on campus with whom her friendship had taken some very noticeable peaks and troughs.

'Looking hot today.' That's what I meant to say anyway. In fact it came out more as a mumbled gurgle, as my throat dried up at the thought of uttering anything that even sounded like a come-on.

But she understood, thanked me, and gave a quick curtsey. 'Thought any more about Dave?' she asked.

'Not in the way you're hoping,' I answered. Then, unable to believe I was saying such a thing, even as the words tumbled out of me, 'but, come on, you must know plenty of cute guys we could rope into this?'

She looked at me curiously. 'I just thought you might want to stay on familiar ground,' she teased. 'But if you're really up for it, yeah, I could rustle us up a few likely contenders.' And, with that, she was off, leaving me inhaling the perfume that trailed in her wake, and begging my mind not to return me to where it swept me last night. At least not until I was back in bed.

Ridiculously, even those words made my heart pound.

I got through the day, and the evening as well. My folks would be home tomorrow and I wanted to make the most of my last night of freedom. Of course Dave came over . . . I cooked, and then we fell into bed, loving and lustful and liquid. And, as my throat closed around the tip of his cock, and I luxuriated, even if it was only for a moment, in the lustful satisfaction of having swallowed him whole, I suddenly knew it didn't matter what Jenny cooked up for the weekend. I'd be able to see it through, no matter what, because I'd shown Dave some of the most wonderful things that any woman can offer, and when I kissed him with a come-filled mouth, that coated our gums and tongues with thick white, I knew that nothing my friends could do to him would ever be anything but second best.

Or, at least, I hoped not.

He was still unlocking his car when I was punching Jenny's number into the phone. She answered on the first ring, and I blurted out the first words that came to my lips. 'Hey, it's me. I've changed my mind.'

I was disappointed when Dave called to say he wouldn't be able to make it on Saturday, after all the planning that Jenny and I had done. But I couldn't blame him. A nasty cold had been circulating campus for a couple of weeks now, one of those virulent little monsters that starts with a sore throat while you're falling asleep, then awakens you in the smallest hours with a raging fever and the distinct impression that your head has just been filled with cement.

I was straight round to his apartment, feeding him up with Cream of Chicken soup, stocking his bedside table with every cold cure I could think of, anything to get him back on his feet in time for the weekend. But it was a losing battle from the get-go and the only positive side of the entire affair was that I could finally quieten the nagging little voice that was asking whether I really wanted to share my boyfriend with not one, but two, of my best female friends? Or was I only going along with it in the hope that I could get inside Jenny's pants at the same time? In my heart, I knew what the answer was.

Jenny shrugged when I broke the news. 'To be honest, I was beginning to wonder whether this was going to work,' she admitted. 'With you and Dave, I mean. Look, let me bring along this other guy I know . . . it's OK, he's cute, smart and discreet, but, better than that, he's practically a virgin. OK?'

I nodded. None of this was for my benefit, anyway. It was Martha was who gagging to slurp up some come, not me . . . no, I'll rephrase that. Ever since I'd discovered how wonderful Dave tasted, I'd had a hard time even allowing him to fuck me, for fear that it was wasting his marvellous mess. I wanted it all in my mouth, to savour and swallow, to drip down my chin till it dropped onto my chest . . . and a couple of nights ago I'd figured out how I could get it. We were screwing, he was speeding up, I knew he had only moments to go . . . so I told him outright. 'Pull out and come in my mouth!'

He was already spurting as he rose above my body, splashing my belly and soaking my face before his pussy-soaked prick slipped between my lips, and he shuddered out the last thick drops deep inside my mouth.

I clung onto him, my hands grasping his butt and holding

him tight while I sucked and suckled the last gasping tremors; when he told me afterwards how much he loved it, how my very words had tipped him over the edge, I knew I'd get no arguments from him in the future. Fuck him, then suck him. It's the best of both worlds, and a few more undiscovered planets as well.

Poor Martha, on the other hand, had been gagging to try it her entire adult life. But a childhood sweetheart who scarcely allowed her to kiss his cock for more than a moment before he plunged it into her pussy was never going to satisfy that urge. So Jenny and I decided to fix it for her, and maybe have ourselves some fun too. And the funniest part of it all was, Martha didn't have a clue what was in store for her.

There again, neither did I. This was Jenny's show, and all I had to do, now that I was no longer expected to supply the man, was be there. OK, I'd probably have to help lower Martha's inhibitions, but Jenny had been working on that for a few days now, and when I arrived at the bar we'd selected for a rendezvous, it was apparent that she was already at work. The two of them were buried deep in discussion, but the shocking pink binder that lay on Martha's lap, and the conspiratorial tone of their whispered conversation, cued me in straight away as to what they were talking about. The binder was where Jenny collected the verses she wrote, the super-erotica she'd been writing for years, just one long rhyming blow job after another. And Martha's eyes were so wide that, if they'd been cocks, they'd have burst out of her pants.

'Not disturbing you, am I?' I sat down quickly and signalled the waitress to come over when she had a moment. Jenny laughed and shook her head, but it was Martha who did the talking.

'No, I've just been reading some of Jenny's poetry. I had no idea there was so much of it.'

'What, the poetry or the sex?' I asked, and Martha smirked.

'Both. Jesus, I thought blow jobs were simply a quick bit of foreplay. This girl's turned them into a three course meal.'

'Best meal there is,' Jenny hit back; she paused in her thought while the waitress took our orders, then finished up. 'Plus, it doesn't matter how much you eat, there's always room for dessert.'

I smirked, Martha blushed. 'Yeah, well,' she murmured. 'The chance would be a fine thing.'

'You just need to pick your moment,' Jenny said softly. 'Or your man. You say Gerry really doesn't like it?'

'I don't know. He's never let me get that far. And the one time I asked, he looked at me like I was charging him money for it.'

'Oh, one of those,' Jenny said, carefully, cryptically, but oddly knowledgeably. 'So you have to go without.' And suddenly the conversation wasn't about sex at all, but about the ways in which relationships always come down to some kind of power play, one partner withholding something or other, regardless of how the other one feels. She was right as well. I've known couples break up – I've heard of marriages breaking up – simply because of something insignificant, in the bedroom or out of it, that grows so out of proportion that it would surely have been easier for someone to give in; that someone, of course, being the partner who says 'no' every time the subject is raised. Just once. Just try it once. Or is your pride, or your fear, or your stupid inhibition more important to you than the love of your life? In too many cases, apparently so.

'Well, I'm not going to break up with Gerry because of it.' Martha spoke slowly and, I thought, just a little tearfully, but Jenny rushed to reassure her.

'I'm not saying you should. Besides, you might try it and discover you hate it. It's an acquired taste, after all. Or so I've heard anyway.'

Martha looked at her curiously. 'What's that supposed to mean?'

'Just that. Not every girl will do it, some don't even want to try, and others have done it once or twice and just don't like it. Right, Chrissie?'

I snapped out of a vivid daydream, in which Dave was filling glass after glass with hot thick come, and I was trailing behind him, draining every one. 'Right. I mean even in porn movies, you'll see girls step back when the guy comes, so as not to get it in the mouth, or even on their face.'

'Where've you seen porn movies?' Jenny reeled around, and I smiled sweetly.

'Around. I do have an older brother after all, and I found his video collection when I was still at High School. I used to invite my friends over when I knew we'd have the house to ourselves, and we'd fast forward through them. But, the point is, a lot of girls don't like it, even if they wish they did. But you never know until you try, and you'll never try . . .'

'. . . unless you do exactly what I say.' Jenny's voice had slipped into a whisper. 'Don't look now, but there's a guy over there who's been staring at you for the last fifteen minutes.'

Martha blushed. 'I know. I saw him a few minutes ago. Do you know him?'

Jenny shook her head. 'No, but he *is* cute.'

I glanced behind me, and saw him instantly: six foot, blond, T-shirt and Levi's. Couldn't tell his eye colour from here, but I'd bet it was blue. A shy smile played around his lips as he noticed us spot him. I wondered whether this was the guy Jenny said she'd line up? I'd been wondering when he'd come into play.

Martha was still blushing. 'How do you know he's looking at me?'

'Because Chrissie has her back to him, and I know he's not gazing into my eyes. Go on, give him a smile.'

Martha shook her head. 'I couldn't. What about Gerry?'

'What about him? I said. 'You're giving him a smile, not a hand job. Go on, before he decides we're a bunch of lesbians and loses interest.'

Ah, the Subtle Art of the Casual Pick-up. I could watch it all night. Who'll make the first move, who'll break the ice, and who will wander casually over and make some absurdly transparent attempt at striking up a conversation, by asking some really dumb question like, 'Excuse me, but could I get a light off you?' Martha had just produced her cigarettes, and the guy was by her side like a shot.

'Sure.' She held out her Bic and flicked it alight; he leaned in close, one hand cupping hers, and Jenny and I exchanged glances. She could as easily have simply handed him her lighter. But no. I flashed on an old movie I'd watched recently, Greta Garbo being offered a light and sharing a cigarette with a suitor. Christ, it was horny. And it's good to see, amid all the anti-smoking propaganda that floats around nowadays, that the art of seduction-by-cigarette isn't quite dead, because Martha was giving her Newport a workout that you'd have to be blind not to comprehend.

The guy, who now introduced himself as Ricky, was certainly entranced and, while Jenny and I forced ourselves into a conversation of our own, we knew that he and Martha were, as they say, 'hitting it off'.

But how far? She excused herself to go to the bathroom; I leaped up to join her and, leaving Jenny and Ricky alone, we went into a huddle the moment the Ladies' room door was closed.

Cut a long story short: she liked him. He was cute, he was funny, he was clearly very shy. But she smelled a rat. 'Is this one of Jenny's set-ups?'

I lied. 'I don't know. I don't think so. Why?'

'Because, well, because. I love her, but I don't trust her. Anyway, I wouldn't put it past her, setting me up with someone and then disappearing into the night.'

'She won't do that. Besides, we've already made arrangements.' My parents, home for three days, had then turned around and gone back upstate to Aunt Lil. So, with the house to myself, I'd invited Jenny and Martha to a sleepover, the first I'd hosted since Junior High. I'd stocked up on videos and a pantry full of snacks, dragged all the fresh linen into my room . . . and laid Dave's photograph face down on the bureau. Just in case.

Martha frowned. 'OK, maybe. But what should I do?'

'What do you want to do?'

There was a silence, so long that I thought for a moment that she hadn't heard me speak. Then a blush. 'I want to fuck his brains out.'

'Then do it.' And that is how, without me even being aware of the fact, my ostensibly innocent sleepover for two of my best friends was transformed into . . . can you call it an orgy if there's only one guy there? OK, a foursome then, three girls and one guy, only he's not going to lay a hand on me because I only have eyes for one person in the room, and I'm going to have her, even if I have to rip that dick out of her mouth myself.

There was very little talking as we walked back to my place. My thoughts were consumed entirely by what I was now desperate to do; Jenny was silent the whole way, and it's hard to say what Martha and Ricky were thinking, side by side, loosely arm-in-arm as though they were both drop-dead terrified of what they were doing, but didn't want the other to know how they felt.

They didn't get any closer once we were indoors either, and I was just beginning to wonder if the whole evening was about to turn into a wash-out when I caught a movement out of the corner of my vision – Martha and Jenny semaphoring one another with eyebrows and smiles and flickers of the eye. Ricky had noticed it too, and looked at me for reassurance; I shrugged and smiled. Guys aren't the only people who can be left utterly mystified by the secret language of the courting female. Other females can be baffled as well, which means I was as surprised as Ricky when Jenny suddenly stood up, stripped off her T-shirt, and declared 'This party is well and truly open!'

For a moment, the rest of us just sat there staring at her, but Jenny didn't care. Her bra came off next, and then she turned to face me, took two steps forwards, then knelt at my feet. 'Come on, Chrissie. You next.' Her fingers reached for my blouse and began deftly undoing the buttons. Two, three, four . . . she was below my breast now, then she stopped, stood up and walked over to Martha. 'You too.' I noticed she didn't offer any assistance though, and my heart leapt inside my chest. Jesus, does this mean I have a chance?

Jenny was kneeling before Ricky now, only he was ahead of her and had stripped off his T-shirt. So she started unbuckling his belt instead.

I watched, spellbound, as he raised his hips slightly, enough to allow her to tug down his jeans. His cock bulged inside his white jockeys, and I watched Jenny trace a fingertip down its length. Her eyes were locked on Martha now, whose own eyes were fixed firmly on that same bulge. I saw her lips part and the tip of a tongue flicker out to moisten them, then linger, poised between her slightly parted teeth. She was hungry.

Jenny's finger was still tracing idly up and down Ricky's

cock, and I could see it beginning to rise now, to harden and tent his underwear, demanding to be released from its cotton cage. But Jenny wasn't paying attention. She just stroked, gently, lightly, distractedly, and her eyes never left Martha's face.

The room was silent. Even the clock on the wall in the hallway seemed to have been hushed, and there wasn't a sound from the street outside. It was as though time had stood still, just waiting for Martha to make her move. And finally, she did, slipping out of the armchair onto her knees, then half shuffling, half crawling to Jenny and Ricky, positioning herself on the other side of his legs, and running a hand up his thigh.

He groaned, the first sound he'd made since this pantomime began, so she did it again. Only this time, instead of stopping at his groin, she allowed the tips of her fingers to graze his balls. Another groan.

Jenny's hand slipped down to join Martha's; a moment later, it was Martha who was caressing that cock, still bound up in its covering, but standing so tall that the elastic was surely approaching its breaking point. She grasped his waistband, pulled it down smartly, and Ricky's prick could finally stand to attention, tall and proud, thicker than Dave's, I noted distractedly, but probably not quite so long. Was that a good thing or a bad one? It might be nice to feel my pussy stretched wider when we fucked, because I'd tried it with toys and it was a wonderful sensation. But then I thought about how sweetly Dave's cock fitted into my mouth, how I didn't need to strain or scrape to accommodate its girth, and how I could even manoeuvre my tongue a little. No, I wouldn't trade that for the world.

Jenny, on the other hand, had no problem. She's a tiny girl, with petite little hands that were straining to wrap themselves around that cock. But her mouth just folded itself over Ricky's helmet and I watched her cheeks sink in as she sucked; heard the faint moist plop as she released it again, and smilingly angled the helmet towards Martha.

There was a moment of indecision, a flash of uncertainty that passed over Martha's face like a shadow. But then it was gone and then she was engulfing that fat purple helmet between her red lips, and so it went on, two girls happily sharing one prick, passing it back and forth like a lollipop at the fairground, while Ricky lay back, his eyes closed in ecstasy. I wondered if he would regret that later, wish he'd kept them open the whole time instead, to record every moment of the magic? If it was me, I'd want the entire event seared into my memory banks forever.

I rose and walked across the room, settled myself between the two girls, and leant in for my share of dick. I could taste my friends' saliva, gently sweet over the hard salt of cock, and then felt Jenny's lips as well, as I kissed the cock from one side and she kissed it on the other, then Martha slipped it away from us and it was Jenny's tongue on mine, twirling and probing while her free hand clasped my breast and mine held her to me, unable to believe it was finally happening, and praying the rest of my dream could come true.

She leant back, away from Ricky, and parted her legs. My finger slipped inside her, deep into that warm wetness. I cupped my hand over her mound and let the pressure of my palm seek out her clitoris, hard against my flesh. I wanted to suck it, like she and Martha were sucking that cock and, when I looked into her eyes as we broke from our kiss, I knew that she wanted me to. She shuffled back a little, raised herself up and, rolling onto my back, I slipped beneath her. Ricky moved too, raising himself to stand up behind me, his feet my bony pillow as my tongue began to explore.

I heard Jenny gasp as my fingers parted her pussy lips and

my curious tongue made its first tentative venture into her moist and so succulent folds. Her taste surprised me. Masturbating alone at night, and licking my fingers clean afterwards, I had long ago grown accustomed to my own flavours. But Jenny's were something else, lightly perfumed and gently salted, like breathing in an exotic incense and feeling it dance on your tongue as well.

She wriggled slightly, guiding my tongue to where she needed it most, and I followed her prompting, moving inside her pussy, swirling it a little while her gentle gyrations encouraged me deeper. I opened my eyes. Ricky was still standing behind me, I could feel his feet beneath the back of my head. But Jenny was no longer sucking on his cock, was barely even stroking it with her hand. She lost herself instead in the sensations that I was driving through her body, and I watched his fist wrap itself around hers, and begin jerking furiously. She leaned forwards and gently enclosed the livid helmet between her lips, but she extracted her fingers from beneath his, and clamped both hands around my skull.

And then she started to ride.

I felt my heart lurch with excitement. This was it. Her cunt lips were dragging themselves over my face, sometimes on my mouth, sometimes my chin or my nose, wet and widening, smothering me in the juices that were suddenly sluicing out of her. She had obviously released Ricky's prick again, because now I could hear her whimpering to herself, short, sweet moans and whispers as she drove herself further. I wished that I could hear what she was saying, the little words and imprecations that she uttered as she drew closer and closer to orgasm, but her thighs only tightened against my ears, and my world was devoured by the delicious, frantic friction of her hot streaming snatch.

I felt a bump as Ricky stepped away, and I lost my headrest.

Cautiously I opened one eye and, at first, all was blurred by Jenny's beautiful body slipping back and forth across me. But yes, I could see Martha now, stepping forwards from between my thighs, and expertly – well, it looked expertly from my peculiar vantage point – taking Ricky's cock in one hand, running her tongue up the red ramrod flesh and then plunging it into her mouth. Her eyes were closed, his expression was radiant. Her dream was finally coming true.

So was mine.

Jenny flipped herself around, and I felt my knees being parted wide, and a slender body worm its way between my thighs, soft kisses on my inner thigh, firm fingers parting my pussy. Jenny did not lick me so much as lap with a long, warm, sweep of flesh that made my cunt yawn wider and my juices flow faster. And then we came, Jenny and I with hitching cries, Ricky with an almighty groan. I tipped my head back as far as it would go to watch Martha, the Queen of Cream, consuming the cock that pulsed in her mouth, scooping up the overflow that ran from her lips. Jenny grasped Martha's dripping fingers and thrust them greedily into her own mouth, then shifted, bent down and kissed me hard, so that I, too, could share in the bounty.

When Ricky finally stepped aside and fell back onto the couch with a shuddering sigh, the side of Martha's head resting on his softening cock, Jenny and I lay back on the carpet, her face on my breast, my arm round her waist.

After all the talk of the last few weeks, all the conspiring and planning and whispers, at last there was nothing left to say.

Misbehaviour features the first appearance of short fiction by Chrissie Bentley in Black Lace.

To Protect and Serve
Kimberly Dean

She was so lost.

With one hand on the steering wheel, Karina held the map higher under the reading light. It didn't matter. She was outside the city, outside the detailed markings of the map, and outside her comfort zone. She tossed the useless guide back onto the passenger seat and tried not to stress. The country road was empty and eerie, like a path to nowhere that locals knew to avoid.

'Come on. Give me a road sign.' A trail of breadcrumbs. Anything!

Her fists twisted around the leather steering wheel. This was not the way to start off a new job. Mr Pearson wasn't going to be happy. She was more than fashionably late for the fundraiser he was throwing for the museum. As the new curator, she needed to be there. But 'new' was the key. She wasn't familiar with the city yet, much less the surrounding countryside. Why had he insisted on throwing this party at his lakeside retreat?

'Damn,' she muttered, chewing her lip. This was not a good showing for her. She patted the passenger seat again to find her cell phone. She'd already called once to ask for directions, but they hadn't helped. There were so few landmarks out here, just rolling hills and looming trees. A bright, thick slice of moon glowed overhead, but it didn't provide any real illumination on her whereabouts. For all she knew, she could be in the middle of –

A long, mournful whine cut through the air, making her jolt. The sound was so loud and foreign; for a moment, she couldn't place it. Yet when her gaze flashed to the rearview mirror, she saw flashing red and blue lights. A siren.

The flinch became tension. As with most people, the sudden appearance of a cop brought caution.

More so, she'd thought she was alone.

Where had he come from? The squad car was right on her tail.

She looked quickly to her dashboard even as her foot eased off the accelerator. She was only going five miles per hour over the limit – or at the least the last limit she'd seen. He couldn't be pulling her over for that, could he? She slowed down even more, hoping he'd go around her. When she eased over to the shoulder to give him room to pass, though, he pulled in behind her. Her stomach tightened when he manoeuvred behind and slightly to the left of her in a text-book police stop.

'What did I do?' She shifted the car into park, but her gaze was glued to her rearview mirror.

She didn't like this. Didn't like it at all, even if . . .

She squashed off the hesitantly whispered thought as the driver's door to the squad car opened. The policeman stepped out and she watched intently. With the flashing lights, it was hard to make out much other than the fact that he was big. Big and solid. His dark form seemed to rise endlessly before coming to a full stand.

She swallowed hard. He was like an oversized dark shadow, meant to intimidate.

Only he was for real.

She licked her lips nervously as he slid his nightstick into a loop along his belt. What should she do? Get out? Roll down her window? Neither seemed like a good idea. His hand settled near his weapon as he started to approach the car carefully, but with purpose. The way he was watching her put her entire body on alert.

Her mind was already there. She was in trouble; that was clear. But what kind? She looked around anxiously and realised again how remote her location was. Her heart began to thud in her ears. She'd read horror stories in the news about situations like this.

She felt a quickening low in her belly that she ignored. *Horror* stories.

She looked to her side mirror, trying to see more of the squad car. From the little detail she could make out, it looked official. A smooth-moving shadow blocked her view, and her breath caught. He was closer than she'd thought. His dark uniform blended into the night, making him seem more prowlerlike than peacekeeper.

More danger than protector.

An enforcer.

She shivered when he came to a stop beside her.

He tapped on her window. 'Ma'am?'

She pried her hand off the steering wheel and pressed the electronic control. The window lowered only two inches.

'Driver's licence and registration.'

His low voice rumbled, making goose bumps rise on her skin. *Everywhere*. Karina cleared her throat. 'Could I see your badge, please?'

Thinking had suddenly become difficult. Her thoughts were zigging and zagging, but as if through quicksand. She had to crane her neck to look up and back at the man. With the way he'd positioned himself, he loomed behind her. He'd done it, no doubt, to protect himself should she pull a gun. But she didn't have a gun. She didn't have anything, and she was out here alone.

She shifted uncomfortably in her seat with . . . uneasiness. Yes, fear was the most pressing concern on her mind. Fear.

The cop watched her carefully, but one eyebrow lifted upwards. The moonlight left most of his face in shadow, but she could see his eyes. They were intent on her as he pulled out his identification and flattened it against the window.

'Do you . . . do you mind if I call it in? Just to be sure?' she asked.

Her gaze flicked meaningfully to their surroundings, never leaving him entirely. There was just something about him that brought up dark thoughts . . . dark voices in the back of her head . . .

'Never ask for permission,' that rough voice returned. 'It's your right.'

She moistened her dry lips. He was for real. Somehow, that made it even . . . better.

Embarrassed, she reached for her cell phone.

She froze when light suddenly lit the interior of her car. Beams streamed through the window as he used his flashlight to highlight her movements. The glare made Karina self-conscious, as if she was on display under a spotlight. And on display, she was. Her short, slinky gold dress had ridden up dangerously high on her legs, and the sharp concentration of light made her bare thighs glow.

Just like her breasts.

Her seatbelt had plumped the rounded flesh against the scooped neckline of her dress. The intrusive light seemed to settle on her cleavage, illuminating all the tiny goose bumps – and other bumps her clothing could no longer hide.

She looked at the officer swiftly, but the light didn't budge. Heat crept up to her face, and that niggling . . . fear . . . settled in the pit of her stomach. Moving more carefully, she picked up her phone.

Taking a steadying breath, she dialled 911. She and the police officer waited tensely as she explained her situation to the dispatcher. Standing as he was, he was a haunting presence. Hidden half in shadows, hovering over her, watching . . .

She glanced at his ID again and read it to the woman on the other end of the line. When the dispatcher confirmed that Officer Steele was with the Caulfield County PD and currently on duty, Karina's reaction discomfited her. She should have been relieved, but she wasn't. She felt anything but.

'Thank you,' she responded.

Steele. It fitted.

She folded the phone, dropped it on the passenger seat, and gripped the steering wheel again.

'Licence?'

'Oh, yes.' Moving more quickly, she reached for her purse. This time, there was no mistaking it. The light homed in on the low neckline of her dress, and the heat in her cheeks became a full-on blush. She had to reach even further to the glove compartment for her registration, and she worried about falling out entirely.

Outside the car, she heard the officer clear his throat.

Was he . . . ? Did he feel . . . ? Mortified with the direction of her thoughts, she passed him the requested information and glanced down nervously. Everything was back in place, but still not covered as much as she would have liked. She felt exposed and vulnerable – and in so many ways.

'Could you step out of the car, Ms Cole?'

Her head snapped towards him, and her thighs clenched hard. 'Out of the car?'

He stepped back a pace.

'Oh . . . OK . . . Of course.' Her hand nearly slipped off the door handle, she was suddenly so nervous. What had she done?

He took another step back as she opened the door, and she felt his gaze on her become more intent. It started on her strappy high-heeled shoe and the expanse of bare leg as she started to get out. The attention made her hesitate. A soft breeze wafted through the car then, caressing her skin and sending a shiver of awareness down her spine. She stood nervously, gripping her car door with one hand and the roof of her car with the other.

The position left her trapped. He was in her personal space, and heat radiated from his big body. She had to tilt her head back to look up into his face. The light still wasn't good. She couldn't see him clearly, but she could tell he wasn't a handsome man. His features were rough-hewn, his jaw strong and his nose just a little crooked. His mouth was tight, but his eyes were alive. Filled with a dark fire, they burned her as he stared at her.

Karina's breaths came harder, her breasts lifting and falling with each sharp inhale and exhale.

He was looking for something in her. What that was, she couldn't tell, she just felt her stomach tighten in response. While that didn't surprise her, the stiffening of her nipples did.

Suddenly, those dark thoughts on the edge of her consciousness couldn't be repressed any longer. They flooded her brain, pushing out common sense and swamping her body with sensation.

The abandonment scared her. She'd never been one to indulge in fantasies. She was too practical and hard-working. Yet here she was, under police scrutiny in the middle of a deserted country road, with her panties sopping wet.

'Where are you headed, Ms Cole?'

He edged closer, and her entire body gave one pulsing throb. 'I'm late for a party in Highland Hills.'

'You're a long ways from there.'

'I'm lost.'

A muscle in his jaw worked. 'Good thing I found you.'

His gaze started a slow journey downwards, gliding over her lips, along the line of her neck, and over her mostly bare shoulders. Her nipples started to ache, almost begging for his attention, and she folded her arms over her chest self-consciously. His observant gaze took in the move – and held.

Karina shifted uncomfortably. Her behaviour disconcerted her. And so did his.

'Why did you pull me over, Officer?'

'You've got a tail light . . .' He glanced down to her hips. 'That's out.'

Her lips parted. The way he was looking at her was suggestive. Intimate.

'And you've been driving erratically.'

That brought her head up. 'I have?'

He gestured inside the car at her map.

'Oh,' she mumbled. Reading and driving weren't a good mix.

She ground the ball of her foot against the pavement, and tiny rocks rasped against the asphalt. It brought his attention right back to her delicate high-heeled gold sandals.

Karina's senses sang. The Indian summer they were experiencing made the night air warm and alive. She could feel it touching her skin and brushing her hair. Her nipples had stiffened into tight peaks and they felt raw against the cups of her bra. An even hotter ache had settled in her core. With every breath he audibly exhaled, she felt more and more reckless.

He finally edged back. 'Let's do a quick sobriety check.'

'*Sobriety?*'

He was in her space before she could utter another word. 'I want to see the way you move.'

Her protests left her with a puff of air.

With his flashlight, he gestured to the white line along the edge of the road. He watched her steadily, almost daring her to defy him. To resist. The nervous butterflies in her chest took flight. She waited for him to get out of her way, but he was planted like a big redwood tree. Big, solid and unyielding . . .

Her pussy squeezed, and she pressed her thighs together tightly. Gathering her nerve, she squeezed by him in the small space left between him and the door. It rocked open that last six inches, but her bottom still chafed against the rubber panel and her breasts rubbed tightly against his hard chest.

Karina barely stopped her moan. The friction felt so good against her tender flesh. So firm and hot. His eyes narrowed, the irises flaring. His cheekbones seemed to harden, and he leant towards her.

She scooted away, stepping back from him.

His chin came up, almost in a challenge.

'Right over there,' he said, aiming his light towards the road markings again. 'Five steps forward along the line, pivot, and come back towards me.'

She smoothed her palms against the slick material of her dress. He had her so off-balance. Was he serious about this? Did he think she'd been drinking? Or had he somehow seen the real secret she was so desperately trying to hide?

The butterflies in her chest flew up higher into her throat. What was going on with her? She didn't do things like this. She didn't play games. She'd never even considered it.

Until now.

She looked at him with his serious eyes, dead-set mouth, and unforgiving jaw. One way or the other, he was the law.

She had to obey.

She turned her back on him. Her dress dipped low in the back, and the flirty flare of the hem covered her only to mid-thigh. Yet her dark hair dipped low on her spine, keeping her modesty intact. Or so she'd thought. When she began to walk, she felt his gaze stroke over her as surely as rough hands.

It made her nearly stumble. She could feel his hot stare on her ass, and the stickiness filling the crotch of her panties began to spread to her thighs. It slickened her skin with each step she took.

She placed her feet more carefully, but almost of their own volition, her hips began to sway. Her hair swung softly, sensitising nerve endings. At last she pivoted on the four-inch heels, but as she came back towards him, his attention turned to her breasts. They became heavy and warm. Achy. Her nipples beaded tightly, and the weight of her bra became bothersome. Too tight and confining.

His eyes seemed darker. Darker and almost fierce now.

Her mind raced.

This was dangerous. Out of control. What was she doing? She should get in her car and hurry to the nearest trace of civilisation. But he was armed. Her gaze went automatically to the gun at his hip – and then to the zipper of his pants. Armed with more than one weapon.

She stopped in front of him, eyes straight forwards. Nerves screaming. Pulse pounding. Need soaring.

His hands were suddenly on her hips. The unexpected touch made her flinch. His thumbs tightened against her hip bones, and his fingers sank almost harshly into her ass. The erogenous zone flared, and a low moan ripped from her throat.

'Assume the position.'

This time, when her heart began to race, it wasn't a flitter-flutter. It was a full-on slamming against her ribcage. 'What?'

He turned her towards her car, his strength an overpowering force. His hand settled against the middle of her back. 'Bend over.'

She went because she had to, and because her knees were suddenly so weak she didn't know if they could hold her weight much longer. 'What are you doing?' she gasped as she braced her hands against the hood.

His breath was hot against her ear. 'Searching you.'

His hands were on her thighs, skin-on-skin, before she could understand his words. The contact was shocking. Reaching back, Karina caught his thick wrists. That didn't stop his hands from sliding up under her dress.

His touch was scorching as it skimmed upwards, lifting her skirt. She went up on her tiptoes when he cupped her ass.

'I'm not hiding anything!'

His hold tightened. 'I'll be the judge of that.'

She moaned. He was rubbing her ass, his thumbs digging deep into the cushiony globes. She tried to shift away, but he was having none of it. He held her in place with a strength that was almost scary, cupping and shaping her until she was fighting for air.

'For all I know, you could have stolen this car,' he murmured.

'Then run the plates.'

His big hands started sliding upwards, tugging her dress up to her waist ... her ribcage ... her breasts ... He cupped her there, his touch inordinately personal and devastatingly thorough.

His weight pressed her down into that scandalous caress, and his lips brushed against her hair. 'You could be transporting dangerous goods.'

Karina couldn't talk. She could barely breathe. He was doing things to her, plucking her nipples through her lacy bra and grinding her breasts in slow circles. Suddenly, the front clasp of her bra turned loose. She pressed her forehead against the warm metal of her car as his touch became even more erotic. Rough callused fingers pinched her sensitive nipples. Hot palms squeezed and petted.

'Dangerous,' he murmured.

He stroked back down her form, leaving her dress bunched high under her armpits. She squirmed as he traced each vertebra of her spine. This was wrong, she knew. She should be screaming bloody murder. He shouldn't be touching her this way, but she was letting him.

Was that why it felt so shamefully good?

The thought brought her up short, and her muscles stiffened. This wasn't her. She wasn't like this.

She pushed herself upwards, but he spread his hand wide against the small of her back and stopped her. She shifted to the side, but froze when her hip bumped against the hard length of his nightstick. It rocked at the impetus, and the tip rapped against her bare thigh seductively. Menacingly.

Steele's voice turned raspy. 'Resisting, Ms Cole?'

Oh, God.

Karina heard a whisper-soft hiss, and she looked back sharply. He'd pulled his nightstick out from the loop on his belt. Her pulse began racing so quickly one heartbeat was indistinguishable from the next.

'Officer,' she panted.

The firm nub at the end of the nightstick slid against the base of her spine, tracing the line of her thong. The touch was gentle, but with the promise of strength behind it.

'I did inform you that this is a strip search,' Steele said quietly. 'Didn't I?'

Karina's arousal took on an edge, and a soft whimper left her throat. Every muscle in her body locked when the tip of that ominous tool slid under the strap of her thong at her waist. It twisted in the fabric and began tugging insistently downwards. The material bit into her skin, clinging, until it gave way over the curve of her ass with an almost audible pop.

He stopped with her panties stretched wide across her thighs and her butt thrust indecently into the warm night air. The exposure made her quiver. The moonlight seemed much brighter than it had before. It left her no secrets, no place to hide.

'What have we here?' the officer said.

She jerked when she felt his hand brush against her inner thigh. She craned her neck and saw him drag his finger along the crotch of her thong.

'Evidence,' he said, rubbing his middle finger slickly against his thumb.

Karina began shuddering in excitement and dread. It was hard to tell which was which, but the combination was potent. He yanked her panties down, using the nightstick on one side and his fingers on the other.

She closed her eyes when he straightened behind her. Her whole body was thrumming, splayed out as it was. He placed his foot in the crotch of her panties, forcing them to the ground, and then nudged her feet outwards even further. Opening her. Making her truly assume the position.

Her pussy squeezed, close to an orgasm. This fantasy had been with her forever, yet she'd never given it credence. She'd refused even to acknowledge it. Yet here it was playing out in full clarity and vivid colour.

Forcing her to recognise it for what it was.

'Hold still, Ms Cole. There will be penetration.'

She bit her lip painfully. God, he was tripping every one of her triggers.

Still, her eyes popped back open when she felt the tip of that hard nightstick caress the back of her knee. The delicate area tightened, then began to pulse.

Her nerves short-circuited when the thick nub slowly cruised up her hamstring. With every millimetre of skin the dangerous weapon touched, it brought that tight, pulsing sensation with it.

The pleasure was too dark. Too daunting. 'Officer, I –'

'If you resist, it will take longer.'

Words deserted her. Reaching out, she caught the edge of the hood near the windshield. Her fingers curled around it until her knuckles turned white in the moonlight.

That firm, inanimate touch on her leg hovered for a moment, and then crept higher. With each stroke it came closer and closer to her vulnerable pussy. Threatening and teasing. Playing and toying. When it finally bumped against her clit, she let out a sharp cry. But the caress didn't go away. It circled slowly, letting her feel it. Every brush brought heat, and that darkness she'd refused descended on her.

Her hips shifted in one last show of resistance. Or was it challenge? Steele caught her by the hip and held her still.

The hard touch of the nightstick became more directed, stroking her slit up and down. Up and down. She was so wet, it glided against her tender flesh easily and with more acceptance than it ever should have.

Karina moaned helplessly.

'Pretty damning evidence, Ms Cole,' Steele said.

His voice was rougher now. Strict. The nightstick stopped against her tender opening, and the edge of the hood bit into Karina's palm. She flailed and caught his wrist at her hip with her other hand. Yet the pressure became more insistent. Not hard, not abusive. Just . . . there. She held painstakingly still, the only thing moving her lungs and her heart.

And her pussy. It was fluttering and squeezing.

Steele pressed just a little harder against her, barely opening her, and her cry wafted over the surrounding hillside. He held the rod there, just inside her, hardly an inch. Her muscles tightened around what little penetration he'd given her, but then it was gone.

Her body began quaking as the hard tip went on the move again. It glided across her delicate, private flesh and massaged her anus. Her body bucked, but the touch continued. Coated as it was with her thick juices, the nightstick slid easily between her butt cheeks. They separated as it stroked endlessly upwards.

Then the hard, cool touch was sliding up her back.

Steele leaned over her, dominating her. His lips touched the back of her neck. 'Body cavity search?'

'Oh, pleeeease.'

His teeth nipped at her ear. 'You're supposed to say no.'

She tried. 'I'll . . . I'll call my lawyer.'

'God, you're hot for it.' The nightstick clattered onto the hood beside her.

'Steele,' Karina panted.

'Fuck.' His voice was almost guttural now. Hard and masculine.

The sound of his zipper was fast and harsh. Karina squirmed, wanting to feel his weight, aching for penetration. He was going to fuck her now, right under the stars and the flashing red and blue lights. His gun belt bumped against her hip, and she creamed.

Yet she was surprised when she heard a jingle.

She twisted around in shock when he caught her wrists and pulled them together behind her back.

'Wait, no!'

But he already had her cuffed.

And the pressure was starting.

His dark eyes gleamed down at her as he started to thrust his big cock into her. Karina couldn't talk, couldn't protest. She was restrained and pinned.

And it set her free.

The pressure increased and she closed her eyes. She pressed her cheek against the car as he surged inside her tight pussy, stretching her and filling her.

'Ahh!'

She'd known he'd be big, but he felt huge. Impossible.

His shoes scraped against the asphalt as he adjusted his stance. He pressed into her wetness determinedly and broached the last inches with grating slowness.

When he finally seated himself deep, Karina came. The orgasm careened through her like a crazy thing.

'Fuck. Me.' Steele caught her hips in both hands and tilted her up towards him. The move pulled her cuffed hands higher, causing a pinch in her shoulders. He began to move in short, shuddering lunges and she lost all semblance of control.

The waves rolled through her, each one more powerful than the last. The pleasure was dark and wild. He fucked her like a madman, pounding in and gliding out. The sounds they made were lewd in the darkness. Wet slurps, the slap of skin against skin, hoarse cries, laboured breaths . . .

Karina's body began climbing again, straining for another peak.

Yet lights flickered unexpectedly in the near distance, brightening the roadside. Soon, they were accompanied by the whir of another engine.

'Oh, no. God, no!'

She struggled, but Steele held her down. A car came over the small hill just then, illuminating them with its headlights. Still, he didn't stop. He thrust his Steele into her, over and over again, fucking her almost roughly.

The car's horn sounded and calls came from inside the car.

'Hey, now that's what I call *cop*ulation.'

'Talk about unlawful contact.'

The young men could see everything. Karina watched as they hung out of the car, grins wide on their avid faces. There was nothing she could do to stop them. Her dress was hiked up under armpits, her panties were strewn on the ground, and her hands were cuffed behind her back. With her legs as wide as Steele had spread them, there was nothing to hide the way his huge cock was pummelling into her – or the way she was straining back for it.

'Use unreasonable force, man.'

Her pussy spasmed. She'd never been so aroused in her life. The feel of it all . . . the total submission . . . the bad girl guilt . . . the exhibitionism . . . Her hands fisted against the metal bracelets and her buttocks clenched.

She cried out and their visitors' horn sounded in a long wail.

Steele's control snapped. With a growl, he began hammering into her. Hammering and grinding. Rutting and humping.

The onlookers in the car pressed him on, yelling out profanities and whooping up a frenzy. When he reached down and flicked her clit, it was over. Karina hurtled into the final orgasm. Behind her, her cop jerked. His hot come spurted into her, filling her until the overflow trickled down her legs.

The men in the car laughed as they drove off. After a long moment, Steele's weight came down heavily on her back. His chest moved raggedly as he struggled to regain control.

'Holy shit,' he panted.

Karina couldn't talk. She couldn't think.

He braced his weight on his hands and lifted himself off of her slightly. 'OK?'

She wasn't sure. She'd just had her deepest, darkest, most unspeakable fantasy fulfilled.

He pulled out of her swiftly, leaving her empty. 'Karina?'

He uncuffed her and turned her around so she was sitting on the car.

'Christ, don't look at me like that. I thought you wanted –'

She caught him by the nape of the neck and kissed him. Open-mouthed and tongue-deep. It went on and on until the need for oxygen made him pull away.

'Damn.' He brushed her lower lip with his thumb. 'I didn't want to mess up your make-up.'

She looked up into his rough-hewn face. He wasn't a man she'd want to meet on a dark, deserted road – but she had. 'How did you know? I mean, why did you . . .'

'Cops have fantasies, too.'

Had it been that clear on her face? She'd worked so hard over the years to keep her reputation spotless. Professional. Dr Pearson and his partygoers would be shocked right down to their precious PhDs if they knew what she'd just done with a total stranger. A cop. A trusted individual, yes, but a stranger nonetheless. People in that crusty stratus didn't misbehave like that.

But she had. And she wanted to do it again.

Steele's face finally broke from that stern, official expression. 'Besides, you know the police motto, "to protect and service".'

She blushed. 'I thought it was "to protect and serve".'

'Close enough.' He pulled her off the car and tugged her dress back into place. 'Follow me. I'll get you to your party.'

She looked around uncertainly as he zipped up his pants, adjusted his gun belt, and snapped the cuffs in their proper place. She spotted her panties on the asphalt, but when she knelt down to get them, he beat her to them.

'Uh-uh. I'm confiscating these as evidence.'

She blanched. 'You can't.'

He tucked the tiny thong into his pocket and leant in close.

'I know that snooty neighbourhood, and you're going to that party bare. It will be the only thing that keeps you awake.'

He was right.

It was late when Karina finally made a break for it. The party was beyond boring, and her body just couldn't take the sedate atmosphere one moment longer. Hiding her lack of underwear from everyone was the only thing that had kept her energised all night.

And it still was.

She rolled down the windows of her car and let the wind stream through her hair as she pulled away from the Pearson residence. She couldn't believe what she'd done tonight, how far she'd let Officer Steele go – how far she'd let *herself* go. She felt sexy and naughty.

A bad girl in a very good way.

The roads were too quiet as she headed back towards town – or at least in the direction she thought would lead her there. She didn't care. Life didn't have to be so regimented, so by-the-book. She followed the path through the rolling countryside, noticing the darkness was even more profuse now that the moon was lower on the horizon. Her headlights were the only light to break the darkness.

Until . . .

A car was suddenly behind her, appearing from out of nowhere. Her gaze flew to her rearview mirror and excitement jumped in her chest. When red and blue lights began to alternate within the car's grill, she pulled over quickly.

He'd waited for her.

Arousal unfurled inside her, and her bare pussy squeezed. Feeling bold and saucy, she opened the door and got out, making sure she made a show of her legs. 'This is police harassment, you know. I could – Oh, God!'

She lurched to a stop and lifted her hands into the air. Simultaneously, the cop coming towards her fell back into a defensive position and his hand went to his gun.

Heart in her throat, Karina lifted her hands higher. 'I'm sorry. I thought you were Officer Steele. Please, don't shoot.'

The cop walking towards her was a stranger.

He watched her carefully, suspicion clear in his eyes. 'Karina Cole?'

She blinked. 'Yes.'

The officer's hand eased away from his pistol, but he still approached her with caution. 'Lieutenant Steele asked me to make sure you got home safely.'

'Oh.' She pressed her hands to her chest, trying to keep her heart where it belonged. Her knees still weren't quite solid underneath her.

The cop kept coming, though, and she stiffened when he got in her space.

She went absolutely rigid when he looped his arm around her waist and pressed her back firmly against her car.

'He told me to take care of any other needs you might have, too.'

His blue eyes glittered as he looked into her face, and she looked back at him in shock. He was shorter and stockier than Steele, a fireplug of a man. Whereas Steele was dark and edgy, this cop was young and eager.

And cute.

'Oh, God,' she breathed.

Her head fell back against the car as he began kissing and nipping his way down her neck. His cock was already tenting his uniform pants and pressing her thin dress into the notch at the top of her legs. In no time, he'd worked the straps of her dress and bra over her shoulder and down her arm. When her breast sprang free, he cupped it in his palm and plumped it for his mouth.

Karina let her fingers sink into his thick blond hair. With a grunt, he wrapped his lips around her nipple and began to suckle sloppily. She let out a shuddering breath, arousal and need building inside her. Steele had sent him for her. To protect and service her. She moaned into the darkness. Caulfield County's finest. She was going to like it here.

Kimberly Dean is the author of the Black Lace novels *Tiger Lily* and *Going Deep*, and of the Cheek novel *High School Reunion*. Her short fiction has appeared in several Black Lace anthologies.

Flexible
Charlotte Stein

There are several steps to becoming sexually flexible. The first one is something unexpected. The first one was me and Quinn in the bedroom of Mary and Chris's new apartment.

'You look so weird like that,' I say to him, because he does. He has come straight from a talk about his new book, and he is Quinn Kaufmann, literary star, rather than just ordinary Quinn. He is bespectacled and tweedy and not in his usual clashing shirts of many colours.

He has shaved, too, where usually he is dirty with stubble. Strangely, he looks even younger than he usually does.

'Like a dork,' he says, and I suppose that's true. But it's also true that I react on some other level to how he looks in the strange whitewashed light of this empty bedroom. I am giddy with this new reaction, and I giggle.

'No,' I reply. 'No, not at all. I love it when you look like this.'

I keep giggling, though, so it definitely cancels out the compliment.

'You do not,' he says, and it only makes the *oh yes, I really do* stronger.

'I do. It just makes me want to . . . rumple you up.'

His mouth quirks up into a smile, and behind the Clark Kent glasses his black eyes gleam. It's the eyebrows though, really, that make him look wicked. He has eyebrows on his eyebrows, and they arch blackly and wickedly over his pretty girl's eyes.

He isn't attractive, exactly. Though I have no idea why I'm thinking about his potential attractiveness now. It's never occurred to me before. Probably because he's gay. He's supposed to be gay. Everyone knows he's gay. The *Chronicle* said he was gay and had a boyfriend named Steve.

And it's true that I've never seen him date . . . well, anyone, really. He doesn't even talk about dating. He is dateless. Sexless. He is a sexless eunuch who sometimes looks interesting in Clark Kent glasses and tweed.

'And how would you go about . . . rumpling?' he says, and I force my mind to concentrate on that *Chronicle* piece I never dared ask him about: *although Kaufmann has never been known to openly refer to his private life, he is notably evasive when directly questioned.*

'Oh, you know,' I say. 'Ruffle your hair. Untuck your shirt.'

'Oooh, dangerous,' he says, and when he does he dips his voice into a vat of faux-wicked.

'Pull your pants down.'

His quirking mouth quirks higher.

'Pull my pants down? That's a little more on the edge.'

'I live dangerously. I'm in the habit of randomly pulling pants down.'

'Start with untucking my shirt and we can see where it goes from there.'

Nowhere, I think. It goes nowhere. You're gay. You love Steve, whoever he is. You and Steve are madly in love.

I reach forwards and tug at the buttons on his tweed jacket. I ruck the whole thing up, and then yank on his shirt until one tail dangles over the front of his cords.

'There,' I say. 'Rumpled.'

'Pants next.'

'You don't really want me to pull your pants down,' I say, and turn my back on him. I do what I came in here to do: look at the things that whoever lived here before left on this dresser. All these tiny bottles of perfume and dozens of little trinkets, glittering and strange.

'Why not?'

'Because you don't.'

I pick up a little bottle shaped like a mermaid.

'I guess I'll have to convince you, then.'

There's a little ship, too, and a turtle. Blue glass junk, Mary called it, but I think it's all rather quaint and lovely.

'Oh, there's no way you could do that,' I say.

'Really? Nothing I could say, or do?'

'Nothing. I'm pretty sure you want your pants to stay on.'

'How about if I begged you?'

'What? To strip you half naked? Nah, I wouldn't believe you.'

'Not even if I talked dirty to you while I begged?'

'That seems unlikely, but even if you did I doubt I would.'

'How about if I sounded desperate, and lustful, and told you how much I wanted you to?'

'I don't think so. I think you'd need something really spectacular to convince me you wanted me to undress you in any way, shape or form. You know, something like a hand on my thigh.'

When he actually puts a hand on my thigh, I contain the jump out of my skin admirably. He's only trying to be funny with me, after all. There's no need to show him that he's getting under my skin in a way that's really itching and irritating.

'Like this?'

'I guess so. But really, what does a hand on the thigh say? Not that much.'

I have absolutely no idea how I got to this place. It's a very weird, heavy-aired sort of establishment.

'So if I did something more? Like maybe pressed up against you?'

'You could do that. But what would that really prove?'

Apart from the fact that he has an erection, of course.

I don't really believe that he has an erection, however. It's just his car keys, pressing into my bottom. It's the banana he has in his pocket. It's something else that is shaped like a hard penis. Thinking anything else will only make me react, and I don't want to react. Reacting will make me seem silly and horny and in love with him.

But I probably am silly and horny and in love with him, so I just do what comes naturally. I press my ass back against him. Not hard. Not rudely. Just kind of like . . . answering a question in a whisper. If the answer isn't the one he was asking for, well, I can just pretend I never said a word!

I can back out at any time if he protests.

But he doesn't protest. In fact, he doesn't say anything at all. This is the most silent I've ever heard him and the silence is pounding on my heart. Or maybe my heart is pounding the silence. I don't know. It's hard to tell.

What isn't hard to tell is him pressing into me right back. He actually does it, and at this point I don't think he's messing around. He seems to be breathing awfully heavy for someone who's just teasing. Plus the hand on my thigh is now on my belly, and although that doesn't seem like a ruder move on paper, in practice it's almost awkwardly intimate. Mainly because I immediately get a sense of why he's moved his hand: so that he can hold me close to him more easily. His hand on my belly makes it absurdly easy for him to curve me into the nice little cup he's made of his groin.

Here's definitely where I should say something, I know. But all that occurs is the very stupid: *I thought you were gay*, and I don't want literary superstar Quinn Kaufmann to be singularly unimpressed by my lack of an open mind. I mean, he's my friend. But he's also just that little bit glittery and powerful and too intelligent, and that kickback of awe makes me not want to seem gauche in front of him.

Not that concerns about gaucheness matter when my body is flicked onto lust autopilot.

To be honest, I didn't even know I had one. And it's frightening to discover, too, because suddenly I don't seem to be in control of myself. I feel a haze descend and then all at once I'm squirming against him. In an obviously designed to make him happy way, too. I rub where I'm plumpest and softest against the stiff thing that's pressing into me, and he sucks in a lot of air.

And still there is silence, nothing but pounding silence. He's not even going to explain any of this to me. Not even a little bit. Instead, he's just going to *unzip my dress*.

I almost cave, when his hand quite clearly goes to the zipper at the nape of my neck. But, oh dear God, it's too sexy to be denied. He has me pinned, hand splayed on my belly, hard cock urging against my arse, and now he's just going to unzip my dress! In Mary and Chris's new bedroom, while they're in the other room trying to hang curtains!

He draws the zipper all the way down to the middle of my back and then parts the two wings to smooth his hand over my bare shoulder blades. His fingers tangle in my curly hair before he sweeps it away to the front of my body.

And then he kisses my back, my neck, my shoulder. I know he kisses these things. I can feel how soft and wet his mouth is, so gentle. Of course I'd like to say here that I always knew he'd be gentle, but then really, how do I know? I've never fantasised about my gay friend. My bisexual friend. My God-knows-what friend.

I can't even care when he kisses like that, and rocking against him feels as good as it does, and any moment we could be caught. I've never done anything sexual where I could be caught, and it makes my teeth chatter.

It makes them chatter even harder when I consider that maybe such a thing is exactly what he gets off on. Being caught. Doing something forbidden. Being corrupt. I think about all those stories about his exploits in college, most of them conflicting with each other and lurid with detail, and wonder. Mainly about myself.

I am his friend. I blush when people talk about sex. I told him last week that I've never had sex in a public place. Or a place with other people next door. Or a place of any interest. I am boring and straight and I've barely had an orgasm with another person in the room.

Jesus Christ – *I'm* something forbidden and corruptible.

And now he's pushing my dress up over my thighs. He's exposing my embarrassing-knicker-covered bottom. Oh God, I think they have a hole in them.

A hole that he absolutely finds and puts his finger into. Oh, if only it were not in such a rude place! Even if I'm glad that it's in such a rude place that when he presses and tests the little tear, he can find the outer edges of my slippery pussy.

I immediately flush when it becomes apparent that I'm wet just that easily, but he doesn't seem to have any problem with it. He moans hotly into my ear, and his breathing becomes harsh and jagged.

He isn't the one trembling so much that all the little blue glass things on top of the dresser are jittering, however.

In a lot of ways, he seems quite calm and measured. Or at the very least, he has a lot of restraint. The way he fluffs up my dress and hooks his fingers into the waistband of my knickers is practically saintly in its patience.

And all the while I say nothing. I do nothing. His weird ambiguity makes me. It's like a mystery – I just want to see what happens next! Surely this is just some sort of prove-I'm-not-gay-for-my-parents thing. Or maybe he wants to enlist me into a threesome with him and his hot boyfriend. Oh dear God, I should not be thinking sexier thoughts.

Or should I? Maybe it's just better to let sexual confusion take you. He certainly seems to think so. He's already working two fingers back between my legs, exploring so thoroughly that I can't decide if it means he's done this before, or finds this all a new and exciting revelation.

When he pushes the fingers inside me, and twists and presses until he finds that little bunch of nerves, I have to go with the former. I buck and moan and only remember that we're not alone when his free hand goes to my mouth. Unfortunately, him gagging me with his palm only makes me moan louder.

Oh, the things I'm finding out about myself today. I like Quinn. I like to be fucked by Quinn whether he's gay or not. I like to be fucked by Quinn in a bedroom while our friends dither next door. And I can apparently be made so horny that I don't care if they hear us or not.

I'm so horny that, when his slick probing fingers leave me, briefly, I wriggle and squirm and try and catch his cock against my bottom again.

'Be still,' he whispers, close to my ear. 'Be still and quiet.'

And then his hand leaves my mouth, too. I almost disobey him and beg him aloud not to stop, but I'm glad that I don't because then I hear him unzipping those boring cords and it's good that I get to hear that. Perhaps before that sound the idea that we're actually going to fuck hadn't solidified. I was still stuck on him playing for the other team.

Now he's on a team where he has to unzip his pants and, even better than that, when I glance over my shoulder I see him slick his rampantly stiff cock with my wetness. He rubs his sticky hand up and down his hard length with some obvious gratification, before realising that I'm watching him.

He meets my gaze with both a ruefulness and a tense pleasure in his expression, and I wonder what cookie jar he thinks he's been caught with his hand in. The girl cookie jar? Should I be a guy, Quinn, but you just couldn't resist a walk on the different side?

He doesn't need to answer, however. It's melting my insides either way. I'm so wet that it's reaching the insides of my thighs, and the insides of my thighs are trembling. All of my legs are trembling. I'm used to lying down when I'm about to have sex.

Though of course I can't admit that, because he's probably never had sex lying down. He probably has it hard and rough up against an alley wall with some big burly guy, frantically tugging on his own prick while his arse is reamed. Panting and groaning and pinching his own nipples through something thin and too tight. Or maybe he likes fucking amid seas of silk sheets, sweating and soft and *holy crap I bet his cock looks gorgeous sliding in and out of the mouth of some rough hot stud.*

Though, really, I have no more idea about what two men do together than I have about the surface of Mars. I previously hadn't really considered the idea. I hadn't considered any of this. I hadn't considered me, and all the ways I might like to bend. But maybe Quinn has.

He's considered it enough that when I reach back for him, groping and too-nervous, my hand encounters slippery rubber rather than the velvety soft of his cock. I sizzle with excitement at the thought that he might have planned this in advance – that he thought to have condoms about his person.

Though maybe he just always carries them – he's doubling his odds on getting laid, after all. Swing both ways and you're never limited to fifty per cent of the population. It's just good sense, I think, caught in a bubble of laughter and sure I'm about to pass out if he doesn't give me something soon.

I'm too strung out. I blush when I stand with my legs wider apart for him and he laughs, deep and wicked – quite obviously at my eagerness – but the blush spreads and grows and heats up my pussy. My clit is tingling and aching – so much so that when he holds my hip with one hand and stirs his cock through my creamy slit with the other, I jerk forwards into the dresser. I can't help it. The tip of his prick bumps my clit and I lose all control over myself.

The only reason I don't shriek is because his hand goes back over my mouth. This time, however, he dips a finger between my lips and I have something to bite down on. And I do – I bite hard and when he gasps a small pained *ah* into the nape of my neck, I make it up to him. I suck and soothe the bite, and taste something that is not me on his finger.

It isn't the tang of his pre-come that excites me, though. I don't think it is. I think it's more about him wanting me to taste that – to know how excited he is and that maybe he isn't just blundering into whatever this is.

Not that I'd want him to stop if he was just blundering into this. I can't even feel any guilt about that, either. I feel nothing about it, except for mindless blistering pleasure and relief when he finally slides his cock into where I'm wettest, and hottest.

My clit immediately misses the fleeting contact, but it's OK, because apparently the groan he vibrates against the softly sensitive space behind my ear goes all the way down through me and pays it special attention. My cunt spasms around his cock and my clit flutters and I actually think Oh God, I'm going to come just from hearing someone groan.

But then it gets worse, because although I'm not allowed to

talk or moan or anything, he certainly is. He says, 'You're so wet and swollen, so excited. Do I excite you, Linnie? Do I make you cream?' And I know I'd just have to rub my clit once or twice and I'd get the release I have clearly been needing forever. But I can't rub myself, because I have to hold onto the dresser or else collapse.

He ruts against me jerkily, jamming his cock right up against all the parts where it's best, but with that messy edge of being-too-far-gone-to-do-it-well. I don't mind being-too-far-gone at all, however. I don't mind, as long as he keeps gasping that he's going to come, he's going to come, oh, Jesus, it feels like he's going to burst.

'Play with yourself,' he groans as both his hands go to my hips and he tugs me back onto his cock – nice and hard and fast. 'Touch yourself, Linnie, please, ah please.'

And I do just as his cock jerks inside me and he makes a sound they're bound to hear. But it's OK, because I make one, too. I press a finger against my clit and a sound stirs all the way up from there, devouring me as it goes.

The second step is less obvious. It's like thinking about him getting fucked by Steve. It's something I never knew I wanted to know about but once I know about it I'm one step closer to bending over backwards for him.

The second step is something unexpected, too. But it's also asked for. I can't deny that I ask for it.

I just blurt it out. I can't stop myself. We're in a bookstore, too, when I do. It's probably not the best of times. But he's just being so normal and blasé about things – it's been twisting my insides for weeks. I need to know. I need to know if he actually *did* blunder into having sex with me.

Great sex with me. The best sex of my life with me.

Still, I'm a little disappointed that the best I can come up with is: 'Are you honestly gay?'

I have no idea why I throw the *honestly* in there. As though he could be what? Dishonestly gay? But then I suppose if he *is* only pretending, that's somewhat dishonest. What are the men who hit on him meant to think when he says Sorry, actually, last week I slept with a bonafide woman?

Of course he looks at me with that mixture of amusement and pleasure. He always looks at me with pleasure now. It's teasing the fuck out of me. It's like he has constant bedroom eyes but I don't know how to say, OK, let's just go to that place your eyes are suggesting.

In case he's gay. He could still be gay.

All right I know – it's really unlikely that he is. But even so.

He could still be gay. It takes him an eternity to answer, after all.

'As though . . . last week my penis just *fell* into your vagina?'

He really seems to consider the idea, too. He formulates theories and rolls them around in his mind. My fears and doubts are his pseudo-science.

Then he sticks his tongue into his cheek and kicks an askew look at me.

'You do know that gay men only sleep with other gay men, right, Linnie? No matter what the sexy books would have you believe.'

'What sexy books?' I ask, both because the sexiest book I've read had nothing like gay men having sex with women in it, and because I'm a blustering idiot. A blustering, horny idiot. All I can think about is his too-big-for-his-skinny-body cock fucking into me with those hard jerking thrusts and his hands on my hips and Mary trilling: 'Are you two OK in there?'

Yes. Yes I'm OK. I'm being tied into knots by a sexually flexible man.

'The ones where women are often the filling in a man sandwich,' he says, and laughs, and puts his book choice back on the shelf – some drippy tale of abuse that he considers to be his competition.

'So I'm guessing you . . . I mean, you don't make man sandwiches, then? The kind with just men in them, anyway? Is that what you're saying?'

I don't know why I expect him to clarify. I don't even know what *I'm* saying.

Whatever it is, though, he seems to think it's hilarious.

'I'm assuming that laugh means I'm being an idiot and you're about as gay as a wet Sunday morning in Suicideville,' I tell him, as he turns to the left-hand side of the book cul-de-sac we're in, and puts his hands in his pockets.

'Stop worrying, Linnie,' he says – so infuriatingly casual!

'I'm not worried.'

'So it doesn't bother you that I might prefer men to women? You're OK with that?'

'I . . .' I start out, but then the sentence just trails off into nowhere.

'Or maybe I just like to try a little of everything, now and then. Does that bother you?'

'Well no, but –'

'Maybe I'm just really fucking horny and not one to pass up an opportunity when I see it.'

He's looking over his shoulder at me now. Eyes bright and mischievous. One eyebrow lifted. That eyebrow says: go on then. Go on, ask.

'What sort of opportunities?'

I almost go with: *Was I an opportunity?* But lurid curiosity wins out. I think he knew it would.

He turns back to face me. He looks even sexier today than he did in the tweed, all skinny-hipped in tight cotton pants, be-stubbled again and louche-looking. I like both sides of him, though, and far more than I ever thought I could, back when he was just my friend. Back when he was off limits and not playing for my team.

'When I was in college,' he begins, and even I know where this is going. The old back-in-college story, where everyone had fun but me. I didn't even know how much I wanted fun until he dared me to want it. 'I was even less attractive than I am now. I was wildly unattractive. I was skinny and short and all my features were too big for my face.'

'A bit like the main character in your *Catcher in the Rye* rip-of – I mean, *homage*. Your *Catcher in the Rye homage*.'

He knuckles my shoulder and puffs out a laugh.

'Cheeky girl,' he says. 'I'll have to punish you for that.'

We both know what punish means in this context. I do not hate myself for shivering and eyeing the subtle shape of something beneath his zipper, as I try to remember what that movie with James Spader in it had to say about punishment.

What if Quinn wants me to bend that way? What if he wants me to do things I've never heard of? Even worse – what if he doesn't? Oh, God, what if he *doesn't*?

'So anyway . . . where was I?'

He's such a storyteller. Though I can't believe he's going to tell me this sort of story in a bookstore. Is it really going to be this sort of story?

'Yes – I was wildly unattractive. And so naturally I was also wildly horny, constantly. I couldn't get laid, I was surrounded by lithe, limber, half-naked girls who nightly smothered themselves in jelly shots . . . I couldn't sleep. I couldn't think. I was masturbating two or three times a day and it still wasn't enough. I was bound to get caught, at some point.'

I wanted to know. I did. But now I'm going to get to know in a place we probably can't finish what he's definitely starting.

My thighs are giving in again. They just can't fight gravity when he awakes the sleeping giant that is my sex drive.

'Who did you get caught by?' I ask, but it comes out so faint that the faraway ding of the till drowns me out.

Not entirely, though, because he leans down close and catches every word, and then whispers back to me: 'My room-mate.'

I have no idea if I knew he was going to say that or not. It feels like both at the same time – I knew but didn't. It's like all the waking up going on inside me. I know myself, but I don't. I know all the old tales, all the sexy stories and all the naughty clichés, but I don't. I don't know them well enough to stop myself becoming aroused by this.

'Of course I was embarrassed. He was this big, wholesome, macho sort of guy. The kind that makes the team and has a sweep of hair and all that sort of stuff. Really clean-cut and buff, and he comes into our room and finds me jerking at my cock. I wasn't even watching anything or looking at anything either. I was just on my bed with my jeans half-tugged down, as though I couldn't wait another second to get off. Even worse – when he walked in and just stood there, staring at me, I came. Him watching me made it so much more exciting – I was overwhelmed. I'd never had another person watch me do myself, or watch me come. It was too much.'

It's too much for me too. I get very close to taking his arm, whispering in his ear: *let's go somewhere else. Let's go somewhere quiet.*

But then he says: 'Do you want me to stop there?'

And my mouth blurts out for me: *no!*

'So there I was, all covered in my own spunk, my cookie-cutter roommate standing over me. I think I babbled something about needing to clean up or being sorry and about how horny I was or something like it, but I didn't get far with that sort of talk. Mainly because he was so sympathetic. He told me all about how he didn't mind at all – he could understand, being as how he was so horny, as well. And he proved it too, because as he talked he couldn't seem to stop himself rubbing the heel of his palm over the tent in his neatly pressed trousers.'

My fingernails are now digging into his forearm. He's practically grinning by now, but I can't fault him for it. He seems to be close to the state I am in – riddled with arousal and not wanting to stand up any more. I want to say to him *you make my knees weak*, but he's a writer. It'll sound so trite to him.

'I remember exactly when I got hard again. It was just as he was about to come, and I realised he was totally planning on spurting all over me. By that point he was pressed right up against my bed, and I couldn't stop watching him jerking off. It wasn't anything like the way I did myself – each stroke was more like a twist, and he worked himself rather than just tugging away. He kept sliding his thumb over the tip too, working his own slipperiness all over the head and down the shaft. I felt embarrassed, that I only ever masturbated in such a perfunctory and dull sort of way. I couldn't imagine what he had found exciting about watching me, but he certainly seemed to be getting off on something. He called out my name when he came. He said that I was so fucking hot.'

'Did you like that?'

'That someone thought I was hot? Yes. I didn't care who or what gender they were – I just wanted someone to want to fuck me. And he did. Of course he played it a little bit coy – we were just two guys, helping each other out. That sort of thing. But it's hard to play it successfully when you're covered in another man's come and he's offering to go down on you.'

'But I'm guessing you didn't mind.'

'Didn't give a crap. There's nothing like feeling a slippery wet mouth around your cock for the first time to realign your proclivities. I don't think mine even needed realigning. I've always been interested in . . . everything.'

Never has the word everything sounded so dirty. Though maybe it's something to do with the flush to his cheeks and the way he's caressing my back up and down, up and down. He's about a millimetre away from rubbing his clearly stiff cock against my leg.

But that's OK, because I'm a millimetre away from rubbing him right back.

'So did he?' I ask.

'Did he what?' he replies, but he knows damned well what I mean. He just wants me to say it, I know.

'Did he . . . suck your cock?'

'Louder,' he says.

'Let me say it quietly and maybe I'll suck your cock, too.'

My clit swells and aches to see his response to that – it's just what I hoped for. His eyes flutter closed, briefly, and his face sags.

'Yes, he sucked my cock. He did it the way I want you to do it, knelt between my thighs, hungry and with your hands all over me.'

'You want me to be greedy for you?'

'Yes. God, yes. Are you, Linnie? Do you want to take my cock in your mouth and suck until I can't stop myself from thrusting, until I spurt on your tongue and everyone in here hears me moaning your name?'

I get very close to saying yes. So close that I have to snap myself back to reality and remember where we are and remember that I'm just not that sort of person. He might be, but I'm not. I'm not.

Not yet.

* * *

The final step happens in a library. It seems we're always hanging out in places that have books and people, instead of where we probably should be. In bed, at my place. In any bed, actually.

Just anywhere.

He's done this on purpose. He's taken my move away from him in the bookstore to heart, and now he's going to prove me wrong on that score. He has only agreed to meet me in chaste places all week, until my body is humming and my head is full of images of things I didn't even know I found exciting. Him and faceless corn-fed guy. Him doing things to me from a million different sexy movies. Him making sandwiches out of me. Him tying me up and tying me down and teasing me this way forever with his ambiguity and his cryptic talk and his smouldering looks.

I don't think it's just the flexibility that makes him suddenly so exciting. It's the mystery too. He could be anything, want anything, he was so horny that he had to masturbate three times a day. He was so horny that he couldn't stop even when his roommate walked in on him.

I mean, he could have made all of that stuff up. As he looks at me over the top of the book he's chosen to read while I study the illustrations in an ancient book of fairy tales, I'm fairly sure he did make it all up.

But that just seems to make the whole thing even more electrifying. So much so that I don't even realise I'm rocking against the unforgiving wood of a library chair until he points it out.

'Something wrong?' he says.

Yes, I think. I've masturbated twice already today and it hasn't done anything for me.

But of course I don't say that. Maybe I should, really, and then we'd have something in common. Or at least, me and his college self would have something in common. Hot, uncontrollable horniness that no amount of touching yourself will solve.

He's turned me back into the teenager I never was, and I love him for it.

'Do you think if you keep rocking like that, it will get you off?'

'Don't be smug. Stop playing with me and let's just go somewhere. Can't we just go somewhere?'

'Why?'

'Because I'm not . . . because I don't think I can . . .'

'Can what?'

'I'm horny, Quinn. Let's just go somewhere and be horny together.'

'If you're so horny, why didn't you just stay home and wait for me to come to you?'

'Would you have?'

He puts down his book and knocks his smile down from that mocking quirk to something warm and lovely. He is more than lovely. He is more all over – far, far more than me.

'Of course I would.'

'Then let's just –'

'But you came here instead, when I asked you to. Even though you can't stop rocking on your chair. What did you think was going to happen?'

I think I go to say something. Something definitely occurs and seems as though it would be a success, coming out of my mouth. But then I realise what he means and I can't say anything at all. I could have just stayed at home and got what I wanted, but I didn't.

I wanted to come out and play instead.

'Naughty, naughty girl. What *are* you going to do in this public library?'

I don't even think about my answer. I'm on lust autopilot again.

'Come,' I say. 'Make me come, Quinn.'

He makes me sit on the edge of a library table with my legs spread, and my skirt up around my waist. Though I say *makes me*, when really I just mean that I desperately want to right now. I don't care – I've never cared. Whatever he is, I want to be it. I want to be flexible and open and daring, I want to make sandwiches with him, and catch each other doing naughty things, and be out in the open up against alley walls and in public libraries.

I'm tired of being straight and boring. I want his mouth on my pussy.

And, oh God, he does it. He presses his face right into the unbearably heated and aching slit of my sex, in the slowly ticking quiet of a musty library. He kneels between my legs as his corn-fed boy knelt between his, that quick sharp tongue licking swirls around my clit.

It doesn't take me long to come. When he reaches up and rubs my tits and my nipples through the material of my shirt, my back arches of its own accord and I grind my pussy into his mouth. My clit jumps and swells, and then hot sensation gushes through me – at last, at last.

So much at last that I don't even care that noise comes out of me. So much noise that it disturbs every layer of dust and every snoozing librarian in the place. But I don't care. I find that I really honestly don't care. I'm bending over backwards. I'm origami.

I want him all the ways I ever imagined him to be.

He looks up at me, smug and satisfied. How noisy I was! Look what he made me do. Now everyone will know what a bad girl I am – oh, how can I bear it?

I can bear it by sticking the heel of my shoe into his shoulder, and ordering him to get up. After all, he can't say no. This is all his fault. He shouldn't have made me this bad, this greedy, this flexible, if he didn't want to pay the piper.

The piper wants him up against the bookshelves. It's not quite an alley, but maybe in some ways this is even worse. There's about five thousand years of prim properness in here, just waiting to be ruffled up. Like his hair, back in Mary and Chris's apartment. Like the shirt I wanted to un-tuck.

I rip his shirt out of his jeans this time. I pin him up against the shelves. Of course he looks delighted, but I can live with that.

'Turn around and spread 'em,' I say, and the delight doesn't fade. Why should it? There's probably nothing I could do that would shock him to his core. Really, I can only shock me to my core.

Which I do, when I make him drop his jeans to his ankles and press myself to his back. I have to stand on tiptoe to whisper in his ear, but I manage it. I stretch myself, I bend, I make myself into something new.

'I'm going to fuck you,' I tell him and the new me does not protest any more than he does.

I think of the man in the alley who I imagined for him. I think of him as I suck my fingers loud enough for him to hear, and slide them down between his soft little ass cheeks. I want to, I need to, I have to. Everything he's done to me demands it.

He turns his head slightly when I circle that pucker I've never even touched on myself – that no one has ever touched – but he doesn't do anything else. He doesn't ask me to stop.

I wish I had something more than my fingers. Though I think they do just fine when I slide them into the webbing and he goes up on tiptoe, and whines for me. I want to eat that whine. I want to eat him.

Instead I thrust my hips against my fingers and my fingers

thrust against and into him, and once I've done it I have to do it again. And again and again and again until I'm all hot and shivery despite the earlier orgasm, and he's all hot and shivery too. He's made me like him, now I'm going to make him like me.

'More,' he says. 'Harder.'

So I do. I do it until he makes a little startled sound and I look at what he is looking at – a librarian at the end of the section, gaping at us. Horrified in lace and lavender.

But even then I don't stop. I don't think he would stop, if it were the other way around. Instead I say what I'm sure he would, as near to his ear as I can get: 'Tell her you're really sorry you're getting fucked in her library. Tell her you shouldn't have driven someone so crazy that she just had to take advantage of you in a public place.'

He doesn't stop staring at the librarian, who doesn't stop staring at us.

'I'm sorry,' he says. 'I'm sorry.'

But he isn't at all. Not that there's anything wrong with that. I'm not sorry, either. Not even when she calls us perverts and storms off.

I think here is where we should be concerned about the police. We should be, but instead all I can feel is him clenching around my fucking fingers, and the sound of his groans getting higher and higher and my own laughter, bubbling up joyous and new.

It's fun, to be sexually flexible.

Charlotte Stein's first single author collection, *The Things That Make Me Give In*, is published by Black Lace in October 2009. Her short fiction appears in numerous Black Lace anthologies.

Visit the Black Lace website at
www.blacklace.co.uk

FIND OUT THE LATEST INFORMATION AND TAKE ADVANTAGE OF OUR FANTASTIC FREE BOOK OFFER! ALSO VISIT THE SITE FOR . . .

- All Black Lace titles currently available and how to order online
- Great new offers
- Writers' guidelines
- Author interviews
- An erotica newsletter
- Features
- Cool links

BLACK LACE — THE LEADING IMPRINT OF WOMEN'S SEXY FICTION

TAKING YOUR EROTIC READING PLEASURE TO NEW HORIZONS

LOOK OUT FOR THE ALL-NEW BLACK LACE BOOKS – AVAILABLE NOW!

All books priced £7.99 in the UK. Please note publication dates apply to the UK only. For other territories, please contact your retailer.

Also to be published in September 2009

NO RESERVATIONS
Megan Hart and Lauren Dane
ISBN 978 0 352 34519 6

Kate and Leah are heading for Vegas with no reservations. They are both on the run from their new boyfriends and the baggage these guys have brought with them from other women. And the biggest playground in the west has many sensual thrills to offer two women with an appetite for fun. Meanwhile, the boyfriends, Dix and Brandon, realise you don't know what you've got till it's gone, and pursue the girls to the city of sin to launch the most arduous methods of seduction to win the girls back. Non-stop action with a twist of romance from two of the most exciting writers in American erotica today.

TAKING LIBERTIES
Susie Raymond
ISBN 978 0 352 34530 1

When attractive, thirty-something Beth Bradley takes a job as PA to Simon Henderson, a highly successful financier, she is well aware of his philandering reputation and determined to turn the tables on his fortune. Her initial attempt backfires, and she begins to look for a more subtle and erotic form of retribution. However, Beth keeps getting sidetracked by her libido, and finds herself caught up in the dilemma of craving sex with the dominant man she wants to teach a lesson.

To be published in October 2009

THE THINGS THAT MAKE ME GIVE IN
Charlotte Stein
ISBN 978 0 352 34542 4

Girls who go after what they want no matter what the cost, boys who like to flash their dark sides, voyeurism for beginners and cheating lovers . . . Charlotte Stein takes you on a journey through all the facets of female desire in this contemporary collection of explicit and ever-intriguing short stories. Be seduced by obsessions that go one step too far and dark desires that remove all inhibitions. Each story takes you on a journey into all the things that make a girl give in.

THE GALLERY
Fredrica Alleyn
ISBN 978 0 352 34533 2

Police office Cressida Farleigh is called in to investigate a mysterious art fraud at a gallery specialising in modern erotic works. The gallery's owner is under suspicion, but is also a charming and powerfully attractive man who throws the young woman's powers of detection into confusion. Her long-time detective boyfriend is soon getting jealous, but Cressida is also in the process of seducing a young artist of erotic images. As she finds herself drawn into a mesh of power games and personal discovery, the crimes continue and her chances of cracking the case become ever more distant.

ALL THE TRIMMINGS
Tesni Morgan
ISBN 978 0 352 34532 5

Cheryl and Laura decide to pool their substantial divorce settlements and buy a hotel. When the women find out that each secretly harbours a desire to run an upmarket bordello, they seize the opportunity to turn St Jude's into a bawdy funhouse for both sexes, where fantasies – from the mild to the increasingly perverse – are indulged. When attractive , sinister John Dempsey comes on the scene, Cheryl is smitten, but Laura less so, convinced he's out to con them, or report them to the authorities or both. Which of the women is right? And will their friendship – and their business – survive?

To be published in November 2009

THE AFFAIR
Various
ISBN 978 0 352 34517 2

Indulgent and sensual, outrageous and taboo, but always highly erotic, this new collection of Black Lace stories takes the illicit and daring rendezvous with a lover (or lovers) as its theme. Popular Black Lace authors and new voices contribute a broad and thrilling range of women's sexual fantasy.

FIRE AND ICE
Laura Hamilton
ISBN 978 0 352 34534 9

At work Nina is known as the Ice Queen, as her frosty demeanour makes her colleagues think she's equally cold in bed. But what they don't know is that she spends her free time acting out sleazy scenarios with her boyfriend, Andrew, in which she's a prostitute and he's a punter. But when Andrew starts inviting his less-than-respectable friends to join in their games, things begin to get strange, and Nina finds herself being drawn deeper into London's seedy underworld, where everything is for sale and nothing is what it seems.

SHADOWPLAY
Portia Da Costa
ISBN 978 0 352 34535 6

Photographer Christabel is drawn to psychic phenomena and dark liaisons. When she is persuaded by her husband to take a holiday at a mysterious mansion house in the country, she foresees only long days of pastoral boredom. But Nicholas, her deviously sensual husband, has a hand in the unexpected events that begin to unravel. She is soon drawn into a web of transgressive eroticism with Nicholas's young male PA. Within this unusual and kinky threesome, Christabel learns some lessons the jaded city could never teach her.

ALSO LOOK OUT FOR

THE BLACK LACE BOOK OF WOMEN'S SEXUAL FANTASIES
Edited and compiled by Kerri Sharp
ISBN 978 0 352 33793 1

The *Black Lace Book of Women's Sexual Fantasies* reveals the most private thoughts of hundreds of women. Here are sexual fantasies which on first sight appear shocking or bizarre – such as the bank clerk who wants to be a vampire and the nanny with a passion for Darth Vader. Kerri Sharp investigates the recurrent themes in female fantasies and the cultural influences that have determined them: from fairy stories to cult TV; from fetish fashion to historical novels. Sharp argues that sexual archetypes – such as the 'dark man of the psyche' – play an important role in arousal, allowing us to find gratification safely through personal narratives of adventure and sexual abandon.

THE NEW BLACK LACE BOOK OF WOMEN'S SEXUAL FANTASIES
Edited and compiled by Mitzi Szereto
ISBN 978 0 352 34172 3

The second anthology of detailed sexual fantasies contributed by women from all over the world. The book is a result of a year's research by an expert on erotic writing and gives a fascinating insight into the rich diversity of the female sexual imagination.

Black Lace Booklist

Information is correct at time of printing. To avoid disappointment, check availability before ordering. Go to www.blacklace.co.uk
All books are priced £7.99 unless another price is given.

BLACK LACE BOOKS WITH A CONTEMPORARY SETTING

☐ AMANDA'S YOUNG MEN Madeline Moore　　ISBN 978 0 352 34191 4

☐ THE ANGELS' SHARE Maya Hess　　ISBN 978 0 352 34043 6

☐ THE APPRENTICE Carrie Williams　　ISBN 978 0 352 34514 1

☐ ASKING FOR TROUBLE Kristina Lloyd　　ISBN 978 0 352 33362 9

☐ BLACK ORCHID Roxanne Carr　　ISBN 978 0 352 34188 4

☐ THE BLUE GUIDE Carrie Williams　　ISBN 978 0 352 34132 7

☐ THE BOSS Monica Belle　　ISBN 978 0 352 34088 7

☐ BOUND IN BLUE Monica Belle　　ISBN 978 0 352 34012 2

☐ CAMPAIGN HEAT Gabrielle Marcola　　ISBN 978 0 352 33941 6

☐ CASSANDRA'S CONFLICT Fredrica Alleyn　　ISBN 978 0 352 34186 0

☐ CASSANDRA'S CHATEAU Fredrica Alleyn　　ISBN 978 0 352 34523 3

☐ CAT SCRATCH FEVER Sophie Mouette　　ISBN 978 0 352 34021 4

☐ CHILLI HEAT Carrie Williams　　ISBN 978 0 352 34178 5

☐ THE CHOICE Monica Belle　　ISBN 978 0 352 34512 7

☐ CIRCUS EXCITE Nikki Magennis　　ISBN 978 0 352 34033 7

☐ CLUB CRÈME Primula Bond　　ISBN 978 0 352 33907 2　　£6.99

☐ CONTINUUM Portia Da Costa　　ISBN 978 0 352 33120 5

☐ COOKING UP A STORM Emma Holly　　ISBN 978 0 352 34114 3

☐ DANGEROUS CONSEQUENCES Pamela Rochford　　ISBN 978 0 352 33185 4

☐ DARK DESIGNS Madelynne Ellis　　ISBN 978 0 352 34075 7

☐ DARK OBSESSIONS Fredrica Alleyn　　ISBN 978 0 352 34524 0

☐ THE DEVIL AND THE DEEP BLUE SEA Cheryl Mildenhall　　ISBN 978 0 352 34200 3

☐ DOCTOR'S ORDERS Deanna Ashford　　ISBN 978 0 352 34525 1

☐ EDEN'S FLESH Robyn Russell　　ISBN 978 0 352 32923 3

☐ EQUAL OPPORTUNITIES Mathilde Madden　　ISBN 978 0 352 34070 2

☐ FIRE AND ICE Laura Hamilton　　ISBN 978 0 352 33486 2

☐ FORBIDDEN FRUIT Susie Raymond　　ISBN 978 0 352 34189 1

☐ THE GALLERY Fredrica Alleyn　　ISBN 978 0 352 34533 2

☐ GEMINI HEAT Portia Da Costa　　ISBN 978 0 352 34187 7

☐ THE GIFT OF SHAME Sarah Hope-Walker　　ISBN 978 0 352 34202 7

☐ UP TO NO GOOD Karen Smith   ISBN 978 0 352 34528 8
☐ VELVET GLOVE Emma Holly   ISBN 978 0 352 34115 0
☐ WILD BY NATURE Monica Belle   ISBN 978 0 352 33915 7   £6.99
☐ WILD CARD Madeline Moore   ISBN 978 0 352 34038 2
☐ WING OF MADNESS Mae Nixon   ISBN 978 0 352 34099 3

BLACK LACE BOOKS WITH AN HISTORICAL SETTING

☐ A GENTLEMAN'S WAGER Madelynne Ellis   ISBN 978 0 352 34173 0
☐ THE BARBARIAN GEISHA Charlotte Royal   ISBN 978 0 352 33267 7
☐ BARBARIAN PRIZE Deanna Ashford   ISBN 978 0 352 34017 7
☐ THE CAPTIVATION Natasha Rostova   ISBN 978 0 352 33234 9
☐ DARKER THAN LOVE Kristina Lloyd   ISBN 978 0 352 33279 0
☐ WILD KINGDOM Deanna Ashford   ISBN 978 0 352 33549 4
☐ DIVINE TORMENT Janine Ashbless   ISBN 978 0 352 33719 1
☐ FRENCH MANNERS Olivia Christie   ISBN 978 0 352 33214 1
☐ NICOLE'S REVENGE Lisette Allen   ISBN 978 0 352 32984 4
☐ THE SENSES BEJEWELLED Cleo Cordell   ISBN 978 0 352 32904 2   £6.99
☐ THE SOCIETY OF SIN Sian Lacey Taylder   ISBN 978 0 352 34080 1
☐ TEMPLAR PRIZE Deanna Ashford   ISBN 978 0 352 34137 2

BLACK LACE BOOKS WITH A PARANORMAL THEME

☐ BRIGHT FIRE Maya Hess   ISBN 978 0 352 34104 4
☐ BURNING BRIGHT Janine Ashbless   ISBN 978 0 352 34085 6
☐ CRUEL ENCHANTMENT Janine Ashbless   ISBN 978 0 352 33483 1
☐ DARK ENCHANTMENT Janine Ashbless   ISBN 978 0 352 34513 4
☐ FLOOD Anna Clare   ISBN 978 0 352 34094 8
☐ GOTHIC BLUE Portia Da Costa   ISBN 978 0 352 33075 8
☐ GOTHIC HEAT Portia Da Costa   ISBN 978 0 352 34170 9
☐ THE PASSION OF ISIS Madelynne Ellis   ISBN 978 0 352 33993 4
☐ PHANTASMAGORIA Madelynne Ellis   ISBN 978 0 352 34168 6
☐ THE PRIDE Edie Bingham   ISBN 978 0 352 33997 3
☐ THE SILVER CAGE Mathilde Madden   ISBN 978 0 352 34164 8
☐ THE SILVER COLLAR Mathilde Madden   ISBN 978 0 352 34141 9
☐ THE SILVER CROWN Mathilde Madden   ISBN 978 0 352 34157 0
☐ SOUTHERN SPIRITS Edie Bingham   ISBN 978 0 352 34180 8
☐ THE TEN VISIONS Olivia Knight   ISBN 978 0 352 34119 8
☐ WILD KINGDOM Deana Ashford   ISBN 978 0 352 34152 5
☐ WILDWOOD Janine Ashbless   ISBN 978 0 352 34194 5

BLACK LACE ANTHOLOGIES

- BLACK LACE QUICKIES 1 Various — ISBN 978 0 352 34126 6 — £2.99
- BLACK LACE QUICKIES 2 Various — ISBN 978 0 352 34127 3 — £2.99
- BLACK LACE QUICKIES 3 Various — ISBN 978 0 352 34128 0 — £2.99
- BLACK LACE QUICKIES 4 Various — ISBN 978 0 352 34129 7 — £2.99
- BLACK LACE QUICKIES 5 Various — ISBN 978 0 352 34130 3 — £2.99
- BLACK LACE QUICKIES 6 Various — ISBN 978 0 352 34133 4 — £2.99
- BLACK LACE QUICKIES 7 Various — ISBN 978 0 352 34146 4 — £2.99
- BLACK LACE QUICKIES 8 Various — ISBN 978 0 352 34147 1 — £2.99
- BLACK LACE QUICKIES 9 Various — ISBN 978 0 352 34155 6 — £2.99
- BLACK LACE QUICKIES 10 Various — ISBN 978 0 352 34156 3 — £2.99
- SEDUCTION Various — ISBN 978 0 352 34510 3
- SEXY LITTLE NUMBERS Various — ISBN 978 0 352 34538 7
- LIAISONS Various — ISBN 978 0 352 34516 5
- MORE WICKED WORDS Various — ISBN 978 0 352 33487 9 — £6.99
- WICKED WORDS 3 Various — ISBN 978 0 352 33522 7 — £6.99
- WICKED WORDS 4 Various — ISBN 978 0 352 33603 3 — £6.99
- WICKED WORDS 5 Various — ISBN 978 0 352 33642 2 — £6.99
- WICKED WORDS 6 Various — ISBN 978 0 352 33690 3 — £6.99
- WICKED WORDS 7 Various — ISBN 978 0 352 33743 6 — £6.99
- WICKED WORDS 8 Various — ISBN 978 0 352 33787 0 — £6.99
- WICKED WORDS 9 Various — ISBN 978 0 352 33860 0
- WICKED WORDS 10 Various — ISBN 978 0 352 33893 8
- THE BEST OF BLACK LACE 2 Various — ISBN 978 0 352 33718 4
- WICKED WORDS: SEX IN THE OFFICE Various — ISBN 978 0 352 33944 7
- WICKED WORDS: SEX AT THE SPORTS CLUB Various — ISBN 978 0 352 33991 1
- WICKED WORDS: SEX ON HOLIDAY Various — ISBN 978 0 352 33961 4
- WICKED WORDS: SEX IN UNIFORM Various — ISBN 978 0 352 34002 3
- WICKED WORDS: SEX IN THE KITCHEN Various — ISBN 978 0 352 34018 4
- WICKED WORDS: SEX ON THE MOVE Various — ISBN 978 0 352 34034 4
- WICKED WORDS: SEX AND MUSIC Various — ISBN 978 0 352 34061 0
- WICKED WORDS: SEX AND SHOPPING Various — ISBN 978 0 352 34076 4
- SEX IN PUBLIC Various — ISBN 978 0 352 34089 4
- SEX WITH STRANGERS Various — ISBN 978 0 352 34105 1
- LOVE ON THE DARK SIDE Various — ISBN 978 0 352 34132 7
- LUST AT FIRST BITE Various — ISBN 978 0 352 34506 6
- LUST BITES Various — ISBN 978 0 352 34153 2

To find out the latest information about Black Lace titles, check out the website: www.blacklace.co.uk or send for a booklist with complete synopses by writing to:

Black Lace Booklist, Virgin Books Ltd
Random House
20 Vauxhall Bridge Road
London SW1V 2SA

Please include an SAE of decent size. Please note only British stamps are valid.

Our privacy policy
We will not disclose information you supply us to any other parties. We will not disclose any information which identifies you personally to any person without your express consent.

From time to time we may send out information about Black Lace books and special offers. Please tick here if you do not wish to receive Black Lace information. ❏

Please send me the books I have ticked above.

Name ....

Address ....

....

....

....

Post Code ....

Send to: Virgin Books Cash Sales, Black Lace,
Random House, 20 Vauxhall Bridge Road, London SW1V 2SA.

US customers: for prices and details of how to order
books for delivery by mail, call 888-330-8477.

Please enclose a cheque or postal order, made payable
to Virgin Books Ltd, to the value of the books you have
ordered plus postage and packing costs as follows:

UK and BFPO – £1.00 for the first book, 50p for each
subsequent book.

Overseas (including Republic of Ireland) – £2.00 for
the first book, £1.00 for each subsequent book.

If you would prefer to pay by VISA, ACCESS/MASTERCARD,
DINERS CLUB, AMEX or MAESTRO, please write your card
number and expiry date here: ....

....

Signature ....

Please allow up to 28 days for delivery.